TARRAGON DREAMS

Book Two of the Tarragon Series

Elizabeth James

Thrall of Darkness

ISBN-13: 978-1-9449-6901-1
ISBN-10: 1-944969-01-2

THE TARRAGON SERIES

CONTENTS

PROLOGUE

Kale awoke with an erection and a burning desire to fly back to Tarragon Academy to join a mating flight. It should have been impossible: he and his dragon were nearly three thousand miles away from his alma mater, yet the desire was growing. Vestis growled and prepared to take flight but Kale forced him to remain still with a powerful command. The dragon reluctantly obeyed. Kale dressed quickly and left his room in search of the other graduates to see if they were experiencing similar symptoms.

The White House was in chaos. Since most of the staff were bonded to dragons and all seemed to be feeling the same bizarre, unexpected lust, many of the guards had snuck off to share intimate moments and even many of the cleaning staff had thrown aside their mops to grab the nearest partner.

Kale wanted to look down his nose at them for their inability to control the strong lust that was even now pulsing through his veins but he couldn't. Their relationships with their dragons were different than his and they had no experience with dragon-born emotions. Kale, on the other hand, was one of the few who could hear his dragon and he was used to feeling every flicker of emotion in his partner.

The President himself was safe, Kale was glad to see, and his body guards, all men like Kale with strongly bonded dragons, were preventing him from seeing anything unusual. The President was completely unaware that his White House was in a shambles. But even though the guards were doing their job, Kale could sense their unease and embarrassment, and he knew they were feeling the same desire to join the mating flight. Kale just prayed none of the dragons would be foolish enough to try a mating flight here, where any unauthorized objects in the sky were shot down without question. He tried to reassure himself that the White House staff, despite their current disarray, was fully trained and would never let such a thing happen. But no one had ever anticipated this.

"Ah, Kale," the president said. "I was expecting you. Is everything all right?"

He was observant for a non-bonded human, perhaps too observant. He suspected them, perhaps he even knew, but he was smart, and trustworthy. He didn't ask, and they didn't tell. It was a good relationship, unlike the last few presidents who had either been completely oblivious or far too nosy for their own good. This president was intelligent and Kale appreciated it. It made his job easier.

"Everything is under control, sir," Kale said, even as his cock throbbed in disagreement. He prayed it wasn't visible. The lust was, luckily, dying down quickly and he could see the relief in the other men. They would undoubtedly find a partner to burn off the residual lust, but the urgency was gone. Kale still was trying to figure out how a mating flight in Portland could affect everyone in Washington DC. It should have been impossible.

"I'll be taking a vacation to Oregon, sir," he said, and then he blinked. He hadn't planned on saying that but now that he thought about it, it was the only rational thing to do. The Academy would never explain what had happened, so if he wanted to find out, he would need to go himself and get answers.

"Well, you certainly have the vacation days for it," the president said with a smile. "I trust that you'll leave me in good hands."

"The best, sir. It will take some time to prepare for my departure, but I estimate I'll leave in about a month."

He always felt so stilted when talking to the president. He hadn't gotten over his childhood awe at the most powerful person in the country, if not the world. Sure, the Tarragon Council might be more powerful, but no one knew about them. The president was a public figure, and Kale was young enough to constantly be overwhelmed by his responsibilities as the president's personal assistant. But he had a month to arrange for a replacement. That ought to be enough time to prepare. And whatever was happening in Tarragon Academy would still be going on, he knew. If there was a dragon so powerful that he felt her mating flight, she wasn't going anywhere soon. The council would hold onto her for as long as they could and it might be up to Kale to help free her from the council's clutches as he had freed himself.

He took a deep breath. It had taken all of his power to escape from Tarragon Academy and the council, and it was madness to go back. But any dragon powerful enough to do this needed help, and he knew it was his responsibility to offer that help. Portland it would be, he thought grimly to himself. In one month.

CHAPTER ONE

Pretending

Mike opened his eyes. Ashton's breath was warm against his back and his arm was cradled possessively over Mike's belly. They had been sleeping together ever since the Queen dragon had flown in her mating flight and both Mike and Ashton had failed to capture her. In order to quiet the lust that inevitably filled everyone who chased the queen, Ashton had taken Mike to his bed.

Now, a month later, they were still spending every night together. Mike tried to breathe quietly so he wouldn't wake Ashton up. At moments like these, he pretended that he meant something to the older man; that Ashton actually cared about him and wasn't just using his body. He knew it was a false hope, but he clung to it anyway.

Ashton's breathing changed and he pulled away from Mike.

"Time to get up," he said, shaking Mike gently. "You have a busy day ahead of you."

Mike winced. He had been training the queen's mate, Scott, for the past month and it was nearly time for the boy to be re-united with Jamie, the queen dragon's human partner. Scott and Jamie were deeply in love and Mike knew that the separation had been difficult for them even though they had been allowed to spend Christmas Eve together. Even though Mike longed for Ashton's love, he had also hoped to use this time to grow close to Scott.

But Scott, unfortunately, had been sullen and unforgiving and if he didn't learn to respect Mike and the rest of the council soon, Ashton would take over his training and Mike would have no way to protect him from the worst of the council's wrath. It was a careful balancing act: he wanted to preserve Scott's sense of independence, but he also needed to teach Scott how to obey the council. Their lessons up until now had been about history, but now they were moving into obedience and Mike worried that Scott would never learn what he needed to know to be reunited with Jamie.

Jamie, on the other hand, had been spending an hour a day with Ashton, learning about queen dragons and a highly edited history of Tarragon Academy. He was far more pliable and naïve than Scott, but Mike suspected that once the two of them compared notes, Jamie's implicit trust of Ashton would vanish.

Ashton slapped Mike's ass when he didn't move, and Mike winced and stood up. They spent the night together, but there wasn't much friendliness in the rough, passionate encounters. Often Mike wondered why Ashton didn't kick him out as soon as they were finished.

Mike dug around the room for his clothes and headed to his room for a shower and a fresh set of clothes before seeing Scott. He wasn't sure if Scott knew about him and Ashton. He didn't want Scott to know. Even though he craved Ashton's attention, he was ashamed of it as well and didn't want anyone to know how much he needed the older man. The other council members knew – they always smirked when he went past – but no one else seemed to have figured it out, or at least no one else had commented on it. It wasn't unusual for two men to sleep together at Tarragon Academy, but sleeping with the head of the council would surely raise some eyebrows and Mike was grateful that Ashton hadn't announced their relationship.

After a quick shower, Mike took a deep breath and headed to the highest level of the dragon canyon where the queen and her mate lived. Or where they would live, once Marisol, the queen,

2

was finished with her training. Right now, Scott and his dragon Narné had moved into the canyon but Jamie and Marisol still lived in the apartment complex on the other side of the campus. Ashton said it was because Marisol was not ready to be moved, but really it was a way to keep Scott and Jamie apart. Since neither boy was in classes due to winter break, there was no way they could see each other without crossing the entire campus and being spotted by at least one council member.

Mike took another deep breath before knocking on Scott's door. Scott answered almost immediately and once again Mike felt a familiar rush of emotions at the sight of the handsome man. Scott was only a few years younger than him and when Scott was a freshman, Mike had been assigned to seduce him. Mike had succeeded, in part, but Scott had resisted and still thought of the encounter as rape. Mike had hoped the weeks of enforced closeness would make Scott realize that it wasn't rape, but Scott was still as skittish and angry as the first day Mike had shown up to begin his training.

"When can I see Jamie? It's been a month."

"There's one more lesson you need to learn, and then Ashton will test you."

Scott's lips tightened. "If I fail that test?"

"You won't," Mike said firmly. If Scott failed the test, then Mike would have failed as a teacher and he might lose Ashton's interest. As much as he enjoyed spending time with Scott, he valued Ashton more. He would make sure Scott passed.

"So what's this lesson?"

"I think it's time we talked about the council."

Scott's eyes brightened with curiosity and he waved for Mike to come all the way in. They sat down near Narné in the massive dragon chamber designed to house two dragons. Sometimes Eraxes, Mike's dragon, joined them, but not today. Narné and Eraxes had become close over the past month, even if their humans had not. At first there had been some tension between

3

them – after all, Eraxes had been just a few seconds away from mating with Marisol when Narné swept in – but they had put aside their differences and become friends. Mike hoped he and Scott would follow a similar path.

"I know you understand a little of how the council works, but you have no idea how much power they really have."

"I have some idea," Scott said bitterly.

"I mean globally," Mike said. "The Tarragon Council isn't just responsible for the school. They're responsible for every graduate across the globe, and they use their connections to control world events to their advantage."

Scott was silent for a moment. "I thought so."

"Well, it's true. And because of that, you are a great risk. You've set yourself up as the queen's mate-"

"I *am* the queen's mate."

"I know," Mike said. "But if Ashton had his way, you wouldn't have that title. There are responsibilities with that title, and a great deal of power."

"Isn't that what you've been teaching me this whole time? My responsibilities? Watching over the other dragons, helping Marisol when she lays eggs, all of that?"

"Yes, but the main responsibility is acting as a counterbalance to the council. And trust me, they are not prepared to let you take on that responsibility."

"They can't stop me."

Mike's hand curled into a fist. "You can't become equal to them yet, Scott. If you try, if you claim your position, they will find a way to get rid of you. If you ever want to leave this training, you need to learn how to submit to the council's will."

"Is that what you're doing with Ashton?"

A flush of heat rushed into Mike's face. He had truly hoped that Scott hadn't noticed.

"We're not talking about me," Mike said firmly. "We're talking about you. You need to learn to pretend to do what the council wants so they'll leave you alone."

Scott hesitated and a crease appeared on his forehead. "Pretend?"

Mike fingered the gold chain around his neck and stared at the ground. The chain was a collar, really, and a gift from Ashton. Now that it was around his neck, there was no way to take it off. He had tried, but the latch had vanished. Eraxes said it was forged by a dragon who had a gift for forging metal together and it would be on Mike's neck until Ashton decided to remove it. It represented his obedience to Ashton, but it also represented his biggest deception.

Mike was a part of an underground group of rebels who were dedicated to getting rid of the current council, specifically Ashton, because of their corruption. Mike had been chosen to attempt to get on the council so that he could make changes from the inside, but instead Ashton had seduced him and collared him. He tried to resist Ashton and pursue the group's goals, but it was difficult. His only chance was to help Scott, but first he had to teach Scott how to get by without attracting the council's notice. Mike had been doing it for over a year now, so he had good experience.

If Marisol laid her eggs and then chose Scott a second time in the mating flight, then Scott's position as the queen's mate would be confirmed and he could afford to make waves with the council, but until then he needed to keep his head down.

"You're not the queen's mate unless she chooses you twice in a row, and some council members won't recognize you until the third mating flight. Until then, you are simply the person who flew with Marisol. If you want to survive, you need to learn to adapt."

"But you said pretend. That's different than adapt."

"The council is... corrupt. You've figured that out by now. Changes need to be made and maybe you're the person to do it.

But this isn't the time. You're not strong enough."

"How do you know?"

Scott was frowning and Mike sighed. Scott was reacting just as he had feared: indignant and angry rather than taking the news calmly.

"Fine. You might be ready to take on the council. You were certainly bold when you stole Marisol from me. But right now, Jamie is in the council's hands and that will be true until Marisol lays her eggs. Marisol is vulnerable right now, and so is Jamie. I know you wouldn't put Jamie at risk."

Scott winced and Mike knew he had played the right card. Jamie was Scott's vulnerability, but unfortunately Ashton also knew this and would use Jamie to keep Scott under control.

"Ashton knows your feelings about Jamie and he will use Jamie against you if you try to go up against him now. Just wait, Scott. Wait and do what the council asks, be as obedient as you can, and then, when the time is right and you and Jamie are both strong enough, then we can turn against them. But if you try it now all of our efforts will be for nothing."

Scott nodded slowly, reluctantly. "Fine. What do I have to do?"

A smile of relief flashed across Mike's face and he felt himself relaxing as he told Scott what the rebels had told him once about how to fool the council members. Most of the council was harmless: either they were so arrogant they didn't expect deception, or they were decent people who had been inured to the corruption around them and didn't even notice it anymore. But Ashton was clever, and would know exactly what Scott was doing. He was the one to fool, and Mike knew it would be a team effort between him and Scott, even though Scott wouldn't like that idea. But without Mike serving as a distraction to Ashton, all of Ashton's energy would be focused on seducing Jamie and destroying Scott.

Scott seemed to take everything in stride until Mike mentioned Ashton, when the man's fists clenched and his eyes narrowed.

"I am not doing anything that man says."

"He's the head of the council," Mike said. "He's the one who matters most."

"It won't work. He'll know I'm faking."

"Maybe. But he'll accept it. He just wants to know that you know your place, even if you aren't happy about it."

Scott was silent for a moment. "So what does it mean to know my place? I have to do whatever he says?"

"Pretty much," Mike said. "I'll make sure he doesn't ask for anything you aren't willing to give."

"How will you do that?"

"Sometimes he does things for me," Mike said cautiously.

In reality, he didn't know how far Ashton would go for him, but in the past the older man had done unexpectedly kind things for him and they had been growing more frequent. It had started before the queen's mating flight when Mike had the responsibility of killing a baby dragon whose human had died. Ashton had done the killing for him, sparing him the terrible task. Then inviting him to sleep together after sex. Ashton called Mike his pet, and he treated him like one, but a spoiled pet. If Ashton had Mike to entertain him and keep him busy, surely he wouldn't worry too much about Scott.

"I'm not sleeping with him," Scott said.

"I wouldn't let you," Mike snapped, then flushed. The thought of anyone sleeping with his Ashton was upsetting.

"I suppose," Scott said slowly, "that I could do what he says. But I have my limits. If he hurts Jamie..."

"Jamie will be fine. He's bonded with the queen, after all. You, on the hand, are in danger if you don't obey."

Scott nodded and his face went pale. He looked incredibly vulnerable and Mike ached with the desire to hold him and kiss

7

him.

"You'll make sure Jamie is all right? You'll visit him and see how he's doing?"

"I'll go today. As soon as we've finished."

CHAPTER TWO

Winter Picnic

Jamie dreamed that he and Scott were together again, lying in bed. There was nothing sexual in the dream – they were just lying together in complete harmony with Jamie's head nestled against Scott's shoulder while they talked about the kinds of things people talk about in dreams. He could feel the flex and pull of Scott's muscles as the other man gestured, and enjoyed the man's musky scent. Even in his dream he knew that the two of them had just made love, but he didn't desire more. This was enough for his dream: lying together in harmony, talking about nothing, being with each other. God, he missed Scott.

He woke up with a heavy heart and when he got in the shower, his mind wandered to what must have happened in the dream before they lay there together. His hand moved across his body as he imagined Scott pushing his legs up against his chest to get a better angle, then entering him so gently and sweetly, kissing him all the time. Jamie's breaths grew shallow in the steam as his hand drifted lower and the vision continued, Scott thrusting against him as his head arched backward in pleasure and a moan escaped his lips. The vision was so real and Jamie was so hard. He stroked himself in the shower, wanting release, but wanting Scott even more.

In his mind, Scott's thrusts were long and steady but in reality, Jamie's hand moved quickly over his body, aching to get it finished and done with so he could move on to another day without Scott. He shut that thought out of his head and focused solely on what Scott must look like above him, kissing him on the lips, the cheeks, nibbling his neck and collarbone as he thrust, thrust. Jamie's hand grew sporadic and his body clenched. His cock exploded against the tile and he let out a long moan. Then it was over and he was spent.

After he was dressed and headed into Marisol's room to check on her, the warmth of his vision still lingered. He missed Scott more than he thought was possible and it was growing worse each day. Marisol said it was because they were a mated pair. She was suffering because she couldn't see Narné but when Jamie had brought it up to Ashton, who was in charge of when they could see their lovers, the older man had dismissed their concerns. Jamie respected Ashton, but he was beginning to resent the man greatly for keeping him and Scott apart.

Marisol was starting to show her pregnancy when Jamie went to check on her and a grin broke across Jamie's face. It was the first day he had been able to notice and the change was abrupt. She had assured him she was pregnant, but until there was visible proof the others wouldn't believe it. Many of the council who stopped by to pay respects to the queen secretly hoped she wasn't pregnant, Jamie knew, because if she wasn't pregnant than the mating flight was void and Marisol would have another mating flight and one of them might win it. Jamie was still frightened by how close he and Marisol had come to choosing someone besides Narné and Scott. They would have to be extra careful in future mating flights, because it seemed like the entire campus was determined to sleep with Marisol.

After brushing Marisol's scales to a sheen and giving her a kiss on the cheek, Jamie headed outside to meet up with his old roommate and best friend Amar and his girlfriend. Jamie still felt guilty about what he had put Amar through – during the mating flight, Jamie had summoned every dragon on campus to chase Marisol, including Amar's dragon Tephis. Amar had found himself in the awkward position of being filled with lust for his best friend – his male best friend – and things had been a little strange between them ever since. But Amar was a good friend and did his best to understand why Jamie had done what he did, and he knew that Jamie hadn't purposefully seduced him or even singled him out. Still, Jamie could appreciate how difficult it must be for a straight man to suddenly be lusting after his male friend for no apparent reason.

Amar's girlfriend had gotten him through the chaos after Jamie's mating flight. Jamie hadn't realized how much his mating flight would affect the campus, but it was worth it, he had come to decide. It was the only way he and Scott could have been together. Jamie headed towards the field beyond the football field to meet up with his friends. They weren't allowed near the dragon canyon and Jamie was still extremely curious what it looked like, but if he went any closer than this field one of the council members always seemed to appear out of thin air to stop him. He suspected it was because Scott was at the canyon and they were determined to keep the two of them apart, but he couldn't figure out the purpose of the isolation.

Still, he spent a great deal of time in the field longing to walk the final half-mile and see Scott. When Amar and Nikki had invited him to lunch he had demurred until they suggested a winter picnic in the field, since they knew he spent his time there. The weather was clear and relatively warm – a brisk 45 degrees – and he had agreed.

Nikki spotted him first and waved. She had a blanket spread out and pita and hummus set up for their picnic. She was vegetarian and Jamie had been learning to appreciate vegetarian food ever since he had tasted her food. He spotted her dragon curled up with Amar's dragon farther down the field and a flash of jealousy overtook him. Both dragons were deep blue, but Tephis, Amar's dragon, was exceptionally beautiful with dark spots over his eyes that looked like eyelashes and an exquisite pattern of stripes along his back. Yanna, Nikki's dragon, was an ordinary blue dragon and while beautiful, she couldn't compete with Tephis for beauty.

Jamie waved at them and trudged over, eyes on the dragons weaving their necks sinuously together, sharing Marisol's longing to do the same to Narné. It wasn't fair. He hadn't done anything wrong. The best dragon had won the mating flight, so how could the council complain? Shouldn't they be rewarding him for being so bold and opening the flight to all dragons? Why couldn't he see Scott? He grit his teeth together and forced a smile for his friends. Only a few more days, Ashton had assured him. Then he and Scott would be together again.

"How are you?" Amar asked. He was always sensitive to Jamie's moods and had been more so since the flight.

"Fine," Jamie said, trying to sound cool and casual. "You?"

Amar smiled uncertainly and Jamie wondered if it was residual emotions from the mating flight or if Amar was unsure how to treat such a vague comment. Either way, he must have decided that Jamie wasn't in the mood to talk about his emotions so he switched topics.

"We found out Tephis's talent today," he said with an undercurrent of excitement in his voice. "It'll revolutionize the campus!"

Jamie smiled sincerely. He doubted any dragon had the skill to fix the problems he had recently become aware of, but he wasn't going to tell Amar that.

"Tephis can look at a person and see their bond, or their potential for a bond. That means when the potential students come to campus next week, he'll be able to spot the ones who can bond with dragons and the ones that will die in the process. Councilmember Eric thinks we can cut casualties completely if we let Tephis into the student recruiting process."

Each of the students who had dragons with special talents had been assigned a councilmember to try and determine what talents their dragons had, and Eric always sounded kind. Jamie was willing to bet he didn't approve of keeping Jamie and Scott apart. Jamie thought about Tephis's gift and wondered if Ashton would allow it to be used. Tephis would probably need to be near the students to tell if they were capable of forming bonds and he hadn't mastered camouflage yet. Plus, what would happen with students like Jamie? When Jamie entered the academy, he had been a virgin and therefore unable to bond. Scott's slow seduction was the only thing that had allowed him to form a bond with Marisol. Would Tephis have seen his potential, or would the dragon dismiss him because he wasn't able to bond when he entered?

"That's great," Jamie said, knowing he had to say something.

"What's wrong?" Amar said. "This might mean that we won't lose anyone."

"What about people like me? The- the difficult cases."

It was the term the council used to describe virgins who didn't easily give up their virginity. Scott had been a difficult case as well, Jamie thought. Ashton had mentioned it at one point, but he had never said who the person was who finally seduced Scott. Jamie couldn't help but feel a little jealous of whoever that person was – he wanted Scott all to himself even though he hadn't been at the academy then.

"I don't know," Amar said slowly. "I hadn't thought of that. We'll have to test it, I suppose. Still, anything that prevents us from dying is a good thing, right?"

Jamie nodded and forced a smile. He glanced over at Tephis and Yanna. Amar followed his gaze and a lightbulb seemed to go off.

"Oh, you're missing Scott. I'm sorry. No wonder you're not excited. I know how hard this is for you."

"I only just got him back," Jamie said. "And then he's taken away again."

Jamie and Scott had been fighting before the mating flight after Jamie had discovered that Scott was assigned to seduce him and it wasn't a spontaneous act of love. Jamie had just forgiven him when the mating flight took place, and then they were separated for a month other than a brief reprieve on Christmas Eve. Jamie would forever be in Mike Ferrin's debt for that one night – the man had insisted that they spend the holiday together even though Ashton had seemed dead set against it. Jamie didn't know what strings Mike had pulled, but the memory of their time together Christmas Eve was one of the few things that kept him going.

And me, said an indignant voice in his head.

Jamie smiled. Marisol didn't often butt into his thoughts but this was probably deserved. Taking care of her the past month was a blessing and kept him pleasantly distracted from his separation. And now that he knew for sure she was pregnant, the council would have to acknowledge Scott and Narné as her mate.

"You seem pretty okay with it today," Amar said. There was a trace of guilt in his voice, because he was the one who instigated the fight between them. Jamie had since persuaded him that Scott was a good person, but Amar's insistence on Scott's guilt was one of the things that had prevented Jamie from forgiving Scott a lot earlier than he had.

"Marisol is pregnant," Jamie said. "She's showing."

Nikki and Amar both brightened.

"That's amazing!" Nikki said. Her dragon, though female, was infertile and unable to lay eggs.

"You're sure?" Amar asked.

"Positive."

"Then we both got good news today," he said with a satisfied smile. Tephis let out a happy snort that could be heard across the field.

"Yeah," Jamie said. "I guess we did."

"Have you told Ashton yet?"

"Not yet. I see him later today and I'll let him figure it out for himself. It's pretty obvious. They warned me that her belly would turn gold and it's definitely changed colors."

"How beautiful," Nikki whispered.

Jamie often wondered if she was jealous of Marisol, or even jealous of Tephis. Jamie and Amar could both talk to their dragons using telepathy and their dragons had special abilities. But Yanna was an ordinary dragon and Nikki could only communicate with her verbally. Yanna had no special abilities, although being a dragon was special enough for most people. There had to be some element of jealousy, but she seemed perfectly content.

There is a stranger coming, Marisol said abruptly.

Jamie squinted at the woods. "Hey, Tephis and Yanna should hide. Marisol says a stranger is coming."

"A stranger? How could anyone get onto the grounds?" Amar asked, but Tephis and Yanna were both vanishing quickly into the woods. They had all learned to hide in the woods, but Tephis had yet to master open fields. Most dragons were able to manipulate the minds of unbonded humans so that the humans didn't notice them, but it took a lot of practice and experience. Plus, some humans were immune, like Jamie. He had been able to see Narné even when Narné was hiding from him.

When the dragons were gone, they looked around for the stranger. Then Nikki let out a startled cry and pointed to the sky. There was a large dragon approaching, and Jamie didn't have to feel its mind to know that it didn't belong.

CHAPTER THREE

Arrival

Kale noticed three young people in the field as he prepared to land. He could just make out their dragons scrambling into the woods to hide. He had forgotten how rarely the campus had visitors. He had chosen the field because in mid-winter he hadn't figured that anyone would be out here, but the three of them had a blanket spread out and it looked like a picnic, of all things. He hopped off Vestis's back as soon as they hit the ground, hoping to calm the clearly panicked students. As he approached them, he was struck by how young they looked. The two men must have been freshmen, he thought, because they exuded youth. The girl seemed a bit older and appeared more collected than the others at the sight of a strange dragon.

As he walked towards them, his eyes caught the younger-looking of the two men and he froze midstep. This was the one. The one whose mating flight had summoned him from Washington DC. There was no question. That auburn hair hanging in loose locks around his face, the wide, innocent eyes and pouting lips. He could almost feel the start of arousal just looking at the face but he forced it away and continued to draw nearer to them. Men who were bonded to female dragons were rare, but Vestis assured him that the boy, Jamie, as Vestis informed him, was indeed bonded with a female.

He is bonded to the queen, Vestis said in awe. *He can speak to me the way you speak to me. He wishes to know who you are.*

Kale nearly stumbled. A queen? It had been decades since the academy had produced a queen, and that queen hadn't lasted long because the bond between human and dragon was so weak. But if this Jamie's bond was so strong that the mating flight could be felt thousands of miles away, it must be a true bond. The implications of the council getting their hands on a well-paired queen were shocking.

Let me introduce myself, Kale told Vestis, who tossed his head and curled up.

The children – for it was hard to think of such young-looking people as adults – looked nervous as he approached but they didn't run away. He studied Jamie until the boy blushed, then turned to examine the other two. The other man had a medium complexion and a hawk-like nose that fit his gleaming brown eyes, and the woman wore her blonde locks loose to her shoulders, framing a petite, pale face.

"My name is Kale," he said, extending his hand to Jamie first. "I'm a former graduate of the school."

The other man pulled Jamie back as if protecting him, then took Kale's hand. "I'm Amar. This is Jamie and Nikki. What are you doing here?"

Another man abruptly appeared in the field, trotting towards them quickly. When he caught sight of Vestis, however, his pace slowed. Kale felt his heart skip as he recognized the man. Ashton. One of the three students must have summoned Ashton. Kale had hoped to get settled before Ashton arrived, because there was always the chance that Ashton would kick him out. Or, worse, would insist that Kale take up his former position and share chambers with the man. Kale unconsciously fingered the gold chain around his neck. It was so dangerous coming back here when he was claimed by this man.

"Kale," Ashton said warmly, and embraced him.

Kale was stiff as Ashton held him close. He would not go back. He would not sleep with Ashton ever again. He would not become a sacrifice for the rest. He still remembered with vivid accuracy the day that Ashton had taken him to the volcanic crater and spoken of sacrifice, of helping the council maintain its power. He would never do those things for the council and it had taken all of his strength and skill to escape the campus afterward. Now he was back, and he was terrified that Ashton would pick up where they had left off.

"What brings you here?" Ashton asked.

"The mating flight," Kale said. Best to be direct and get this over with. He had never been able to lie to Ashton. "We all felt the queen's mating flight and I came to investigate."

"How did you know it was a queen?"

"I recognize the boy," Kale said, gesturing at Jamie who went pale and hid behind Amar. "And Vestis just informed me there is a queen here. Who else would have that kind of power?"

"Six years you've been gone," Ashton said, letting his hand trail across Kale's cheek and drop to the collar around his neck. "I thought you were hiding from us."

Kale blushed. Ashton's hand should not feel so good against his skin. He had been hiding, in a way. He had been doing the council's work indirectly – the council sent instructions to Vestis and Kale obeyed – but there had been no direct communication between Kale and the council in years.

"Please," Ashton continued. "Stay with us a while. There are rooms available in the apartments or in the canyon."

Kale let out a sigh of relief. Ashton wouldn't insist that he sleep with the man. He could have his own quarters and pretend not to be Ashton's favorite. Unless Ashton had a new favorite, he thought suddenly. A new favorite who was sleeping in Ashton's quarters, receiving Ashton's favors, being prepared for the same talk on the volcano that had scared Kale into running away for six years. If there was a new favorite, it was one more person Kale needed to save.

"The apartments would be nice," he said, wanting to be as far from Ashton as possible.

Jamie and the others packed up their picnic and followed Ashton and Kale back to the main campus. Vestis followed in the air above, and two beautiful blue dragons emerged from the forest to circle him. The smaller one, a male, was exceptionally gorgeous and must have belonged to Amar because he butted his head against Vestis playfully and had little of the seriousness that dragons developed as they aged. He seemed, if anything, determined to play with the much larger green dragon and wasn't going to take no for an answer. To Kale's surprise, Vestis let out a snort of amusement and gave in to the little blue, circling him and butting against him as if he were a hatchling again.

Kale and Ashton walked side by side with the other three following, but it was Jamie that Kale wanted to talk to. He slowed down and Ashton seemed to guess what he was doing because he gestured for Amar to take Kale's place at his side as they walked. Kale studied Jamie, who blushed and looked at the ground.

"I'm sorry," Jamie said. "I had no idea so many people would be affected."

"You have a powerful gift," Kale said, already thinking of all the ways the council could manipulate it. This boy had to break free from the council. "What is your dragon like? The queen?"

A bright smile lit his face and he looked at Kale fully for the first time. Despite being so young, he was truly beautiful, Kale thought idly. If Kale were a few years younger he would have pursued the boy himself.

"She's huge," Jamie said proudly. "Much bigger than the males. She barely fits in the apartment."

"Shouldn't she be in the canyon? I thought there was a special room set aside for the queen."

He wasn't actually sure whether or not that was true, since it had been so long since they had a queen, but the rooms in the canyon were consistently larger than the apartment. Surely the council knew this. They must have some reason for keeping the queen in the apartments and as the boy's face fell, he knew he had stumbled upon something.

"I can't go there yet," Jamie said. "Not until Scott is ready."

"Scott?"

"The queen's mate."

The phrase, so innocently uttered, sent Kale's heart pounding in a swift tattoo. The queen's mate. The only man equal to the council, a counter-balance to their power. Every rebel knew about it, but no one had ever suspected that a queen would be born, let alone live long enough to mate. And above all, no one had ever suspected that the council would let anyone claim the title of queen's mate. It was a title that reached back into Tarragon history, back when there were gatherings of dragons across the globe and each had their own queen and mate. Back then, the queen took care of her nest and the children and dragons who served her, while the queen's mate made sure that the outside world stayed away.

As the queens started dying off and weren't replaced, however, the last great queen's mate had formed a council of elders who would protect the dragons from the outside world. The mate ruled the council, but the council ruled the other dragons. When the last queen died, all power went to the council.

Having a new queen was change enough, but the queen's duties had always been at home and that was no real threat to the council's power. In fact, they were probably glad to cede the responsibilities to someone else, as many council members thought they distracted from their primary goal of manipulating world events. The queen was not a threat, but anyone who claimed the title of queen's mate was setting himself up to be the leader of the council and surely Ashton wouldn't allow that. Ashton was far too power-hungry to let anyone mess with his authority and Kale wondered what would happen to the unfortunate person who had made the mistake of claiming the powerful title.

"Do you know when Scott will be ready?" Kale asked, wondering if Ashton would ever let an intruder take the title.

"Soon," Jamie said with bright eyes. "Marisol will have to be moved soon."

Ashton, walking in front of them, must have heard the last comment because he turned and placed a casually possessive hand on the boy's shoulder.

"Why do you say that, Jamie?"

"She's showing," Jamie said happily. "Her scales turned to gold overnight."

Ashton's face went pale and it was interesting to watch, Kale thought. It was rare that the composed, powerful man ever showed emotion other than cruelty but he seemed genuinely concerned.

"We'll need to move her immediately. Today. I only hope it isn't too late."

"It isn't," Jamie said. "She said she can still move for a little longer."

Ashton turned to Kale. "Kale, I would love to show you to your quarters but there are things I have to do. I'll send someone to take care of you. Until then, please feel free to speak with Jamie and his friends, and meet the queen for yourself. She is quite impressive," he added with a smug smile, as if he had anything to do with it.

Kale nodded and watched the man head to the dragon canyon. He hoped Scott, whoever he was, was ready for Ashton because if he failed, Kale knew Ashton would have no qualms about killing him to prevent a threat from taking over the council. Silently, he prayed that this Scott would have the common sense to keep his head down and do whatever Ashton told him, because once the queen's mate was in place, the rebellion might gain a powerful new ally that could succeed where they had failed for decades.

CHAPTER FOUR

Ashton's Test

Scott listened to Mike list the council members and how to deceive them with more than a little awe. He had no idea that Mike had been playing a double-game, but Mike was a master at deception if what he was saying was true. And Scott had no reason to doubt him. His descriptions of the council members that Scott knew were spot-on and eerily accurate, and Scott had used some of the same techniques himself to avoid suspicion.

He remembered just a few weeks ago when he almost let slip to his instructor, a council member named Eric, that he was planning on violating the council's order and entering Marisol's mating flight. A bit of flattery and distraction had worked wonders, and that was the strategy Mike was outlining for most of the council.

Ashton was different, though, and Scott could see how much trouble Mike was having when talking about deceiving Ashton. He knew Mike and Ashton slept together, and he wondered if Mike realized that he wasn't deceiving anyone about his feelings for the man. When Mike mentioned Ashton's name, his face lit up and a small smile appeared at the corners of his mouth.

He was falling hard for the man but if what he was saying about Ashton's history was true, there was little chance the man shared his feelings. Ashton sounded like a cold-hearted killer, capable of wiping out most of the planet if he ever decided to flex the council's power. And yet Mike was caught by his superficial charm like a fly in a deadly spider's web, thinking he was in control while in reality the spider moved in closer for the kill with each passing second.

Scott hated Ashton. Not just for what the man was doing to him and Jamie, but also for what he was doing to Mike. Scott would never admit it to Mike but he cared for the man; after all, Mike had been his first. Even though their encounter was horrific and he still believed that Mike had raped him despite Mike's occasional protests otherwise, he still cared for the man. He didn't want to see Mike get hurt the way Scott had been hurt, and Ashton was only capable of harm.

"Just remember," Mike said. "Do whatever Ashton wants. You can manipulate the others but not him. He's too smart. He doesn't care about whether you truly respect him – appearance is everything. If you obey him in public, you'll be fine. Just don't question him or disobey him. That's how people get killed."

"Even if he asks me to do something I can't do?"

Mike was silent for a moment. "He'll push your limits," he finally said. "But he has a good sense of what will truly break people. He won't alienate you completely, he'll just punish you. After all, at some point he is going to have to acknowledge you as his equal, so there can't be too much bad blood between you."

"Let's hope you're right," Scott muttered. He could think of a thousand things Ashton could command that Scott would refuse, and he wasn't sure that Ashton would be able to think so clearly about their future relationship.

Narné lifted his head. *There is a stranger.*

"A stranger?" Scott repeated more for Mike's benefit than anything else. "Where?"

Heading to Jamie. He is not a threat, Narné added. *He brings hope.*

Mike was watching him, waiting for him to repeat what Narné said and he did, quickly.

"I have to make sure Jamie's alright," Scott said. "Even though

Narné says he's not a threat-"

"Trust your dragon," Mike said. "I'll go check on Jamie and you stay here. Or did you learn nothing from our lesson today? You can't see Jamie until Ashton gives you permission."

Scott stood and scuffed his toe against the ground, frustrated. "Fine," he said. "But have Eraxes tell Narné if anything is amiss."

"I will."

Mike headed out through the human door and Scott was tempted to tell him to ride Narné to the field where he knew Jamie was. It would get him there quicker and Narné wouldn't mind carrying him, but Narné snorted and told him again that the stranger was not a threat. He brought hope. Scott pondered that as he paced the room. He paced and paced, waiting for word from Eraxes. Nearly twenty minutes passed until there was a knock at the door. He exploded out of his pacing and opened the door, expecting to see Mike, Jamie, or the stranger. Instead, Ashton stood outside.

"May I come in?" Ashton asked, pushing against him and coming inside before he could respond. He knew his face was revealing his disappointment but didn't care. Ashton knew he wasn't on the list of people Scott wanted to see and even though Scott would do his best to obey Ashton, he didn't have to like it.

"Today is your test," Ashton said.

Abruptly, Scott straightened and invited Ashton inside properly, showing him to the living quarters and getting him a glass of water to drink at the man's request. The test. After a month had passed with no sign of the mysterious test that would allow him and Jamie together again, Scott had assumed that it would be put off indefinitely. He wondered if perhaps the stranger had something to do with the rush. Perhaps Ashton wanted the campus to be as strong as possible with a stranger on campus and he knew that the best way to do that was to allow Scott and Jamie to be together.

"What has Mike taught you?" Ashton asked.

Visions of the day's lesson flashed before his mind before Scott pushed them aside. Ashton didn't mean that; he meant what Mike had been teaching him this past month about Tarragon Academy and his role as the queen's mate.

"My role is to care for the queen and her partner," Scott began. "To make sure that she produces eggs, cares for her eggs, and to assist in the hatching of those eggs. In the future, I will also be in charge of preparing students for the first year exam and teaching students to bond with their dragons. I will be in charge of keeping track of all of the dragons after they leave the academy and making sure that they understand the laws protecting our existence."

He paused. There was so much more, so many intricate details about how to go about doing these things, but Ashton already knew the details. Currently the council was in charge of all of this and Mike hadn't really been able to tell him how much of this would fall to him and how much would remain with the council. Keeping track of graduates would almost certainly remain with the council, because it was how they maintained their grip over the major political figures across the globe. But the first-year exam would probably go to him, unless he delegated someone else to handle it. Mike had volunteered to take the job, since he was already doing it.

He wondered if he should expand on his knowledge, or add on about the more personal responsibilities that went with caring for the queen, but Ashton was nodding his head and looked satisfied. Apparently he had given a sufficient answer.

"You understand that not all of these powers will go to you?"

"Yes," Scott said. "The council was formed to take on these powers after the last queen's mate died, and they've handled everything for centuries."

Ashton paused. "You understand that your role will be subordinate to the council?"

Scott could almost hear Mike pleading with him to agree, but he couldn't do it. Not fully. "For now," Scott said. "I don't think I could take on all of the responsibilities now and I understand that I am subordinate. But I won't always be that way."

Ashton looked amused, not upset. "I see. Well, you have the correct knowledge to begin your duties, but your attitude is questionable. Your true test will take place next week."

Scott winced. Had he done that poorly? Another week without Jamie?

"There's a boy, the son of two graduates. He'll be starting at Tarragon Academy next fall and coming to the prospective student weekend next week. A virgin," Ashton said, emphasizing the word as Scott's heart sank. He already knew what was coming. "I want you to seduce him while he's here. His parents have requested it. You'll have two days, but if you fail, you'll go back into training and you won't see Jamie again for months."

Scott brightened slightly. "Does that mean I can see Jamie until then?"

"Yes," Ashton said. "As a gesture of the council's goodwill. But if you fail…"

Scott nodded. He wouldn't fail. He would have to explain it to Jamie, explain the deal he had made with the council all those months ago when he had promised to seduce other young men if they would assign him to Jamie exclusively. He hoped Jamie understood, but they didn't have much choice if they wanted to be together.

"I'll do it," Scott said.

"Good. Marisol and Jamie will be moved into these quarters later today. She's pregnant," he added casually. Scott's heart leapt.

"Pregnant?"

"Arion confirmed it. She'll need all of your attention, and Jamie's too. This is the first time a queen has been pregnant in centuries and I hope you realize that caring for her takes precedent over all of your other duties."

Scott nodded again. Ashton's message was clear. Scott would be acknowledged as the queen's mate as long as he didn't interfere with the council and limited himself to caring for Marisol. He didn't mind. He didn't want anything else – the thought of caring for Marisol as she gave birth to his and Narné's eggs was enchanting and he knew it would be a full-time job. According to Mike's lessons, Jamie was traditionally in charge of the pregnancy but he was so new to life as a dragon's partner he would undoubtedly need help and Scott was more than ready to be there. Despite the brief interlude with the other student's seduction.

"When can I see him?"

"Soon. I have business to attend to, but I expect you'll wait here until he arrives."

Scott heard the command in that suggestion.

"I'll get ready for Marisol and Jamie," he said.

A faint smile crossed Ashton's lips and the man ruffled Scott's hair affectionately. Scott tried not to react, but his distaste must have been obvious because Ashton chuckled.

"Mike has done a good job teaching you," he said. "I shall have to reward him. Your reward, Jamie, will be on his way shortly."

"Thank you," Scott said, pulling away from the man's touch as soon as was polite. Ashton smirked, then left the room. Scott grinned. Jamie was on his way!

CHAPTER FIVE

Dragon Canyon

Marisol flew to the canyon first, slowly lifting her red and gold body into the air and flapping her wings in steady, determined strokes so as not to disturb the eggs growing inside of her. She assured Jamie and the others that she was fine to move for several more hours. She was already a little grumpy about her upcoming days being unable to fly or move around while the eggs developed. No one knew how long her pregnancy would last, but Marisol thought it would be several months.

Jamie was bouncing on his toes as he packed his personal items. He was so excited he barely even thought about the stranger, who was now settling in next door after greeting Marisol and giving her an appropriate number of compliments. Amar and Nikki were back in Amar's room and for once Jamie wasn't jealous of the two of them together – in less than an hour he would be in Scott's arms again!

Most of the items in his apartment belonged to the academy, but some were personal items, such as his clothes, his books, and his computer. The computer was the most valuable thing he owned in terms of money and he packed it carefully before hesitating over an unopened box. Inside was something far more valuable to him than the computer, even though the computer had greater monetary value.

He opened the box and reached inside, pulling out the snow-globe and staring at it. Inside was a house with a tiny family out front. His father had given it to him after his mother had died. At first, the house had lit up when Jamie flipped a switch on the bottom and he often stared at the lit up house with the family outside, remembering what it was like to live a normal life.

After his father died, he had spent nearly every night with the snowglobe by his bedside, acting as a nightlight. His aunt had tried to get rid of it once and he had taken it back by force, nearly hitting her in the process. It was one of the reasons she hated him so much. Jamie flipped the switch on the bottom but as had been true for years, the little house no longer lit up. He had worn it out and new batteries didn't make a difference. The house and the people were trapped in darkness with the snow falling around them. Until now, Jamie thought. Now he had someone who loved him, someone who would be his new family. Scott couldn't replace his parents and he certainly didn't want him to, but he could be a support in the world.

Jamie carefully wrapped the snowglobe back in the bubble wrap and put it in the box. This was the only thing he cared about, the only thing that mattered from his old life. Everything else from his old life could be thrown away, even his computer, but he would never lose his memories of his parents. He would never forget what it felt like to be loved. And Scott would help him recapture that feeling every day for the rest of his life. Jamie closed the box again and carried it into the living room where his belongings were stacked in neat boxes.

It seemed like he had just unpacked everything and in reality, he had. He had only moved into this apartment a little over a month ago before the winter break. Some of his belongings were still in boxes and he was happy about that – less time packing, more time with Scott. The rest of his belongings were thrown into boxes haphazardly. He hoped this would be the last time he packed; he wanted to spend the rest of his life with Scott and couldn't imagine the council letting their queen leave.

According to his lessons with Ashton, the queen lived on campus her entire life and watched over the other dragons, while the queen's mate often traveled to protect the dragons who lived off campus. The council had taken over the queen's mate's job, and Jamie hoped that meant that Scott would be staying at his side.

A foolish grin lit his face as he pushed the last box into the hall where the movers waited. They were older students who had offered to help him move and they undoubtedly hoped to increase their reputations by helping the queen, but he barely even noticed them. All he cared about was that now that he was packed, he could go straight to the canyon without waiting for his things. He could see Scott, finally, for the first time since Christmas Eve.

His smile softened as he thought of Christmas Eve. Mike had pleaded with Ashton on their behalf and Ashton had finally caved and allowed them to be together. Scott had been so gentle with him, and so sweet as they lay together. Even though they knew their time was limited to a single night, that night had been perfect. He would forever be in Mike's debt, and Ashton's as well for allowing it. Now, though, they would have more than a night together. They would have a lifetime and nothing had ever felt as right.

Jamie started the hike across campus to the dragon canyon. He still hadn't seen it and was looking forward to it, but not nearly as much as he was looking forward to seeing Scott's smiling face. When he reached the field where he, Amar, and Nikki had begun their picnic only a few hours ago, he kept going, half-expecting a council member to appear and prevent him from continuing as they always did. But no one appeared, and he strode forward with rapidly increasing steps until he was nearly running. He reached the top of a hill and staggered to a halt. He had reached the dragon canyon.

It was incredible, like a vision from a dream or a movie. Dragons soared around freely, without fear of being spotted, and the sky was filled with blue and green blurs as they navigated the airspace. Some had humans on their backs, most didn't, but all moved with a sinuous grace that young Marisol had yet to gain. Along the walls of the deep canyon were rows and rows of holes cut into the rock: entrances for dragons into the housing that lined the walls. The canyon stretched far into the distance and Jamie couldn't even imagine how many rooms there were. Thousands, perhaps. Ashton had said that nearly two thousand dragons lived on or around the campus, but it was one thing to hear that number and another to see the living spaces and the majestic creatures filling the sky.

The canyon lay along the side of Mount Tarragon and Jamie knew from maps that it circled most of the mountain and had been built into the dragon canyon by centuries of dragon and human workers. At the highest point of the canyon, he saw a massive hole decorated with gold and silver. He knew without asking that this was the queen's quarters. His new home.

Jamie's hands trembled as he stared up at what would be his new home. Normally, he would have asked Marisol to carry him up, but she was already there and wasn't capable of flying much anyway due to her pregnancy. He would have to find the way up on his own.

"Beautiful, isn't it?" a voice asked.

Jamie turned to see a council member at his side. He was tall and handsome, incredibly well built with a chiseled face and chocolate hair that spiked upward. Jamie recognized him as Eric, the council member who worked with Amar.

"Yeah," Jamie said. "I'm not sure how to get around, though."

He felt a trace of embarrassment admitting that, but Eric was a teacher and teachers usually didn't mind helping others.

"There's a system of paths along the canyon. You're not afraid of heights, are you?"

He asked the last with a laugh and Jamie laughed too, but he wasn't sure if it was a joke or not. He wasn't afraid of heights, but the thought of climbing a rugged path up the side of a canyon was a little frightening.

Once he reached the path, though, he saw that he had nothing to fear. The path was wide and well-worn, and they weren't the only ones walking around. People stopped and stared at him as he went by, and Eric clasped a hand on his shoulder. Jamie wanted to shrink into his skin and hide.

"They know that you're partnered with the queen," Eric explained. "That's the only reason they're looking."

"You're sure it's not because of the mating flight?"

Jamie remembered what the stranger had said, that he had felt the mating flight even though he was far away. He had recognized Jamie instantly and Jamie was terrified that when he sent out the call to all of the dragons, his face had somehow been projected to them. Did everyone know him? Did they resent him for interrupting their lives with the mating flight? Did the straight men hate him for making them feel lust for a man? Amar had forgiven him, but even with him there was still an awkwardness. What about the others? When Jamie had opened his flight, he hadn't realized that thousands would respond. And if people off-campus had felt it, who knew how many people had been drawn into his lust?

Jamie slunk along the path. At least he would be with Scott soon. Ignore the rest, he told himself. Just think about Scott.

Scott is waiting for you, Marisol said. *He is very happy.*

Jamie smiled and tried to straighten his shoulders and ignore the looks everyone was giving him. Eric released his shoulder and gestured for him to take the lead down a pathway that had gold engravings along the wall.

"This leads to the queen's chambers," he said. "Your things will be along in about an hour. Congratulations on the pregnancy," he added.

"Thank you," Jamie said, hoping Eric knew he meant for the congratulations and for the help getting to his new rooms. He was grateful that Eric wasn't planning on coming in or even being at the door when he first saw Scott. He didn't want any distractions from his lover.

Eric left and Jamie went down the hallway until he reached an elaborate door with gold plating. Idly he wondered how much it was worth, but then his hand was reaching up of its own accord and he knocked. The doors opened and Jamie's face lit up. Scott was standing on the other side in loose black pants and a grey shirt with a fetching black vest. He looked healthy and happy, and his eyes glittered and reflected his joy more clearly than the grin on his face. He held his hand out to Jamie and Jamie took it. Scott pulled him into a hug and held him, Jamie's head cradled against his shoulder.

After several minutes just holding each other, Scott traced a finger along Jamie's cheek and pulled his face into a kiss: a chaste, sweet kiss. Jamie opened his lips against the kiss, wanting more, and Scott dove into his mouth and took possession of him. Scott gripped him tightly as if afraid that Jamie would disappear again, then began rubbing his hands against Jamie's body, sneaking under his shirt to rub against his bare skin.

Jamie moaned into the kiss and pushed them into the room further, pausing to close the door behind them. He barely looked around at all – his entire field of vision was Scott. Scott kissed him again and again, letting his hands explore the body that had been off-limits for so long. Jamie boldly slipped his hands under Scott's shirt to feel him as well, and the hard muscles twitched against his touch as if unused to such tenderness. Scott paused to take a breath and then he stripped his vest and shirt off, exposing his tan body. Jamie could feel himself hardening as he struggled to follow suit, but his hands were trembling too much and he got tangled into his shirt.

Scott laughed and pulled his shirt off over his head, then leaned down and kissed him on the shoulder, licking and biting the spot until Jamie moaned in pleasure. Scott held out his hand and gestured to what must be the bedroom. He hope Scott hadn't been waiting long, because he was ready for more. Jamie nodded and kissed Scott on the lips one more time before allowing the other man to lead him to the bedroom. Inwardly, his heart was glowing. He was with Scott again.

CHAPTER SIX

Ashton's Favorite

Mike headed straight towards the apartments where the stranger was settling in. He still didn't know anything about the man, but he had passed Ashton on the way and Ashton had warned him not to meet the stranger. Normally he would obey Ashton, but he had promised Scott to find out who the stranger was and his curiosity was a stronger force than obedience today.

The stranger's room was in the most luxurious open room, right next to Jamie's. Mike noted with pleasure that Jamie was moving out of his room; a note of concern also crept into his heart as he realized Ashton must have been heading over to the canyon to give Scott the test. He had no idea what kind of test it would be, but he knew it would test Scott's submission in addition to his knowledge. And Scott was not the type of man who submitted easily, even for something as important as this, even after Mike's warnings.

The fact that the stranger got such a nice room meant that he was important in some way, perhaps an honored alumni who was returning for a weekend – or longer – as occasionally happened. Mike knocked on his door and wasn't surprised when it opened immediately: the stranger was no doubt waiting for someone to show him around campus.

He was handsome, with a warm, wide face and shaggy hair that fell enticingly over his brown eyes. Despite his hair, however, his stance was all business and he held himself like a cop, or some other profession where body language could be the difference between life and death. But as soon as Mike's eyes got past that handsome face, all of the air left his body and he had to clutch the doorway to remain standing as his eyes fixated on the man's neck. There was a gold collar around his neck identical to Mike's, and there was only one place he could have gotten it. Did Ashton have two pets?

"Are you all right?" the man asked. He reached out to help Mike and Mike was too stunned to shove the offending hand away. The man drew him into the room and then seemed to notice the collar around his neck.

"Oh," he breathed. "He did pick another."

Mike felt something snap within him. "I am not *another*. I am his, and I don't know who you are but you are not welcome here."

"You're Mike, right? I remember you from school. You were a year younger than me. I'm Kale."

Mike scowled, mentally placing the handsome man. He did remember Kale, but the man had grown more beautiful with age. He also remembered that immediately after graduation, when Mike had left for a few years before he returned to teach, Kale had stayed on campus. Was that when Ashton had made him his favorite? And was he still Ashton's favorite? Unfamiliar jealousy was eating away at him as he remembered Ashton telling him not to bother the newcomer. Did Ashton not want him to know that he didn't really matter, that he was about to be replaced?

Kale fingered his collar and Mike scowled further. He should be the only one able to do that. He should be the only one wearing Ashton's mark. He should be the only one in Ashton's heart.

"Look, Mike, I don't know how much Ashton has told you but this collar doesn't mean what I think you think it means. It doesn't mean anything good."

A shimmer of hope spun down into Mike's jealous heart.

Perhaps Kale hadn't appreciated Ashton the way Mike did, and that's why he had left. Perhaps Ashton hadn't cared for Kale the way he cared for Mike. Because he did care for Mike, Mike assured himself. He did so many little things for Mike, and let him sleep with him every night. It had to mean something.

"Maybe not for you," Mike said. "But for me it means everything. I'm sorry I intruded. I'll be leaving now."

"Wait, Mike. We need to talk more."

Mike sniffed and turned his back on the man. He ignored Kale's offers of conversation and left the apartment, shutting the door firmly behind him and getting into the elevator without a word. Two students were moving some of Jamie's boxes and they smiled at him shyly.

"Hi, Mr. Ferrin," the girl said.

"Good morning, Greta. Helping out with the move? That's awfully generous of you."

"It's nothing, really. I just wanted to meet the queen and her partner."

"Did you get a chance to see the queen?"

"Yes," Greta said, eyes lighting up. "Just before she flew to the canyon. She's incredible. Do you think next year's students will choose her eggs?"

"I think a lot of people are asking that question," Mike said with a smile.

Marisol's pregnancy must be showing; that was the only thing that would cause Ashton to let Jamie and Scott move in together. But the thought of Ashton, normally such a pleasant thing, brought an unpleasant chill to his heart now. Kale had the same collar and had undoubtedly shared the same perks that he now enjoyed, yet Kale had left the academy and Ashton for years, long before Mike returned. Why had he left? He needed to talk to Ashton, and he hoped Ashton would be open with him.

He reached Ashton's chambers but no one was inside. He

reached out to Eraxes, who said that Arion was greeting the new dragon, Vestis. Mike felt his hands clench into fists and he looked around for something to punch. He had just settled on the stone wall when the door opened and Ashton's familiar form strode in.

"Good morning, Michael. I was just about to look for you. You did an exceptional job training Scott and I think you need a reward."

His voice was light and lilting and Mike smiled despite himself, but Ashton must have noticed his distress.

"What's wrong?"

"I met Kale."

Ashton's smile vanished. "I told you to leave him alone."

"I was curious."

"Of course you were," Ashton said wearily, wiping a hand across his forehead. "Well, I don't know what he told you-"

"He didn't tell me anything," Mike said, spinning to face Ashton. "What I saw was enough. He had – this thing," Mike grabbed his collar and lifted it, not sure whether to call it a necklace or collar.

"You didn't talk to him?"

For some reason, Ashton sounded relieved.

"I thought I was – I thought we were-"

Mike trailed off, his eyes filling with tears. It felt so stupid to say all of this out loud. Of course Ashton would have other lovers. He was notorious for the number of lovers that he took. He and Arion frequently took part in mating flights across campus, but Mike had thought they were different, special. After all, Arion hadn't been in a single mating flight except Marisol's since Ashton had given Mike the collar. And while Mike had at first thought negatively of the collar, he now viewed it as Ashton's pledge to him, a pledge to be loyal and loving. With that pledge broken, his whole world was falling apart and there was no one to catch him.

"Hush," Ashton said, swiftly enveloping Mike in his strong arms and pulling Mike's head beneath his as he cradled Mike. "Kale didn't appreciate what I gave him, but he left before I could take my gift back. It means nothing, pet. You are my only concern."

Mike clutched Ashton desperately, needing his words to be true with a ferocity that surprised him. He knew Ashton was a liar, but these words rang with truth. He believed Ashton. Needed to believe Ashton. A tear fell, then another, as Mike relaxed into Ashton's arms. Ashton murmured comforting words until Mike's tears stopped and he gained control of himself again.

Kale was nothing, he assured himself. A past lover. Of course Ashton would have them, but he had never thought he would react with such jealousy or anger. But it was alright; the man meant nothing now. Mike was Ashton's only lover.

Ashton pulled Mike's head back until they were face to face and wiped his tears with his thumbs. There was a sincerity in his gaze that nearly broke Mike's heart and he knew he would never doubt Ashton again.

"Are you alright now, pet?"

"Yes," Mike whispered.

"I was going to reward you," Ashton said with a mischievous smile. "But since you disobeyed me perhaps I should punish you instead. Which would you prefer?"

Mike's mind flew back to the spanking Ashton had given him once, and the incredible pleasure he had gotten from it. He felt his cheeks flush and knew he would never be able to verbalize the request, or even think it to himself, but the thought of Ashton's hand on him was irresistible. He felt like he needed to be punished for thinking such unloyal thoughts about Ashton.

Luckily, Ashton seemed to know exactly what he was thinking because his smile widened to a grin and he pointed to the bed.

"Strip and lay down. Let's see how much punishment you need."

Mike was already hard as he obeyed, and he lay on his belly as he watched Ashton undress in a more leisurely fashion. Despite his age, Ashton was incredibly toned. Being partnered with a dragon extended life and youth, so no one knew exactly how old Ashton was. Most people estimated that he was at least a century old, but Ashton himself never spoke on the issue and instead let his age add to the air of mystery that surrounded him as the head of the council.

His muscles were hard and rippled under his body as he stripped, making a show of it once he realized Mike was watching. Mike held his breath as his pants and underwear came off and his penis was slowly exposed. The first time he saw it he had been frightened, on his knees and exposed before the entire council. Now he was alone with Ashton, far more experienced, and he could admit that he loved Ashton's cock more than any other. Sometimes he would feel an ache in his body and know that only Ashton could soothe it, and he would have to hope Ashton was in a soothing mood. He closed his eyes and inhaled deeply, searching through the scents of the room for the familiar musk of Ashton. It grew strong quickly and he opened his eyes to see Ashton right in front of him, erect cock nearly touching his lips.

"Here, pet," Ashton said, grabbing Mike's hair and tilting his head to achieve the best angle for sliding his cock down Mike's throat.

Mike knew better than to struggle; Ashton knew what he was doing. Instead, he attempted to make himself comfortable and luxuriated in the feel of the smooth, musky flesh filling his mouth and throat. He made circles with his tongue along Ashton's shaft as the man thrust in and out slowly and Ashton petted his head. It was difficult taking it in so far but Ashton kept his hand on Mike's head and guided him when his gag reflex kicked in, refusing to let him withdraw. He breathed through his nose as much as he could, but soon black stars were dancing across his vision and he knew he needed air. But Ashton was close – his eyes were shut and his head thrown back as he thrust in deep and moaned.

The base of Ashton's cock spasmed and something wet splashed down his throat. Mike gagged, then swallowed. It tasted of musk and salt and it was exactly what he needed. Ashton pulled out and Mike inhaled deeply to get rid of the stars in his vision.

"Good boy," Ashton murmured. "Now let's start your punishment."

CHAPTER SEVEN

Reunion

Scott could feel Jamie quivering with excitement as he pulled the young man into the bedroom and straddled him on the bed. Jamie's face was flushed and Scot was intensely aware of Jamie's hard on, as it matched his own. He had dreamed of this moment for so long, ever since Christmas Eve. He leaned in to kiss Jamie sweetly but Jamie yanked him tight and responded with a desperation that surprised Scott. Jamie must have missed him more than he had anticipated and was prepared to skip the foreplay, because he was already pulling at Scott's pants and his own.

In minutes they were naked together and Jamie rubbed against him and moaned. Scott kissed his beloved Jamie's shoulder and sucked hard enough to leave a mark. He wanted the whole world to know that Jamie was his, and they would belong to each other forever. Jamie tangled his legs around Scott's and arched his back.

"In me," he whispered. "I want to feel you."

Jamie's words sent his cock twitching and without thinking he lifted Jamie's legs to get a better position as he pressed against Jamie's opening.

"Relax," he whispered.

"Faster," Jamie whispered.

He wanted to go slow – after all, this was only Jamie's third time and he knew the experience was still new and painful, but

Jamie's words drove him forward and he plunged into the sweet tightness of Jamie without thinking. Jamie cried out but when Scott tried to stop, he pressed himself against Scott and whimpered for him to go faster, harder. He could feel Jamie's lust in his mind as clearly as he could feel his own and as he finished sliding inside, their minds connected and both men gasped at the unexpected pleasure. Scott was within and without, penetrating and being penetrating, and he instinctively began thrusting into Jamie as sweat poured off both of their bodies.

Scott leaned up to get a better position and ran his hands over Jamie's chest, pausing to massage the man's nipples and tweak them, feeling phantom hands tweaking his own nipples through the intimate bond that had formed between them. He could feel Jamie's astonishment and explosive pleasure as he continued slow, steady thrusts that had them both panting. He knew they were both close to completion but he wanted to extend it, wait for release until they couldn't bear it anymore and the pleasure overwhelmed them. He slowed further and Jamie squirmed beneath him, desperate for his strokes. Scott threw his head back and moaned as the doubled sensations increased in intensity. Then he let himself fall forward onto his lover and kissed Jamie fiercely, finally giving in to his body's desires and increasing his speed. Jamie shifted beneath him in perfect harmony and for a long moment their rhythm was flawless.

Then Jamie cried out and his cock spasmed. The incredible sensation of Jamie's orgasm pushed Scott over the edge and he plunged deep into Jamie as his own cock exploded like strings of pleasure being pulled out of him into his lover. Black spots appeared in his vision and he kept kissing Jamie again and again until the pleasure subsided and he went limp.

Neither of them moved or spoke for a long moment. Their minds were still connected but they were too spent for words, and all that Scott could manage was a muzzy happiness and pleasure at being with his beloved again. After several moments passed, Scott reluctantly pulled out of Jamie, trying to be as gentle as possible. The connection between them broke, but Scott didn't need to feel Jamie's mind to know how he felt. Satisfaction was written across the young man's face, his eyes shut and a small smile playing around the edges of his mouth.

"Feel good?" Scott asked, rearranging so that he was spooning his Jamie.

Jamie cuddled against him and nodded.

"I missed you so much."

"Me too," Scott whispered. "But we're together again, forever."

"Just us," Jamie said. "No one else will ever come between us."

Scott was grateful they were no longer connected, because his mind went to the boy he was supposed to seduce. The boy wasn't a threat to their love, but he would come between them.

"What's wrong?" Jamie asked, twisting out of his arms to face him.

"Just thinking," Scott said. "Jamie, there's something we need to talk about."

"I knew it," Jamie said, sitting up and distancing himself from Scott. "I knew they wouldn't let us be happy together. You're not leaving, are you?"

"No, sweetheart, I'm here to stay. But if I want to stay, there are certain things that I agreed to do. I agreed before I was with you, in order to be with you."

"What things?"

"There's a boy coming to the student orientation. I have to seduce him."

Jamie went pale, then turned his back to Scott. Scott put his hand on Jamie's shoulder, desperate to see what Jamie felt about this, what he thought, but Jamie shoved his hand away.

"Don't touch me," he hissed.

Scott felt a trickle of fear run down his spine. He had not expected this extreme a reaction.

"How could you touch me, knowing this? How could you pretend to love me, knowing you would cheat on me? How could you do this to me?"

Jamie whirled to face him on the third question and there was open rage in his eyes, along with the fear and betrayal that Scott had expected. Scott backed to the edge of the bed, the remnants of their lovemaking cold between them.

"I trusted you," Jamie continued. "I thought I could count on you. I thought it would be us against them. How can I possibly do all this alone, without you?"

"You aren't alone," Scott said. "You'll never be alone. I'll always be with you."

"Yeah, when you aren't off with some other boy."

The statement stung because he knew it was true. Ashton could extend his test infinitely, make him a whore for the council, and he would have no real recourse or way to object. If he wanted to stay with Jamie, he would have to obey.

"What would you want me to do? Refuse? The only reason you and I are together right now is because I agreed."

"No, the only reason is because Marisol is pregnant with Narné's babies and no one would dare risk her health by keeping her in the apartments."

"Jamie, they would have had me move out if I didn't agree."

Or worse, he thought. Ashton might have sent him away from campus, or even killed him. Who knew what the limits of that man's evil were, now that Mike had warned him about Ashton's duplicitous and corrupt nature?

"But you said you agreed before you even met me."

Scott winced. "Yes," he admitted. "In order to be assigned to you, I had to agree to certain things. This was one of them."

"One? This was just one of them? What else did you agree to? What other bombshells are you going to drop?"

"The others don't matter. I had to switch instructors for

my dragon training class and, well, I had to sleep with my new instructor."

Jamie flinched. "Who was it?"

"Does it matter?"

"Isn't Eric your instructor?"

Scott nodded. It hadn't been an unpleasant experience. Eric hadn't seemed to understand the command, either, but had followed it gently and Scott had been grateful for his kindness. Because Eric had been so gentle with him, there was very little awkwardness between them. In fact, most of the time Scott didn't even remember that he slept with the man. He trusted Eric in a way that he didn't trust any other council member. In fact, he was almost looking forward to see him again for their lessons. Eric was a good person put in a bizarre situation, and Scott hoped Jamie didn't form any negative impressions of him.

"Eric helped me get here," Jamie said. He didn't sound as angry. "He seemed like a good person."

"He is," Scott said.

"So you have to sleep with whoever the council wants, whenever they want?" Jamie shook his head. "No. I can't live with that. If they want me as their queen, they're going to have to change that."

"Jamie, they've only asked me this one time. We can get through it."

"And the next time? And the one after that? They won't stop, you know it as well as I do. They want us apart and every time I imagine you with someone else-"

He shuddered.

"Just this once, Jamie," Scott promised. "I can't refuse. But after this, we'll talk to them. Together. We'll make them see that this can't continue. Is that okay?"

"Will you enjoy it?"

Jamie stared at him with vacant, vulnerable eyes from across the bed and in an instant, Scott was cradling him. "Of course not. You're the only one that I love, the only one that I want. I'll do what I promised I would do, and nothing more."

A tear ran down Jamie's cheek. "When is it happening?"

"Next week. They arrive on Thursday and stay until Sunday. Sometime in there."

"I don't want to see you during that time. I don't want to see him. I don't want to know about it."

"All right," Scott said, still cradling his lover as more tears came and Jamie began to sob.

"How can this happen? I just got you back, again, and already they're pulling us apart. Why can't we have any happiness?"

"We will have happiness," Scott said firmly. "But it looks like we'll have to make it ourselves and not wait for it to arrive. Classes start tomorrow. Do you want me to wait for you after your classes the way I used to?"

"Is that how you'll meet him?"

The silence stung. Jamie knew exactly how to hurt him. He remembered how carefully he had seduced Jamie, but it had been done with love in his heart, nothing else. He had waited outside Jamie's classes, met him for lunch, and eventually started hanging out after class. And then one day, Jamie had initiated things and confessed his feelings. Scott still remembered the joy he had felt when Jamie admitted that he had feelings for Scott, and he could finally confess that he loved the younger man. Things had moved rapidly from there, interrupted by the eggs hatching and Jamie nearly dying, and then Jamie had discovered that Scott had been assigned to seduce him and they had fought. Just when they made up, the mating flight had started and afterwards they were separated again. And now, when they were finally together for what looked a more permanent basis, Ashton's test was going to drive them apart. He was not about to let that happen.

"It doesn't matter how I'm going to meet him," Scott said,

kissing Jamie's forehead. "We have five days until it happens and we're going to make each one count."

Jamie nodded, but pushed him away. "Maybe you should check on Marisol. This fighting isn't good for her."

Scott stood up. Jamie probably needed some time alone to process everything that was happening. He went to the bathroom and cleaned himself up before getting dressed, and in the bathroom he stared at himself in the mirror. He didn't deserve someone as sweet as Jamie, and he had no idea how he was lucky enough to have captured Jamie's heart, but he would do everything in his power to protect Jamie. He just wished there were more that he could do, and that it didn't involve sleeping with other men. He shook his head and pulled on his clothes. Once dressed, he went to the dragons' chamber where Marisol was still getting settled.

Marisol had found her way to the massive queen bed and Narné was cuddled around her the same way Scott had been cuddled around Jamie before the argument. Since the dragons were affected by the emotions of their partners, they had undoubtedly been affected by the sex, though oddly the argument didn't seem to have registered. Scott had forgotten how strongly the dragons would be affected by his and Jamie's actions and made a note to himself to remember to warn the dragons before they made love again. He hoped they didn't mind, because he wasn't about to stop sleeping with his love just because it made them uncomfortable.

We will deal with it, Narné said in an amused voice. *You have more pressing matters. Is Jamie all right?*

"I was hoping you could tell me," Scott said.

Marisol says Jamie is resilient and he loves you, Narné said.

Scott reached up to rub his dragon's neck and plant a kiss on Marisol's large cheek. She was more beautiful than ever: far larger than Narné and a brilliant red except for her belly, which shimmered gold with her pregnancy.

He wondered what her eggs would be like, and when she would lay them. Would she fly away to one of the nesting grounds, or would she lay them here in the canyon? No one knew for sure what happened since it had been so long and the ancient records gave conflicting reports and the previous queen wasn't a good comparison. And would the new freshmen go to her eggs, or to the other eggs?

It was common knowledge that the longer an egg had been in a nesting ground, the stronger the dragon. When students went out to find their dragon partner, students who ended up in ancient nesting grounds nearly always ended up with dragons who had special abilities, including the ability to speak telepathically to their dragon. However, records from the days when queens were common stated that everyone could speak to their dragons like that, and the newest dragons were the strongest.

The subject was covered in one of the advanced history classes and Scott's teacher had come to the conclusion that eggs were extremely potent for about a year after hatching, then they lost their potency and it was only regained as decades passed and the egg absorbed energy from the surrounding environment. He had never been able to prove it, of course, because there were no eggs to test, but it was a commonly held belief. If it were true, and if the next class of students ended up at Marisol's eggs, then the academy was about to get an extremely powerful class of students. Usually only one or two students had dragons with special abilities; with Marisol's eggs, the entire class of one hundred students might have a chance.

Stronger students, of course, meant a stronger academy and stronger graduates, which made the council even stronger. Scott wondered if Mike and the rebellion he claimed to represent had thought of that, or if they were too delighted about the queen to think of the possible repercussions. He wasn't sure how he felt about the rebellion: on the one hand, he despised Ashton and wanted him gone, but on the other hand he hated the fact that they had sent Mike without any backup to do their work.

Unless the newcomer was backup, he thought. He hadn't heard anything about the stranger yet except Narné's assurances that he brought hope, and hope was exactly what was needed to save Mike.

A polite knock sounded at the door and Scott opened it to find several of his classmates outside carting Jamie's things. He helped them move everything inside and thanked them before shooing them out. He found a place for Jamie's computer and set it up, then went through the other boxes and put away as much as he could. The clothes were easy, as were the kitchen items, but some of it he didn't know what to do with. Mostly sentimental things. He paused over a snow globe. There was a switch at the bottom but it must have been broken because nothing happened when he switched it on. It seemed important, though, so Scott brought it to the bedroom and set it on the dresser.

He then turned to the bed and his face relaxed into a smile. Jamie was asleep, sprawled on his back, half-covered by the comforter, with just a hint of a snuffling snore escaping on every other breath. It was the most beautiful sight Scott had ever witnessed and he knew he would do anything to keep Jamie safe so he could sleep with this abandon. Scott got into the bed and Jamie curled onto one side as if inviting Scott to spoon, and Scott happily obliged after brushing a strand of hair from Jamie's forehead and planting a kiss. He had never felt so happy or fulfilled in his life, but he could feel an edge of terror and fear in his happiness. On Thursday, this happiness would vanish and only time would tell if Jamie would be able to accept him after he had been in another man's bed. He cursed Ashton as he shut his eyes and tried to focus on the beautiful love in his arms.

CHAPTER EIGHT

The Best of Them

Kale paced his room after Mike left, wondering if there was even a chance of saving him. Mike seemed entirely under Ashton's control. Kale took a deep breath and tried to calm himself, but inside his heart was falling to pieces. He felt lonely, in a way he never could have imagined. It was being back in this place, he knew. Once, he had friends here, and lovers, and warm memories. It had all ended when Ashton had taken him to the top of the volcano and told him that he wanted Kale to sacrifice his life for the sake of the academy. He shivered as he remembered how he had seriously considered killing himself to please Ashton. But instead he had fled, and now almost everyone who had helped him leave was gone, either killed or run away themselves. Now this place was a tomb and he couldn't bear to be back here alone.

There was a knock at the door and he opened it, bracing himself to see another unfamiliar face or, worse, a familiar face twisted under Ashton's control. Instead it was Eric, the only person who had helped him run who was still here. They shook hands formally, then Eric hugged him and Kale clung to him for a long moment, needing the reassuring touch of another person in this lonely place that had once been his home.

"Kale, I'm so glad to see you. I never thought I would see you again."

"I had to return, after the mating flight. I knew another boy was in trouble and I had to help."

Eric squeezed him gently and pushed him far enough away to meet his eyes. "Jamie isn't in trouble, Kale. He's holding his own."

"What about his mate? I heard they're not allowed to see each other and I can't imagine Ashton allowing someone to take the title of Marisol's mate without a fight. And what about Mike?"

Eric's face twisted into a disapproving frown. "What Ashton does with Mike is not my concern."

"But you're worried, aren't you? He'll do the same thing he tried to do with me, only Mike will do it. Mike will kill himself to help Ashton."

"I doubt Mike will go to that extreme," Eric said. "I think he'll react the same way you did. But I don't think it'll get that far. If their relationship gets out of control, the council will step in. The council may have looked away in the past, but we won't anymore. Not after you."

"Ashton will kill again. He said it's the only way the academy can survive."

"Ashton lies. The academy survives because of the dragons, not because of some volcanic ritual."

Kale was silent. The memory of the volcano was clear. Ashton had flown him to the peak of the mountain on Arion's back, telling him he had a special treat. But Ashton had intended to fly back alone.

Tarragon Academy was built on the slope of Mount Tarragon, an occasionally active volcano just outside of Portland, Oregon that was continually surrounded in a mist that prevented outsiders from coming on its grounds and discovering its secrets. Most people in Portland didn't even know it existed, or if they did they falsely assumed they were looking at Mount Hood. It seemed impossible that such an enormous mountain could exist so close to a large population center, but Ashton explained that the mountain had been the home of the Tarragon tribe for thousands of years and the ancient Tarragonians had used magic to seal the mountain in mist as protection for the dragons.

In modern times, Ashton explained that the protection of the mist only worked if the ancient magic was revived every once in a while, and it could only be revived with a blood sacrifice. Ashton told him that the only way for the academy to survive and remain protected from the outside world was for Kale to sacrifice himself to the volcano. Since there was no longer any lava at the volcano as there had been in ancient times, he would have to slit his own throat to appease the ancient magic.

He had loved Ashton and he had raised the blade to his throat, but just before he pressed against his skin, he thought of his dragon. He knew he had to say good-bye to his dragon first, so he begged Ashton to let him leave and return. He had sworn to return, promised that he would come back, and Ashton had let him go. But when he reached Vestis, the dragon had lifted him into the air and refused to land until he came to his senses. Confused, he had gone to Eric to ask for guidance and Eric had sent him to several other people, now dead, who had smuggled him and Vestis out of the campus.

And now he was back, as he had promised Ashton so long ago. Kale's mind caught on the way Eric had phrased his response – the council had looked the other way in the past.

"Were there other boys before me?"

"Every few decades, Ashton would choose a pet. Most of the time, that boy would go on to join the council. But every once in a while, he would disappear and his dragon would die. But there was never any proof that Ashton was involved in the deaths, not until you. Now that we know he's the cause, he won't get away with it."

"But how will you stop it? You're certainly doing nothing to separate Ashton and Mike."

"It will work itself out."

Kale shook his head at the callousness Eric was displaying. Had Eric really become so immune to Ashton's evil in the last few years, or were there protections in place that he couldn't talk about with Kale? He hoped for the latter, because he couldn't bear the thought of Eric becoming an unfeeling monster like most of the council seemed to be.

"And the queen's mate? Will that work itself out as well?"

"It already has. Jamie and Scott are together again as we speak. Scott won't be allowed to take on the position of queen's mate until he's a bit more mature, of course, but we would wait for anyone his age. His dragon is still perfecting fire-breathing and is only on the brink of full maturity, and he's still a student, a junior, not ready for the responsibility."

Kale nodded. That actually sounded reasonable. He hadn't realized the other boy was so young. It must kill Ashton to have been beaten in a mating flight by someone with so little experience, he thought, and Ashton was a vengeful person. He would find ways to make the boy's life miserable. Perhaps Kale would find him to be a sympathetic listener, since everyone else on campus seemed to be completely under Ashton's spell. He had expected it from Eric, since Eric was on the council and that required obedience to Ashton, but Mike's attitude had surprised and disappointed him. Even Jamie, in the brief moments they had talked, seemed to not recognize Ashton's duplicitous nature. There had to be someone on the campus who could hear the truth about Ashton, and Kale was determined to find them and help them, if they needed it. His nature demanded it.

He was still committed to helping Jamie, of course, since the boy would need all the help he could get with a pregnant queen dragon, a complete lack of knowledge about Tarragon society, and the council trying to manipulate him. But now his help was likely to extend to Jamie's mate as well, and perhaps to Mike if Mike wanted the help. He knew deep down that Mike was the one he wanted to help the most, but he knew that Mike couldn't be helped if he had fallen in love with Ashton, as Kale had done when he was Ashton's pet. A man in love was difficult to reason with and if Mike saw him as a threat, there wasn't the slightest chance of helping him.

"Would you like to see the campus?" Eric asked, snapping him out of his reverie abruptly.

"I'd love to," Kale replied, even though he didn't care.

Seeing the place where he had once been a carefree boy would be difficult, but necessary. His past was dead and gone, and all that remained was the loneliness and isolation he felt in this awful place, surrounded by people who were blind to the obvious truth all around them. But perhaps he would find someone who saw past the shining exterior into the gritty realism and he could help them escape before the council ensnared them in promises and oaths.

He was one of only a handful of graduates who had never taken an oath to the council and he worried that they would take this chance to rectify that, but he would leave rather than swear obedience to them. They were corrupt and he would never serve them, especially since they had a tendency to kill or cripple anyone who disobeyed them. Graduates of Tarragon Academy were some of the strongest, wealthiest, and most powerful people in the world but all of them were bound by their allegiance to the council. All except Kale and the few others who ran away.

Eric led him around campus, showing him improvements from when he was a student: larger apartments for students, new dorms, improved classrooms with high-tech equipment, everything a college needed to keep up in the fast-paced world around it. Whoever was in charge of keeping the college current was doing an excellent job, and as Eric explained their courses it sounded like students received an education equivalent to any traditional college, with the added benefit of learning about dragons as well. It was no wonder graduates of the school went on to become successful in whichever field they chose, because the college had everything a student could want.

Kale knew that a group of prospective students was coming soon to examine the college and spend the night in the empty dorms, seeing what it would be like to be a student at Tarragon Academy. The dragons would all be hidden, of course, and students were forbidden from mentioning anything having to do with dragons. Communication into and out of the campus was forbidden as well, and there was no cellular reception or internet on campus, which probably scared off some prospective students, Kale guessed. But knowledge had to be tightly controlled, especially in this day and age, when the slightest slip could have drastic and immediate effects if students could access their usual information channels.

He realized he was fingering the collar around his neck as they walked, and he snapped his hand to his side. He had managed to forget about the collar these past few years working in the White House and no one had ever asked him about it, but now that he was so close to Ashton he could feel it tingling against his skin. He thought of Mike again, and how proud Mike had been of his collar. Had he ever been like that, proud of his own degradation, proud of the collar that was intended to lead to his death? He hoped not. But he remembered how the council had looked at him in those days, as if they knew something he didn't, as if they were mocking him for his love of Ashton. They had known what Ashton intended to do, he was sure of it. And everyone except Eric was content to let it happen.

As the tour of campus finished, Eric brought him back to the apartments and kissed him softly on the lips. Kale returned the kiss hungrily, needing to feel the one man who had always respected him and listened to him. When they broke apart, there was a sadness in Eric's eyes.

"I know I've disappointed you," Eric said. "But you don't understand what it's like to live here. You escaped. I never can."

"You'll never disappoint me."

Eric laughed. "I know you're lying, remember?"

Kale stroked his cheek and kissed him again. Eric and his dragon had an extremely useful yet limited gift: he could tell when someone was lying, but only if he had slept with that person. Kale knew that his gift was the reason he had been admitted to the council in the first place, and he knew that Eric had slept with almost everyone the council considered dangerous. His gift gave them warning when any of their enemies started plotting against them.

No one outside of the council was supposed to know about his gift, but he had told Kale when he helped Kale run away. It was one of the things that bound them together, because Kale's ability to sense danger to those he cared about was very similar. Luckily, though, Kale didn't need to sleep with his targets, only care about them. He was one of the best bodyguards in the business because of this sixth sense, and it was why he was the President's personal assistant. Or had been, before this vacation that he sensed would become a permanent break from his previous life. There were too many people in danger here, people he needed to protect.

"You're still the best of them," Kale said, stroking Eric's face. "And you know that's true even without your gift."

Eric kissed him again, and then left. Kale stared at the room he had been assigned and collapsed into an armchair. He was alone again, but with Eric nearby he wasn't as alone. Eric had disappointed him, but the man was right: he couldn't escape. Would the same thing happen to the sweet freshman bonded to the queen? Would young Jamie become as hard-hearted and callous as the council just from living in a world corrupted by Ashton? There had to be others on campus who hated Ashton as much as he did, and Kale was determined to find them.

CHAPTER NINE

Preparations

Mike stood in front of the class and lectured on the importance of keeping dragons a secret from the soon-to-arrive prospective students. Between his classes he also stood, and his feet were beginning to get tired, but it was nothing compared to the stinging in his ass from where Ashton had thoroughly punished him. When Mike asked his students to get into groups and role-play being prospective students with each other, he let his mind drift back to that evening and tried to hide the pained smile that he knew curled his lips every time he thought of it.

Ashton had been ruthless. First, he had tied Mike to the bed on his belly spread-eagled and blind-folded him. Then he had begun spanking him, hard. The first blow should have been the most difficult as Mike adapted to his punishment, but it wasn't. Ashton started out easy and waded him from light slaps to the kind of gut-wrenching pain that had him begging for mercy after every blow, only Ashton was merciless. And Mike had loved every minute of it. What kind of person was he to enjoy such treatment?

He came back to the classroom with a start when the groups started to die down in their hubbub and he heard the conversations turn to gossip about what the prospective students would be like. He allowed them to gossip for a few minutes. One of his goals was to build community in his classroom, and gossiping was one way to do so. They thought he couldn't hear that their conversations had shifted, but in reality he knew everything that they said and he just allowed them to talk about non-academic topics for several long minutes before calling them to order again.

As first year students, most of them wouldn't have too much contact with the prospective students. Each visiting student would be assigned an upperclassman to escort them around campus and get a feel for whether or not they would do well. The upperclassmen were carefully selected and this year, most had done it before so there was little chance any prospective students would stumble upon the school's secrets. It happened occasionally, but a quick visit to Yasmina would fix that.

Yasmina was one of the oldest dragons on campus, second only to Arion, and her talent was making people forget things. Luckily, it only worked on people who were not partnered with a dragon, but most people on campus were still highly suspicious of her and grateful that she lived on the sister campus. Her partner, Margot, was the president of the girl's college, and it was said that she and Ashton used to be together, but Mike didn't believe it. Ashton was far too interested in men to have ever been in a serious relationship with a woman.

This year, Amar would be allowed to meet the prospective students to see if his dragon could predict which students would be able to form good bonds and which ones wouldn't. Mike had pushed hard for Amar to meet them, and Ashton had eventually given in despite his reservations about letting a first-year student into the process. Mike just hoped Tephis's talent proved true.

He finally called the class to order and there were a few last-minute giggles as the students broke up their groups and focused back on him. He went over the rules for the visit again, and dismissed them to their dragon-training class. They filed out of his room and Mike was surprised to see Jamie waiting at the doorway, and even more surprised when Jamie didn't meet up with Amar but instead came into the classroom. Jamie, being bonded to the queen, was receiving private instruction from Ashton for the next few weeks and then would join the regular classes again, so it was unusual for Jamie to even be on campus instead of in the dragon canyon.

"Mr. Ferrin? Can I talk to you about something?"

"Of course, Jamie."

Mike shut the door to the room. He was finished for the day and grateful that he didn't have another class, because otherwise he wouldn't be able to talk to Jamie and Jamie looked upset. He remembered another conversation with Jamie in this classroom and wondered if Jamie and Scott were on the rocks again.

"Is this about Scott?"

"You know?"

"Know what?"

Jamie scuffed his shoe on the floor and looked down. "Scott has to sleep with one of the students who's coming and I don't know what to do. I've tried to ignore it, pretend it isn't happening, but they're coming tomorrow and I can't ignore it anymore. How am I supposed to get through this?"

Mike shook his head, wondering if this was Ashton's test. He had thought that Ashton gave in and let the boys move in together too quickly. He wondered for a moment if he could offer to seduce the boy instead of Scott, but suspected Ashton wouldn't allow it. He knew it had to be Scott, and the purpose was to destroy Scott and Jamie's relationship just like it seemed to be doing.

"He doesn't have a choice in the matter," Mike said, knowing it didn't help. "I would stay away from the prospective students, like you're supposed to."

"I thought I didn't want to see him, but maybe it would easier to have a face in my nightmares."

"Let me meet him first, Jamie," Mike offered. "Then I'll tell you if there's anything to worry about."

There wouldn't be, and Mike already knew it, but hopefully this would help Jamie. Jamie didn't realize how much Scott was in love, and how no man in the world would ever compete with Jamie in his heart. Mike was more than a little jealous, since he doubted Ashton cared for him half as much as Scott cared for Jamie. He and Ashton had been monogamous as far as Mike knew, but he had never asked because he didn't want to learn that Ashton had been sleeping with anyone else. That knowledge would crush him, just as it was crushing Jamie.

His mind flew to Kale and for a moment he wondered if Ashton was sleeping with his former pet again, despite his protestations that Kale meant nothing anymore. Ashton was a liar, after all, even though his words sounded so true and Mike wanted so much to believe them. No, he told himself, Ashton was not sleeping with Kale. For whatever reason, Kale didn't seem thrilled by Ashton's attention so even if Ashton were willing, he doubted Kale would be. But why was Kale even here? Why was he staying? What purpose could he possibly have if not to steal Ashton's heart from Mike?

"Is everything okay?" Jamie asked.

The boy reached out and touched Mike's shoulder and Mike realized he was on the brink of tears just thinking about Ashton's former pet.

"I guess I'm in a similar situation," he admitted. "Only my boyfriend isn't honest with me. At least Scott told you what he had to do. He isn't lying to you and sleeping around behind your back."

"You mean Ashton?"

Mike nodded, since words were beyond him. If he spoke, he would cry and he would not cry in front of one of his students.

"I don't think he's cheating on you. Arion hasn't been in any mating flights since Marisol's," and the boy blushed a beautiful peach color, "and there haven't been any rumors."

"It's that stranger, Kale," Mike admitted.

Jamie hesitated and the blush grew deeper. Not for the first time, Mike wished he had been the one to seduce Jamie. It would be delightful to chase that blush with kisses all the way across his cheeks. He wondered if the blush extended down his body, as sometimes happened with pale-skinned men. Jamie was so beautiful, such an extraordinary catch, and if Narné hadn't pulled that stunt during Marisol's mating flight, then he and Eraxes would be Jamie's partner right now, not Scott and Narné. He had come so close to claiming the boy for his own.

"I didn't mean for him to come," Jamie said. "I didn't realize he would hear me."

"You have a powerful gift," Mike said. "The council will try to use it to their advantage."

"Well, I won't let them use anything if they ever ask Scott to sleep with someone else again. It isn't right. Will you tell the council that?"

"It might sound better coming from you."

Jamie shook his head. "They think I'm a child."

"Ashton doesn't, and he's the only one who matters."

Jamie was silent, then he shrugged and stared at the floor. "I didn't think Ashton knew about it. Scott said he did, but I didn't want to think Ashton would be involved in something like this."

Mike let out an explosive sigh. How could Jamie be so naïve? "Of course Ashton is behind it. He's behind everything the council does. He is the council."

"But you love him."

"Yes," Mike said, and he felt the beginnings of a headache starting between his eyes. "I do love him. Look, Jamie, you should be the one to tell Ashton. He'll listen to you and respect you. As for the prospective student, I'll find out who it is and I'll tell you if you need to worry or not. But right now I have to get ready for tomorrow's class. I'm sorry."

Jamie apologized as well and scurried out as Mike shook his

head and pressed his hand against his forehead. He hated being rude to Jamie but his head was pounding and rapidly descending into a migraine. He hadn't had a migraine in years but he recognized it instantly. He needed to get home, somewhere dark and quiet, before the real pain set in.

The migraine was caused by his cognitive dissonance, he knew. By his split opinion of Ashton. On the one hand, he knew that Ashton was scum, the worst of the worst, the embodiment of evil that the council represented. He had told Scott as much, and even Jamie. But on the other hand he loved the man and would do anything for him. Even though he was evil, he made Mike feel alive in a way nothing else did. When they were together, Mike forgot that he was a lying, cheating bastard and only thought of him as his sweet lover. How could those two things coexist?

He heard Eraxes grumbling in his mind and knew his headache was extending to his dragon as well. So much for a ride back to the canyon. He would have to walk, in the bright sunlight, or hole himself up in the classroom and hope no one asked questions. Eraxes was settling into the dragonbed at home and Mike sent a wave of jealousy towards him. Eraxes mentally nudged him in affection and sympathy, but there was nothing either of them could do.

Mike sat at the desk, wincing as the pain from his spanking days before was unabated. Then the door opened and Ashton walked in. He shut the door behind him and pressed his palm against Mike's forehead.

"Are you feeling all right?" Ashton asked. "Arion said Eraxes wasn't feeling well."

"Migraine," Mike managed.

"I'll carry you back to my room and take care of you," Ashton said, helping him stand. "Arion is just outside and can lift both of us."

Mike clung to Ashton, his brain hurting even more than

before. This man was helping him in his time of need without asking anything in advance, but this was the same man who was forcing Scott to sleep with a prospective student against his will. How could such things coexist in the same person? How could a cruel, cold man like Ashton have such a sweet side to him? He relaxed against Ashton and let the stronger man help him onto Arion's back, and soon he was tucked into Ashton's bed with a cold compress over his eyes and Ashton rubbing soothing circles on his hand.

"Tell me what you need, Mike," Ashton said.

"You," Mike whispered. "I just need you."

CHAPTER TEN

New Danger

Jamie kept his head down as he meandered through the campus, avoiding the areas where he thought Scott might be. He wanted to be alone, or at least separate from Scott for a while. They had been pretending that nothing was going to happen, laughing and holding each other and cuddling as if everything was all right, but every time Scott tried to kiss him or the cuddling began to get too intense, Jamie froze up. He could only pretend so much. He couldn't forget that soon, Scott would be cuddling and kissing someone else.

As he walked, he noticed Kale sitting on a bench overlooking the main campus. It was at the top of a large hill and he started heading up the hill. Maybe he could find out if Kale was sleeping with Ashton and reassure Mike, just as Mike was trying to reassure him about the visiting student. Kale spotted him right away, but didn't move from the bench. It seemed almost like he had been expecting Jamie. When Jamie reached the top of the hill, he bowed his head awkwardly and kicked the ground.

"May I join you?"

"Of course," Kale said, gesturing to the bench beside him.

Jamie sat down and stared at the campus stretched out below them. It was a beautiful campus, with brick buildings coated with ivy in a square with a large field in the middle – the knoll, everyone called it. The football fields were just visible beyond the buildings and the dense forest that sloped up the mountain and were lost in the mist. The dragon canyon was much farther away and completely shrouded in mist at this time of year, or so everyone said. Jamie couldn't imagine the mountain without its veil of mist.

"Beautiful, isn't it?" Kale asked. "And so many secrets."

"I'm amazed no one's ever found it before."

Kale glanced over at him with an amused look in his eyes. "Oh, people have found it. But the council has ways of taking care of them."

"By killing them?" Jamie nearly shouted, thinking of all the movies he'd seen and the ways villains "took care" of their enemies.

Kale laughed. "No. Just by erasing some of their memories. You certainly don't have a high opinion of the council if you think they're capable of murder."

Jamie's head dropped to his chest and he rubbed his hands against his pants. "They're not my favorite people right now."

"Can I ask why?"

"It's private."

"Something to do with why you and Scott weren't allowed to see each other?"

"How do you know about that?"

"I make it my business to know about the wrongs that the council has committed so that I can find ways to right them."

Jamie reassessed Kale. He seemed honest enough, even though Mike saw him as a threat. And if he wanted to undo the damage that the council was causing, that was more than enough reason to like the man.

"Why did you leave the academy?"

"Most people do," he said, shifting in a way that made Jamie think he'd stumbled on something Kale didn't want to talk about. But Kale took a deep breath and continued. "Ashton wanted me to do something that I wasn't prepared to do, and the only way out was to escape."

When Kale said 'Ashton,' there was a clear undercurrent of hate. Jamie perked up a little at that. He would get to tell Mike not to worry, that Kale wasn't a threat to him. Of course, it also meant that Mike was in love with someone who made unreasonable requests, but Mike himself had said that Ashton was a bad person, so he knew what he was getting into. Jamie didn't think they were right for each other, but he wasn't one to judge. He would just be happy that Ashton wasn't having an affair with Kale.

"So," Kale said. "What trouble is the council causing you?"

Jamie sighed. Kale was a stranger and he didn't like spilling his heart to a stranger, but no one else seemed to care. He couldn't talk to Scott, who would only feel horrible, and talking to Mike had ended with Mike being the one in tears. He was afraid to talk to Amar, since he wasn't sure how Amar felt about him and Scott being together ever since Amar told him that Scott had been assigned to sleep with him. Amar had been supportive while they were separated, but Jamie got the impression that Amar was grateful that Scott was kept away and thought they were better off separate.

He didn't have many close friends, especially now that he was the queen and everyone was in awe of him, or lusted after him thanks to the mating flight. He still couldn't be around large groups of students because it reminded him too strongly of the mating flight when everyone had swarmed and overwhelmed him. And many of the students still had feelings for him, even though they usually tried to hide it. He'd already been approached by nearly a dozen students asking if he needed companionship. He had politely refused the way that Ashton had taught him and he was grateful that his daily lessons with Ashton were so useful.

He still didn't believe that Ashton was behind Scott's assignment, but it was seeming more and more like an inevitable fact. Ashton, as Mike had said, was the council. They didn't do anything without his say. Jamie's lessons with Ashton the past week had been strained as Jamie had tried to control his resentment of the man, but he knew he was just waiting to explode. He suspected as soon as the prospective students got on campus and this nightmare became reality, he would unleash his helpless anger on Ashton.

Kale was still waiting for his reply, he realized with a start. The man was waiting patiently, as if he knew how hard it was for Jamie to talk about this. Jamie's hands curled into fists and he stared fixedly at the ground.

"The prospective students are coming tomorrow."

Kale nodded.

"When they're here, Scott has to seduce one of them."

The other man nodded again, slowly, as if pieces were coming together in his head. "A test," he said. "To see if Scott will be obedient. If he refuses, he'll never see you again. Ashton is as cruel as always."

"Why does everyone think Ashton knows about it?"

"Because it's right out of his playbook," Kale said. "If you know him – the real him and not the act he's putting on for you – you know that this is exactly the kind of thing he does on a regular basis. He uses sex to control people."

"But it's not like he insisted that Scott have sex with him," Jamie said, shuddering at the thought.

"No, that would be too direct. He uses sex indirectly. By forcing other people to have sex with who he wants, he can control their actions and reactions. It's a far more subtle evil."

"I think I get it," Jamie said, thinking of how upset he had been when he found out Scott had been assigned to seduce him, and how upset he was now that Scott was assigned to seduce someone else.

If Scott had been forced to sleep with Ashton, Jamie would have instantly hated Ashton and turned against him. But because Ashton was only indirectly involved, Jamie was more angry at Scott and the unknown student than at Ashton. Evil was perhaps a strong word, but Jamie understood what Kale was saying and for the first time, he realized that Ashton was truly not a good person. He shivered and wondered what Mike could possibly see in the man. Or what Kale had seen years ago.

"As long as Scott goes through with this," Kale said, "He won't be in any danger. But I sense that if he is unable to seduce this student, his very life is at stake and there will be little you can do to save him."

"What do you mean?"

"I can sense danger to people," Kale explained. "You are safe. I suspect that as the queen, you will rarely be in danger. But Scott is at a crossroads and this decision will determine whether he lives or dies. I know this is a difficult time for you, but you must let him do this. You can't stop him in any way."

"I wasn't going to," Jamie said miserably.

Stopping Scott had been an option, of course. He had dreamed of running into the bedroom where Scott was seducing the student and shouting for him to stop. Scott would look up with tears in his eyes and confess that he only loved Jamie, no one else, and then he would fling the student to one side and he would kiss Jamie wildly. Or Jamie would be awake one sleepless night when Scott would walk in and tell him that he couldn't do it, couldn't break their love by sleeping with another man, and Jamie would welcome him back into his arms and never let him go. So many options of Scott turning away from his mission, all of them carefully envisioned in Jamie's mind. Would they really get Scott killed?

He wasn't sure he believed Kale, but he had learned to trust dragon gifts. In his limited experience, they were always correct. He reached out to Marisol to confirm Kale's gift and she did. She added that the new dragon was very large and very polite, and was visiting her at the moment. With a rumble of pleasure that reverberated through his body, she added that he had brought her a gift of a rabbit. Since she was unable to fly, her food had to be carried to her and her appetite was voracious, so the rabbit was no more than a tidbit, but still a nice gesture.

"Even if I don't stop Scott," Jamie said, "He might not do it."

"He has to. Otherwise you might lose him forever. I'll fight to protect him, but I can only do so much."

Jamie nodded slowly. He would have to convince Scott that it was okay to seduce the student. But what if the knowledge that his lover was sleeping with someone else killed him on the inside? Kale's assessment of his safety was not quite true – he might be alive, but he was in serious danger of losing his heart or his mind if Scott did go through with this.

It is only one night, Marisol said, entering his mind abruptly. *You were prepared to sleep with someone else during the mating flight. Now you must give him permission to do the same.*

But it's not the same, Jamie insisted. *The mating flight was different. I didn't have a choice.*

Scott does not have a choice either, Marisol reminded him.

Jamie sighed. "All right. I'll talk to him and – and try to make things better. Will you talk to him?"

"I'll wait until this is over, I think. But I'll be nearby in case he gets in trouble."

"Why are you helping him? And me?"

Kale reached out to squeeze Jamie's hand. "You, I help because you're the queen. And Scott, I help because I think he will be a valuable ally. I don't want to lose him so early."

"Ally in what?"

Kale just smiled. "You should go. I'll see you again."

Jamie waved before descending the hill, pondering Kale's words. An ally. Narné had said that Kale brought hope, so whatever he was doing here, it was something good. Jamie could get behind that.

CHAPTER ELEVEN

Prospective Students

Scott and the other upperclassmen waited in the gymnasium as the prospective students nervously filed in. The students had just finished the mandatory informational session about Tarragon Academy and many of them had already formed groups and were chatting with each other. Scott tried to figure out which student would be his, but one had already caught his eye.

The student in question was handsome and bore a striking resemblance to Ashton if he were decades younger, with dark hair swept back from his face and dark eyes in a classically beautiful face, almost like a sculpture come to life. But it was his attitude that caught Scott's attention. He flitted between the groups like a butterfly and each group looked awed to have him as he laughed and joked and got to know his fellow students. He was more than outgoing, he was radiant and many of Scott's classmates were already talking about him and how they hoped they were assigned to him.

Scott would have preferred one of the quieter students, but as soon as he saw the boy with his arrogant, cocky smile dipping from one group to the next, he knew without question that this was his charge. The only question was how such an outgoing, confident young man was still a virgin.

There were about forty prospective students, a larger number than usual. Scott noticed Mike and Amar talking with the different students as they filed towards the upperclassmen to find their partners for the weekend and he wondered why Amar was allowed to meet them. But he was busy holding the sign that read "Derek Everly" and waiting for his student to find him. He kept an eye on the outgoing student and sure enough, the dark-eyed boy read his sign and then fixed on him with a smile.

They shook hands and introduced themselves, and Derek looked a little relieved as he sized up Scott. Scott wondered what he was expecting, and whether he knew what was going to happen this weekend.

Once all of the upperclassmen had found their younger partners, they split up to show the younger students to the dorm rooms where they would be staying for the weekend. Scott helped Derek shoulder his backpack and they headed to the dorms with everyone else. They talked about the campus for a little bit in the vaguest terms, since Scott couldn't give many specifics, and once they reached the dorm room Derek shut the door behind them and sighed. The glowing, outgoing act he had been exuding vanished and he looked lonely and a little frightened.

"My father told me what was going to happen," he said. "I'm glad it's with you. You seem nice enough."

Scott was taken aback. "Is your father a graduate?"

"He's on the council. The head of the council, actually."

"Ashton is your father?"

It shouldn't have surprised Scott as much as it did. Ashton was in numerous mating flights and wasn't the type to use protection, so it wasn't surprising that some of those women would have gotten pregnant afterward. But somehow the thought of Ashton as a father was mind-boggling and he couldn't process it.

"He's not much of a father," Derek admitted. "He's never really been there for me. But he set up this visit."

That made more sense, and Scott's heart went out to the young man. He thought of how hard Derek had tried to be outgoing and wondered if that was his personality or if he were trying to impress his father. Derek was going to have a very difficult time at the college, but there was no other place for him to go. He was destined to bond with a dragon.

"Well, Derek," Scott said, returning to Derek's initial comment, "As for what happens between us, that's private. If you want something to happen, then it will. If you don't, then it won't. I won't push you."

Derek looked surprised. "I thought that was the whole purpose of bringing me here."

"No, the purpose of this visit is to make sure you like the college. My role is secondary."

His role. Scott cursed Ashton for the fact that he even had a role in this matter. And how could Ashton do this to his own son, and worse yet, tell his son about it? It would have been better to let Scott seduce the boy naturally rather than tell Derek that he was going to have sex with Scott. Plus, there were fewer alleys of escape this way. Ashton's son. He shook his head. If it were anyone but Ashton's son, he could lie and say he slept with the boy even if he hadn't, but Ashton would ask his son and his son wouldn't lie about it. Ashton had trapped him in an impossible situation.

And worst of all, he now wanted to give Derek a proper seduction because he felt so bad for the boy who had gotten no love so far in his life. He was so much like Jamie in that regard. If he had to seduce Derek, and he did, then he was going to do it right. He reached out and took Derek's hand. He stroked it, turning it over and running his fingers lightly over the palm of his hand.

"What do you think of the college so far?"

Derek blushed. "It's beautiful. You know I've never- I mean, this is the first time-"

"I know," Scott said.

He pulled the boy closer to him until they were nearly nose-to-nose. He leaned forward and kissed Derek sweetly. The boy resisted for a moment, then opened his mouth and wrapped his hands around Scott. He either had a lot of experience kissing or else his instincts were spot-on, because the kiss was incredible and Scott found himself hardening. He had been worried that he wouldn't be able to perform with anyone besides Jamie, but Derek had skills.

He gently pulled away from the boy. That was enough for today. He didn't want to frighten him, and he was a little confused by his own reaction. Surely it shouldn't be so easy for him to be aroused by another man.

"Aren't we going to, you know, do it?" Derek asked, tilting his head towards the bedroom.

"Not yet," Scott said. "I don't want to rush you."

"You're not," Derek said. "I've been waiting for this for so long."

He leaned forward and kissed Scott and again Scott was impressed by his skill. This was not a blushing virgin, this was an experienced kisser. Something was not adding up. Scott allowed the kiss because he knew he had to, but he had no intention of taking Derek back to the bedroom so soon after meeting him even if that's what the boy expected. And wanted. When they broke apart, Derek's cheeks were flushed and his eyes were bright, and there was a mischievous smile on his lips.

"Come on," he said. "Take me. I want you."

Scott frowned. This couldn't be the same boy that had protested that this was his first time just a few minutes before.

"Derek, you're awfully – forceful."

He laughed and threw his head back. "Oh, I can't keep up the act. You're too good a kisser. How can I pretend to be shy when I can feel your body responding to me? I want you so bad right now."

Scott chilled and drew back from him. "What are you talking about?"

"My father told me you went for shy boys, so I decided to pretend to be shy and innocent and sweet. But I just can't keep it up. It isn't who I am."

"And who are you?"

"I don't know, I'm just me. And I know you want me, I felt it when we kissed. I know you have to do this, too, or else something bad will happen to you, so stop pretending to be a gentleman and just take me already. I've waited my whole life for this and I'm dying to know what it's like."

Scott felt betrayed and drew back further. Derek had pretended to be shy just to get his attention? It had certainly worked; Scott had been drawn in like a moth to the light and now he was burned. What kind of creature was capable of such deception? Ashton's son, a voice told him. Of course Ashton's son wouldn't think twice about manipulating the people around him.

"You're just like your father," Scott said.

"People tell me that," Derek said with a shrug. "But as I said, I barely know the man."

"I'm surprised you're still a virgin if you want it so much."

"My father told me that if I waited until my trip here, he would make sure I was taken care of by someone who knew what he was doing. It's been hard, and I've had to pass up some good opportunities, but as soon as I saw that you were assigned to me I knew it was worth it."

Scott scowled. He was quickly beginning to hate Derek and that would make it very difficult to seduce him. There had to be some redeeming quality in the boy, something that made him worthwhile as a person. He was a liar, just like his father, and a manipulator, but surely there was something sincere about him.

"You're so beautiful when you're angry," Derek said, reaching out to stroke Scott's cheek. He allowed the gesture, since it wouldn't do to strike Ashton's son. The boy's touch was gentle and a little hesitant. He kept his palm on Scott's cheek and drew forward for another kiss, but this one was chaste and apologetic.

"I'm sorry I lied about who I am," he whispered. "But I wanted to be someone you would like. I wanted you to like me as much as I liked you and I didn't know if you would like who I actually am."

There was the sincerity, Scott thought. The insecurity that had caused the deception in the first place. Ashton manipulated without a second thought, but at least this boy realized that what he had done was wrong and felt bad about it. It wasn't much to go on, but Scott could work with that and slowly recover his trust in the boy, and eventually allow himself to seduce the other.

"You made a mistake," Scott said. "But either way, we're not having sex today or tonight. We have a tour of campus to attend, and then dinner with the other prospective students. Your father would not want you to miss either."

"I don't think he would mind, if I were with you."

Scott secretly agreed with Derek, but he wasn't about to say that out loud.

"Well, I don't want you to miss them. Getting to know your fellow students is vitally important. It's one of the main reasons we bring you here, especially students like you who are already committed to going to the university. You need to know who you'll be working with."

"Will you still be a student next year?"

"Yes," Scott said. Another year when Ashton could order him to sleep with whomever he wanted. "I'll be in my last year."

"Good," Derek said with a bright smile.

The boy was beautiful, with that dark hair and those engaging dark eyes, and he shone like a star when he smiled. He was so different than Jamie's auburn hair and green eyes, and Jamie's quiet beauty that glittered like a diamond only under the proper lighting. When Jamie smiled, the whole world lit up.

When Derek smiled, though, it was like the rest of the world went dark and a spotlight shone on him so that all attention was on him and nothing else. It was a selfish charm, but a beautiful one nonetheless.

"Shall we start our tour, then?" Derek asked, bouncing up on the balls of his feet with an energy that surprised Scott. "I can't wait to see what you want to show me."

He winked and Scott flushed. This was going to be a long weekend and he couldn't figure out if it would be less painful to seduce Derek sooner or later, but now that he knew Derek was Ashton's son one decision had been made for him: he wasn't slipping out of this trap. He would have to have sex with Derek before the boy went back home.

CHAPTER TWELVE

Rumors and Gossip

The rumor reached Jamie long before Mike came to see him and tell him about Scott's prospective student. Scott had been assigned to Ashton's son. Jamie's hands curled into fists and he was tempted to punch the wall in his quarters, even though it was solid rock and he knew it would probably break his hand. He wanted to punch something. What he really wanted to punch was the student – Derek, they said his name was – but he knew he couldn't get away with punching Ashton's son.

So instead Jamie paced and fumed and waited for the next person to enter the room so that he could explode at them. He didn't know who it would be. Mike, Ashton, maybe even Kale, it didn't matter. He just wanted someone there to yell at. Marisol was keeping a low profile to avoid his wrath. When he first overheard the other students gossiping, Marisol had tried to soothe him and he had turned on her in a rage. She had quickly stopped communicating with him and now cowered on the dragon bed. He felt bad about lashing out at her, but he couldn't help it. Scott was assigned to Ashton's son. That was as bad as being assigned to Ashton himself. How could Ashton do such a thing?

If Narné were nearby, he would have gotten all of Jamie's anger, and rightfully so. But he had snuck out much earlier in the day, probably as soon as he realized who Scott had been assigned to. He could see the future, after all, and would have known the dangers of staying around Jamie in this mood.

Jamie circled the room again, looking for something to hit. He had already punched all the pillows and it did nothing to calm his anger. Or his fear. It was really fear that drove him, under all the anger. Fear that Scott would like Ashton's son more than him, and that Ashton would win a victory that couldn't ever be undone. Kale had said that Jamie wasn't in physical danger, but Kale had vastly underestimated the importance of Jamie's state of mind. What good was being alive if Scott wasn't at his side?

He had first overheard the gossip when walking back from class. The two students, both upperclassmen, were talking about the new students with an air of excitement. One student in particular had caught their attention and from the way they spoke of him, he had caught everyone's attention. Derek, his name was, and he was a gorgeous, outgoing, confident boy that even the other students had started to worship. He would be class president for sure, one of the upperclassmen said. The other went on at length about the beauty of his dark eyes, and how they sparkled when he smiled. Both students sounded absolutely smitten. Then a third student joined them and revealed that this Derek was actually Ashton's son. Jamie had tried to move closer to the group when he heard that, because warning bells were going off and he suspected what was going to come next. The first student asked if anyone knew who had the good fortune of being assigned to the beautiful student and the third student said, with jealousy, that the queen's mate had that honor.

Jamie had slunk off the path after hearing that, not wanting the students to spot him and bombard him with questions about his mate's assignment. So Scott was assigned to a beautiful, outgoing boy. What if Scott liked him better than Jamie? After all, Jamie was so flawed. Everything about him was quiet and reserved and broken in some way, why wouldn't Scott want something beautiful and pure? Jamie's thoughts had started in a downward spiral as he made his way home to the dragon canyon and he had been spiraling in self-loathing and self-doubt ever since.

He wandered into the bedroom and saw his snowglobe set up. He hadn't set it up, so Scott must have done it. For a moment he smiled, then his smile withered. The snowglobe was broken, just like him. Everything about him was wrong. He rubbed his shoulders where his scars were hidden by his shirt, his scars that he thought Scott had accepted but what if he hadn't? Or what if Scott had only reluctantly accepted them while secretly hoping for someone without any flaws? Someone like Ashton's son? Jamie was willing to bet that Derek's body was flawless. No son of Ashton's would ever suffer from depression or have the desire to cut himself. Ashton would make sure that his children had perfect lives.

Ashton's son wouldn't have nightmares about his parents dying in fiery graves; he would be well-cared for and well-loved his entire life. He wouldn't have an aunt who scorned him and locked him out as often as let him in to his own home. He wouldn't have any of the horrors that had scarred Jamie mentally throughout the years and made him hesitant and shy of human contact. No, this Derek was quite the opposite – a social butterfly, it sounded like, happy and joyful and confident around others. What if that was what Scott really wanted?

There was a knock at the door and Jamie's head snapped up. Finally, someone to vent to. He almost felt sorry for whoever was on the other side, because they were going to get yelled at, he could already tell. He almost hoped it was Ashton, because Ashton was the only one who deserved to get yelled at, but it was too early for their lessons and there was no other reason Ashton would stop by. He opened the door and Mike stood on the other side with a wary look on his face. Good. At least he knew what he was in for.

Jamie invited him into the living room politely, managing at least a modicum of control before he let loose. The instant Mike was seated, Jamie whirled to face him, hands waving wildly as he launched into a tirade about what he had overheard from the other students. All of his doubts and fears about Scott's love came tumbling out and he was unable to stop them. Mike listened patiently, occasionally trying to interrupt but for the most part letting Jamie talk. And talk. And talk. Jamie talked himself out, sharing all of his worries that had filled his mind before Mike had knocked on the door, and soon he was in tears.

He collapsed on the couch beside Mike and circled his arms around the other man's neck. He heard Mike's sharply inhaled breath before the man embraced him in return, and there was something almost sensual about the way he stroked Jamie's back. Too late Jamie remembered the mating flight that had made everyone on campus lust for him, but he didn't care. Scott was off with some other man, so why shouldn't he be in the arms of another man as well? At least he wasn't going to sleep with Mike, like Scott was doing with Derek.

Another sob escaped and he pulled closer to Mike, needing the comfort of another body pressing against his. Mike's hand carded through his hair as he held Jamie close.

"You have nothing to worry about," Mike whispered. "Scott loves you, and that will never change."

"He was assigned to me, just like he's assigned to Derek. What if he falls in love with Derek the same way?"

"He won't," Mike said. "Derek is not his type."

"How do you know?"

"Because Derek is a lot like me, in some ways, and Scott would never think of me that way."

Jamie heard the sadness in Mike's voice and found himself rubbing the other man's back in sympathy, even though he would never want Scott and Mike to be together. Still, Mike was a decent guy, at least as far as Jamie could tell. Did that mean Derek was a decent guy, too? Jamie's heart dropped.

"So he's a good guy?"

"Derek? No, Jamie, I'm saying the opposite. He's a liar, a manipulator, a – a bad person."

"But you're not those things."

"I have been. Did Scott ever tell you how I met him?"

"No," Jamie said, leaning out of the caress to meet his gaze. Mike looked infinitely sad and remorseful.

"I was assigned to him," Mike said, and Jamie's eyes opened wide. "I seduced him, but I didn't expect to fall in love with him. He was a lot like you, back then. He didn't have the confidence he has now. He's really blossomed," Mike added with the hint of a smile. "No thanks to me."

"What happened?" Jamie asked breathlessly.

He realized that while Scott knew all sorts of things about his past, he knew almost nothing about Scott. Scott hid from his past almost as much as Jamie did, although he had never realized it before. Jamie felt suddenly selfish for never asking about Scott's past before. He hoped it was okay to hear about it from Mike, because he wasn't going to let Mike stop talking now.

"I was assigned to seduce him," Mike repeated. "He was a virgin and the first year exam was only days away. I was desperate, and he wasn't giving any ground. One day, when we were in the classrooms after everyone had left, I – I got a little forceful. I pinned him to the wall and kissed him, and I didn't let him leave. I had sex with him, Jamie, right in the hallway and against his will."

Jamie shivered. "You raped him?"

Mike flinched. "He says that I did, but I had no choice. He would have been killed in the exam and I couldn't let that happen. He was my charge and I had to have sex with him before the exam. The exam happened the next day, you know, I only barely saved him. But I remember the betrayal on his face, the rejection…"

Mike turned his head away from Jamie but Jamie could see tears forming in the other man's eyes.

"There's no way he would have agreed?"

"He did, Jamie. At the end, he said yes. I think that haunts him more than anything. He gave in to me."

Jamie backed up out of Mike's arms and started pacing again. He didn't know how to react to the information. On the one hand, he was horrified by what Mike had done. His Scott, forced into sex by someone he trusted. Raped right in the school where he was supposed to be safe and protected. He must have felt so betrayed by Mike, so frightened, and then so ashamed that he couldn't control his body and felt aroused by Mike's assault. Jamie remembered his mating flight and how he would have slept with anyone if they had only touched him. He still had nightmares of coming out of that lustful trance and finding himself with a stranger. Sex was a powerful thing and it made men want things they couldn't always control, and for Scott to have such a conflicted first time was horrifying.

But on the other hand, Mike looked truly upset by what he had done to Scott. There were tears in his eyes and his voice had trembled with pity and self-loathing as he had spoken. And it was true that Scott wouldn't have survived the first year exam if he were a virgin. Jamie didn't understand why that was exactly, but he knew that Marisol would have killed him if he and Scott hadn't had sex before the exam. There was something about the ability to connect intimately that was necessary for the dragons to communicate, and virgins were incapable of it. Jamie hated what Mike had done to Scott, but he could understand Mike's desperation as the days ticked down and the exam drew nearer, yet Scott was still a virgin. But surely there was a better way to do it.

"Please forgive me, Jamie," Mike said. "Perhaps I shouldn't have told you. But it's how I know he only loves you. After what I did to him, he withdrew from romance. He had a few flings, but nothing serious. He was too afraid of being hurt. And this new boy, Derek, is exactly the type of boy that would hurt him. He's far too smart to invest any real emotion into him. He'll sleep

83

with the boy because he has to, but other than that there will be nothing between them. I know it."

"You think Derek will hurt him?"

"He'll try. He's Ashton's son, after all. Deception runs in that family."

Jamie shut his eyes and wished again that Scott didn't have to do this. He wished he could run into Scott's arms and tell him to lie, to find someone else to bed the boy, to find some way to get out of the ridiculous situation they were in. But if the council found out, if Ashton found out, then Scott might die, according to Kale. How accurate were Kale's predictions, he wondered. Was there another path that Kale hadn't considered? After all, he had said Jamie would be safe but Jamie's mind and heart were exploding in a million different directions.

He couldn't bear the thought of some stranger hurting Scott, especially someone whose mere existence was a pain to Scott and Jamie. Derek could have been the sweetest person alive and he would hurt Scott, but the thought that he would purposefully hurt Jamie's boyfriend was insult upon injury.

He needed to save up his rage for his class with Ashton, so that Ashton could receive the full bulk of it and would finally understand that he and Scott were not chess pieces to be moved around at will but instead living, breathing humans with minds and plans of their own and Ashton was no longer in charge of them.

Jamie opened his eyes and saw Mike before him, looking at him with an expression of shame and hope. Did he forgive Mike? It was too confusing. He would have to talk to Scott first. He couldn't focus on anything until he was back with his boyfriend.

"I don't know if I forgive you," Jamie said. Mike nodded and his shoulders straightened, as if that were a better answer than the one he'd been expecting. "But I do have some good news for you. Kale is not interested in Ashton and would never even consider sleeping with him."

"You talked to Kale?" Mike's voice was sharp.

"He's a good person. Marisol agrees."

"Maybe I misjudged him," Mike said. "He wanted to talk to me, but I jumped to conclusions when I saw his – necklace."

Mike was fingering his necklace and Jamie realized it must have been a gift from Ashton. But Ashton was cruel and deceptive, as Mike had said. Ashton deserved all of Jamie's rage. Mike may have raped Scott, but he was still a mostly good person, too good for Ashton.

"You shouldn't be with Ashton," Jamie said.

Mike winced. "I know. But he's so kind to me. You haven't seen that side of him. No one has, except me. And maybe Kale."

"Well, he'd better show that side soon because right now I'm pissed at him. The next time I see him I'm going to tell him what's what about me and Scott, and I'm not going to take no for an answer."

"Good," Mike said. "I think you should. Why not tell him right now? I'll walk you over to his quarters."

"Um, now?"

Jamie's mind whirled. Was he ready for a showdown with Ashton?

"No time like the present. You should strike while you're still angry, but calm enough to think clearly. I think this is a good time."

"You're right," Jamie said, straightening his shoulders and taking a deep breath. "Let's go."

CHAPTER THIRTEEN

Heart to Heart

Kale shut his eyes and focused on his dragon, Vestis. Vestis was flying back to the White House to check on things and make sure the other dragons and their partners were surviving without him. One of his duties at the White House, aside from protecting the president, was to keep the other dragon partners in line and without him, the task had fallen to a junior member of the staff. Many of the staff had already expressed concern about her age to Kale before he left and despite his assurances that she was fully qualified, they were hesitant to obey her.

Kale had agreed to send Vestis every couple of weeks to make sure things were going well but now that Vestis was gone, he regretted the decision. Without a dragon, he felt helpless somehow, as if he were missing a valuable asset in his silent war against Ashton. He had noticed Arion keeping a close watch on him ever since Vestis had left and he worried that Ashton would try to hurt him when he didn't have a dragon to protect him.

His ability to sense danger to others didn't, unfortunately, extend to himself, so he couldn't tell if he were in danger or not, but he was keeping a close watch on the others on campus. He especially kept an eye out for Mike, Ashton's current pet. There was a spike in potential danger to the man just recently, and Kale was on his way to intercept Mike from doing whatever potentially deadly thing he was about to do. Mike may view Kale as a threat, but he had no idea how much Kale cared about him.

Mike was more than a person to protect and a man in the same position that he had been in years ago. He was a beautiful, charming young man that deserved better than anything Ashton could give him. Kale had been observing the campus lately, paying particular attention to Mike and his activities. Mike was a devoted teacher, always taking time out for his students and even the first year kids who weren't his students, and they swarmed around him. Clearly he was a favorite.

Kale had heard stories about Mike's handling of the first year exam and was impressed by the low number of casualties – in Kale's year, fifteen students were killed and it was considered an average year. He had even heard that Mike demanded a moment of silence for the three students who were killed, the first time any such remembrance was held on campus. Clearly, Mike was doing good things. And he was so beautiful.

Kale found Mike with Jamie, and the two of them were headed in the direction of Ashton's quarters with grim looks on their faces as if they were about to go into battle. When they saw Kale, however, they stopped. Kale could practically see the danger swirling around Mike. If he continued on his path to Ashton's room, he would likely be killed in the near future, or at least face death. Something would happen and Ashton would bring him to the volcano, and Mike was too much under Ashton's spell to refuse. Kale needed to get Mike away from Ashton, and quickly.

"Good day," he said, trying to sound casual, as if he had just happened to run into them. "What brings you here?"

Jamie lifted his head, his face set with determination. "I'm going to tell Ashton that he can't boss me around anymore."

Kale's eyes widened. No wonder the two of them were in danger. But Jamie was not in serious danger, only partial danger. He would survive the incident and probably come out on top. There was no reason to stop him from seeing Ashton; in all likelihood, the talk was long overdue and would benefit the queen's partner and his mate. But if Mike went in there with Jamie, he would be considered a traitor and Ashton would feel that he needed to speed up his plan to trick Mike into sacrificing his life. After Jamie left, Ashton would take Mike to the volcano and Mike would give up his life. Kale could feel it with a certainty that was reflected in the aura of danger radiating off the handsome young man.

"I think that's a good idea," Kale said cautiously. "But why are you here, Mike?"

"Ashton will listen better if I'm there," Mike said.

"Are you sure?"

Mike glared, but Jamie looked hesitant.

"Is that – I mean, can you see something?"

Kale let out a sigh of relief. The boy believed in his gift. That would make this a little easier.

"Yes, I see that if both of you go in, you won't be successful. But if you go in alone, Jamie, the chances of getting what you want are quite good."

Jamie looked thoughtful but Mike let out a bark of laughter. "I suppose now you can see the future like Narné. Your dragon's not even here, Kale, how can you see anything?"

"I see danger to people I care about, whether my dragon is here or not. And there is only danger if both of you go in. Think about it, Mike. Ashton will lose respect for Jamie if you accompany him. You can talk to him privately, if you want, but being there to support Jamie only makes Jamie look weak. You know that."

Mike scowled and Kale knew his words had rung true with the man. Mike looked at Jamie.

"Jamie, I know I said I would go with you, but…"

"It's all right," Jamie said. He squared his shoulders. "I can do this."

Kale nodded in approval and clapped Jamie on the back.

"Good luck, Jamie."

Mike embraced the boy and shooed him towards Ashton's quarters, then turned his attention back to Kale. He was scowling, but Kale could see the curiosity in his eyes.

"So who are you, really, and why are you here?"

"Why don't we walk and talk?" Kale responded, not wanting to talk about sensitive matters so close to Ashton. He knew Ashton would soon be occupied with Jamie, but Arion might be listening and he couldn't be sure that Ashton was above using common spies to listen to his enemies. And Kale was definitely considered an enemy, or at least he should be.

The two men left the dragon canyon and wandered towards the forest where the path split into the nesting grounds. Once they reached the split, they stopped. Kale sat on a mossy log and gestured for Mike to sit as well, but the man remained standing with his arms crossed. Mike fingered the collar around his neck. Kale decided to be the one to talk first, and he would start with Mike's questions.

"To start with, you know who I am. I was once Ashton's pet just like you, but he demanded something of me that I couldn't give and I had to run away."

"You didn't care for Ashton like I do," Mike said softly. "I would do anything for him."

"Even die?"

"He would never want me to die," Mike scoffed. "He loves me."

Kale shook his head sadly. He remembered thinking the same thing, until Ashton had taken him to the volcano. He had been shaken and hurt realizing that Ashton wanted him dead, but he had been willing to do anything for the man so he had promised to kill himself. He was just lucky Vestis had more sense and had taken him back to the campus, where Eric and the others had helped him escape.

"What if he did, Mike? What if he told you that the only way the school would survive was to sacrifice your life?"

"That's insane."

Kale shook his head. "That's what he told me, and because I loved him, I was ready to die. Just because he wanted it, I was prepared to give up my life. One of the reasons I'm here is because I can't let that happen to you. I can't let him kill another man."

"Another?"

"Yes, another. I was not his first pet. Every decade or so, he takes a pet, spoils them, then kills them. I only recently found this out."

Mike turned his back on Kale. "You're lying. You just want Ashton to love you again, but he won't. He's mine."

"He's not yours, any more than he was mine all those years ago. He manipulates people, Mike, he's not a good person."

"Fuck," Mike said, whirling around and gesturing wildly. "You think I don't know that? I've been telling Jamie and Scott how horrible he is for weeks now! But with me he's different. There's this whole other side of him that no one else sees, that he can't show anyone else."

"I know," Kale said. "He's a bastard, but he's sweet to you. Did you know that that's a brainwashing technique? Alternating cruelty with kindness until the person's spirit breaks and they become completely dependent on the other? He's grooming you, Mike, and I know you can't see it but you have to trust me."

"No," Mike said. "You're lying. He loves me, I know he does."

There were tears in Mike's eyes and Kale knew that Mike was fully aware of the truth of the matter and was choosing to disillusion himself. Mike leaned against a tree, then collapsed to the ground.

"When the resistance chose me to try and join the council, they warned me about Ashton," Mike said. "They told me what he would make me do, what he would force me to do. They never warned me that I would like it, that he would be so kind to me. Sometimes I think he knows I'm with the resistance and he's just toying with me for the fun of it. But other times he genuinely seems to care for me. I joined the resistance because I wanted to get rid of Ashton, but now I don't know what I want anymore."

Kale drew in a breath. Mike was with the resistance? No wonder Ashton had chosen him as a pet. Mike's assessment of Ashton was correct: he undoubtedly knew that Mike was with the resistance and took great pleasure turning their agent against them. Ashton had spies in the resistance and the resistance itself was carefully monitored by the council. It was their way of rooting out traitors.

They allowed the resistance to exist because it was a good way to discover anyone with anti-council sentiments and the resistance itself was mostly useless, so anyone who truly hated the council was on their own. Like Kale. There was almost no way to connect with other true rebels because the council had so many spies in place. What they needed was someone who could communicate with other dragons without the council knowing.

Jamie had that gift, but it was untrained. He had sent out his lust to every single dragon in the world, as far as Kale could tell. There had to be some way to narrow his focus and allow him to communicate only with dragons who hated Ashton and the council. If Jamie could limit his gift like that, he would be truly invaluable. Unfortunately, Jamie was in the council's hands and it was unlikely that he would ever get free of them, so the chances that he would be properly trained were slim. Unless Mike, as his teacher, instructed him on the sly.

"I know you love Ashton," Kale said. "But there are so many other options for you. You don't have to abandon Ashton now, but be aware that if he ever asks for your life, you can refuse. Other people care for you. Other people want you. Other people love you."

Mike dried his eyes and cocked his head at Kale. "And you?

How do you feel about me?"

Kale looked down. Mike was so beautiful, and seemed like such a good person. "I care for you," he said carefully. "I think it could be more, if you were ready."

A hint of a smile crossed Mike's face. "I thought so. You are jealous, just not of me. You're jealous of Ashton."

It was Kale's turn to blush. Was he jealous that Ashton held Mike's heart? Maybe a little, but it wasn't his motivation in breaking them up. He was trying to save Mike's life, not get Mike into his bed. Although he wouldn't mind Mike in his bed, he thought as he admired the handsome young man. Mike's blond hair sparkled darkly in the sunlight and he leaned towards Kale seductively. Kale got off the mossy log he sat on and placed his hand on Mike's shoulder.

"Perhaps I am jealous," he said in a husky voice. "But my reasons in getting you away from Ashton are not based in jealousy and you know it."

Mike's face fell and he stared at the ground. Kale moved away from him.

"We should get back," Kale said. "We need to find out how young Jamie did."

With a heavy sigh, Mike climbed to his feet and nodded. The two of them set out towards dragon canyon, and Kale was pleased to note that Mike followed so closely their hands brushed on several occasions. He didn't know if he had gotten through to Mike about Ashton, but at least Mike no longer saw him as a threat and that was worth everything.

CHAPTER FOURTEEN

Confrontation with Ashton

Some of Jamie's confidence leaked away as Mike left him to talk to Kale and he was left alone, marching towards Ashton's chambers. He understood Kale's concerns but once again, Kale seemed not to understand the effect his actions would have on Jamie's mental state. He was getting scared now, not just angry, and he was afraid that Ashton was going to talk his way around Jamie's concerns and then Jamie and Scott would never be free of the man's interference.

Jamie reached the door to Ashton's chambers and paused, unwilling to knock and begin the confrontation. He didn't have a plan, after all, and he hadn't rehearsed what he was going to say. Maybe he should take a few steps back and rethink this whole confrontation until he was more prepared. Then he heard a voice inside, and felt a voice in his head. Ashton and Arion were talking and he was close enough to eavesdrop.

He pressed his ear against the door and opened his mind to Arion's comments, which were clearly directed to Ashton but the dragon hadn't expected someone with Jamie's gift to be nearby, so Jamie could make out what he was saying.

"I'm not going to ask again," Ashton said. "Stop the bond between Kale and his dragon."

No, Arion growled. *Vestis is obeying the council's wishes and is keeping the large white house safe. He needs to be able to communicate problems to his partner.*

"His partner is interfering and needs to learn a lesson."

Do it in another way. I am not going against the council's will in this matter.

"Arion-"

I am not your servant, nor your lesser. I do not take orders from you. You would wise to remember that.

Jamie's eyes were wide. Ashton and his dragon, having an argument? He wondered how often this happened, since both of them seemed weary of the conversation as if they'd had it before. And Arion's last line rang through the room and through Jamie's mind with a strength that surprised Jamie. He had never really thought of how the dragons saw the relationship with their partners, but he, like most humans, had assumed that they were the subservient ones in the relationship.

Marisol, after all, mostly did what he asked and when she didn't, it was either because she couldn't or because she didn't want to and she was still young enough that it didn't bother Jamie or make him reexamine the relationship. But then again, Marisol had deliberately withheld information from him in the past, and seemed quite capable of making her own decisions. She wasn't a pet by any means; she was a highly sentient creature who just happened to be bonded to Jamie.

There was silence in the room and Jamie braced himself and knocked. Most of his anger had leeched away but he hoped that at the sight of Ashton it would come rushing back.

"It's open," Ashton called.

Jamie pushed open the door and gaped at the sight in front of him. Ashton was cradling Arion's head with an expression of love and tenderness that Jamie had never seen or even imagined the man capable of, and Arion's eyes were lidded in pleasure. Clearly their argument was over. The image of the two of them was so sweet and so pure that Jamie couldn't step further into the room; he was trapped, knowing he would never be able to yell at a man capable of such tenderness. Why didn't Ashton use that tenderness on people?

"Ah, Jamie," Ashton said, giving Arion a pat before the dragon made its way into the dragon's sleeping quarters. "I didn't expect to see you until later today. To what do I owe this pleasure? Is everything all right with Marisol?"

Jamie briefly thought of Marisol cowering on the dragon bed while Jamie raged and some of his anger returned. What Ashton was doing to him and Scott was hurting Marisol, and nothing should be allowed to hurt Marisol.

"I want to talk about Scott," Jamie said, curling his hands into fists as adrenaline began pumping through his veins again. This was dangerous territory and he might actually make it worse for Scott if he messed this conversation up, but he was determined.

"I see. I've been waiting for this conversation," Ashton said, and gestured to a low-slung couch nearby. "Why don't we sit?"

They both sat on opposite ends of the couch and Jamie found that his leg was jiggling constantly. He couldn't seem to control it. The adrenaline was rushing through his body now and demanding that he fight, but it wasn't used to fights with words and his body didn't know what to do with itself.

"You can't do this to him ever again," Jamie warned, deciding to start with his basic requirement for how things were going to be in the future.

"What am I doing to him, exactly?" Ashton asked. "I need to know, if I can't do it again."

"Making him sleep with someone besides me."

Even the words twisted in Jamie's mouth and he tried not to think of what Scott could be doing that very instance. It was late, after all, it was perfectly possible that Scott was entwined with someone else that very moment. Jamie scowled and fought the brief urge to vomit. Scott touching someone else, moaning at someone else's touch, Scott stripping for someone else, pulling off their clothes slowly, Scott entering someone else, someone else feeling that intense, almost painful pleasure that came with sex. He couldn't think about it, not now.

"I see," Ashton said. "Unfortunately, Scott already agreed to sleep with whoever I choose for the next year, so you really have no say in the matter."

Jamie's lips tightened. Was that true? Is that what Scott had promised in exchange for getting to be with Jamie? Well, it wouldn't happen. Jamie wouldn't let it.

"And you are going to choose no one," he said with as much confidence as he could muster. His head was pounding and he could feel a droplet of sweat forming on his forehead but he tried to sound as convincing as possible despite his body's weakness.

"Why would I do that?" Ashton asked with an amused smile.

Jamie thought about making moral arguments, or practical ones, or relying on Ashton's kindness as a human being, but he knew all of those would fail. Other people had tried them and Ashton was still in control. No one got out of Ashton's deals. But there was one argument that Jamie could make that no one else had ever been able to make, that might just make Ashton reconsider.

"Because it upsets me, and when I'm upset Marisol is upset. Already her belly is churning with acid and who knows what that will do to the eggs. She doesn't think a single exposure will kill many of them, but who knows what a second dose will do? She has to care for them constantly or they die. And trust me, if I am distressed about Scott, she won't be caring for them."

Ashton's skin was white and Jamie knew his threat had hit home, but then Ashton shrugged.

"She'll have another batch in time," he said but his voice was unsteady, as if Jamie's threats had rocked him. "Perhaps next time she'll have a better suited mate."

"No," Jamie said. "It will always be Narné and you know it."

"You say that with such confidence, but you've only been in

96

one mating flight. You don't know how they work."

"I know Narné, and I know Scott. I know you, too, and I know you won't let the first batch of dragon eggs in centuries die from something you can prevent. The council certainly won't."

Ashton's lips quirked into a moue of distaste. Jamie could hear Arion shifting around in the dragon chamber and guessed that the dragon was now eavesdropping on them, wondering what his partner was going to do.

Ashton stood up and paced for several minutes in silence while Jamie sat, clenched in fear with a droplet of sweat beginning its path down his face. He was burning hot but not from the heat of the room; the stress was affecting him severely. His hands trembled and his knees couldn't keep still. His heart was pounding heavily in his ears and he could barely hear over the noise.

"You know that he has to go through with his current assignment, don't you?" Ashton asked with his back turned.

"Yes," Jamie said with gritted teeth. "And I know it's your son."

"He's a good boy. It shouldn't be hard for Scott. After that, however," Ashton turned, then frowned. "Are you alright?"

Jamie shivered. The stress seemed to be getting to him because now the room felt icy cold. He was still sweating, though, and his hands kept clenching and unclenching. His stomach churned and he realized with shock that he was on the brink of vomiting.

"No," he managed, and gestured that he was going to throw up.

Ashton brought him a trash receptacle and he grabbed it just in time, before his body locked in place and his stomach tossed its contents up while he watched helplessly. He hated the feeling of losing control when he vomited, and it was even worse with Ashton patting his back and making soothing noises. When his stomach was empty, he coughed and wiped his mouth.

"I didn't realize the stress was that bad," Ashton said, moving the trash receptacle to another room before sitting beside Jamie and stroking his back again. Jamie was in tears. "You just need to get through this weekend. After that, I won't require Scott to sleep with anyone else. Is Marisol okay?"

Jamie reached out to his dragon. She was also feeling sick but had handled it better than Jamie. She sent him a happy thought that he had gotten what he wanted from Ashton, then asked him to please return so he could take care of her.

"I have to get back to her," Jamie said.

"Why don't I come with you," Ashton offered. "I want to make sure you're feeling better and I want to check on Marisol as well."

"Alright," Jamie said weakly, allowing Ashton to help him up.

He cursed the fact that he had to lean against Ashton as they walked, but he tried to remind himself that he had gotten what he wanted. Scott would never have to sleep with anyone other than Jamie again. He just wished he could feel better about it. Ashton's hand on his back, though a necessary support as he stumbled down the hallway, was anything but comforting.

It was strange to think that just a few days ago he had trusted Ashton and thought of him as a good person, and he hadn't believed that Ashton had anything to do with Scott's assignment. His view had certainly changed. Even though Ashton was being kind to him now, Jamie could see that he was only acting to protect the queen. He had no real sympathy for Jamie.

"You're burning up," Ashton said as his skin touched the back of Jamie's neck. He felt Jamie's forehead as well. "You have a fever. Have you been eating and drinking enough? Getting enough sleep?"

"Of course not," Jamie nearly shouted. "How am I supposed to sleep knowing that Scott is with someone else?"

Ashton stared at him with blank eyes, then shook his head. "You are supposed to be taking care of your queen, not worrying about Scott. Haven't you learned anything in your lessons? Marisol's health depends on yours."

"Once Scott is with me again, I'll be fine. And you already said this would never happen again, so Marisol won't be in any trouble again."

"She shouldn't be in trouble now," Ashton snapped as they reached the doors to Jamie's chambers.

Ashton pushed inside and hauled Jamie to the bed. He pressed Jamie into the bed, then his body seemed to lose some of its stiffness.

"I'm sorry, Jamie. I'm just worried about you. Both of you. You have no idea how precious you are to me, to the school, to our whole society. It's troubling that you fall ill so easily."

Jamie flushed. He hadn't realized that he had a fever, though he was freezing cold and sweating profusely and felt like his head was going to explode. He had assumed it was stress and anger, and then adrenaline. He didn't know how someone could go from being perfectly healthy to weak and feverish in such a short period of time, but he was grateful that Ashton was there to tuck him into bed even while he hated Ashton for being the cause of his discomfort.

"Marisol," Jamie said. "Check on Marisol. I don't want her to get ill."

"Of course," Ashton said. "Now drink this water and get some rest. And stop worrying about Scott."

Jamie drank the water Ashton handed him and laid back in the nest of pillows on the bed. Scott loved having dozens of pillows of all shapes and sizes on the bed, even though most of them got kicked to the ground while they slept, and Jamie cuddled around an especially large pillow and tried to pretend Scott was beside him, asleep. His eyes drifted shut and he reached out to Marisol drowsily. She was fine, he sensed. Ashton would baby her appropriately. Ashton may not care about Jamie, but he did care about Marisol and she was pleased to have the head of the council serving her.

Jamie smiled and felt himself relax. Scott was free from Ashton's control, and Marisol was happy. Then Jamie's smile slipped. Scott wasn't free yet. There was still Derek, the prospective student. Ashton's son. Jamie's fists clenched and his headache roared back to life. Sweat dripped from his forehead and Marisol growled in sympathy. Until Derek was gone, Jamie knew his body was going to rebel. He would just have to try to sleep through the worst of it and hope the weekend ended quickly. Jamie shut his eyes but even though he was exhausted, sleep wouldn't come.

CHAPTER FIFTEEN

Shared Dorm

The dorm next to Derek's was supposed to be where Scott slept during the prospective student's weekend, but it was inexplicably locked and the RA in charge of the floor couldn't get it unlocked. When the RA suggested that he share a room with Derek, Scott knew that the room was locked on purpose to make sure that Scott went through with his task. He wished the whole school didn't have to know about his infidelity, but he'd already heard the other upperclassmen talking about how he was lucky enough to get Derek for his partner and what they would love to do to the poor kid.

Scott almost felt sorry for Derek, except that Derek had come here planning on losing his virginity and was looking forward to it. He still remembered how easily Derek had played on his sympathies and anger rose up in his belly. He would share a room with Derek, but he would be sleeping on the couch. There was no way he was falling asleep in the same bed as that deceptive-

"Something wrong?" Derek asked, interrupting his negative thoughts and jarring Scott back to reality.

"I'll be sleeping with you tonight," Scott said, then winced when Derek's eyes lit up. "I mean, I'll be sleeping in the same room. Not with you."

"It's my father, isn't it?"

"What?"

Derek looked down and suddenly seemed very vulnerable, though he tried to hide it by flashing a wide smile.

"He abandons me my whole life, then promises me one thing and now you won't give it to me because of who I am. He's ruined everything, even the one thing he promised me."

"That's not it at all," Scott said, surprised by the pain in Derek's voice. This was not faked, he could tell. Now that he knew how deceptive Derek could be, he was on the lookout for lying but this was utterly sincere.

"It is," Derek said, tears forming in his eyes. "If I were anyone else, you would have no problems with me. Tell me that isn't true."

Scott was silent for a moment. Was it true? How much was he letting his hatred of Ashton affect his feelings for Derek?

"I would have a hard time with anyone," Scott finally said, reaching out to squeeze Derek's shoulder. Derek leaned into the caress. "You see, I already have a boyfriend."

"Then why are you doing this?"

Scott shut his eyes. "Ashton."

A single word was all that was needed. When he opened his eyes, he saw Derek's understanding.

"I hate him so much," Derek whispered. "He's ruined everything for me, and now he's chosen someone who could never give me what I deserve. I've waited my whole life for this night but instead of choosing someone who could love me, he chose you. Why?"

"It's a long story," Scott said. "But don't give up hope."

Scott spotted two drinks set out on the counter – water. He started to reach for one when Derek stopped him.

"Don't drink that. My father instructed me to put something in the water to to help you agree to sleep with me."

Scott withdrew his hand like it had been burned. "You were going to drug me?"

"He said it made people compliant. I didn't want to do it but he said if you didn't show signs of wanting to sleep with me, to give it to you. I don't want my first time to be like that, though."

"But you still mixed the drink."

Derek shrugged and turned his face away from Scott. "He said it would help. But what does that say about me, that I can't even get a guy unless he's drugged?"

Derek kept his face turned away and his voice was rough. Scott reached out to pat his back, but inside Scott's mind was whirling. Ashton had a drug to make people compliant? He had to warn Jamie. He sent a thought to Narné but the dragon was silent. Damn it, he thought. Arion was interfering with their connection and he couldn't send messages to his dragon. But why wouldn't Arion want him communicating with Narné right now? Was the dragon aware of something that Ashton didn't want him to know, or did he just want Scott focused on his son?

Scott shook his head to rid himself of those thoughts. They wouldn't change the fact that Narné was out of reach for now. And they wouldn't change the poor boy in front of him. Derek was being sincere, for once, and he seemed weary and beaten. Just a kid who was tired of pretending to be someone else all the time, tired of manipulating others to serve his will. He had the potential to become like Ashton, yes, but he still had the seed of a good person in his soul. Ashton hadn't trampled it out of him yet.

And Scott was attracted to him, though nothing could compare to Jamie. He thought of all the other students that Derek might have ended up with. It would have been so easy for Derek to get raped, but Ashton had specifically chosen Scott. Perhaps Ashton really did care for Derek, because Scott was the only student on campus who would be sure to get Derek's complete cooperation and consent first. Scott took a deep breath.

If he was going to do this, commit to Derek and seduce him, he needed to put all thoughts of Jamie out of his mind temporarily. He thought of Jamie's sweet smile and looked at Derek, fearful and full of bravado before him. Then he closed his eyes and imagined all of his time with Jamie going into a box, to be taken out later. Their first, gentle kiss, the sweet taste of Jamie's skin, the mating flight and earning the right to be Jamie's mate forever, sleeping next to him while Jamie curled into his body perfectly, all of it went into the box in his mind until his mind was clear and he could look at Derek without seeing Jamie's shadow.

Then he reached out to caress Derek's cheek, drawing the young man into a kiss. Derek went easily, clutching Scott's shoulders as the kiss deepened. Scott wrapped his hands around Derek's waist as he felt the boy's knees weakening, but he refused to pull out of the kiss as he mapped the boy's mouth, full of honey and sweetness. Derek's hands clenched and un-clenched convulsively on his shoulders and Scott smiled into the kiss as he knew Derek had never been kissed like this before, so passionately or deeply. The knowledge drove him to extend the kiss further until Derek moaned against him and Scott could feel his arousal pressing against his thigh like a molten bar.

"You don't need to drug me," Scott said. "You're beautiful and desirable just the way you are."

"But – your boyfriend," Derek said, gasping for breath.

"He understands," Scott said, praying that is was true. He stroked Derek's cheek and felt just the slightest hint of stubble. Jamie would understand. He had to.

Scott pulled him into another kiss and marveled at how skilled the boy was. And how sensitive. He carded his hand through Derek's hair and the boy moaned against him, while his other hand stroked the boy's back and snuck under his shirt. The skin of his back was warm and smooth, like silk left in the sun, and Scott found himself wanting more. He broke apart from the kiss and peeled off Derek's shirt, revealing a lightly muscled and astonishingly beautiful torso with hazel-brown nipples and well-defined abs. Derek blushed and attempted to cover himself, but Scott pulled his hands away and ran a finger down the center of the boy's chest, from his sternum to the dark hair that formed at his belly button and led to his pants. When he reached the button on Derek's jeans, Derek's breath hitched.

"Wait," he said. "Are we really doing this? Shouldn't we be in the bedroom?"

Scott glanced at the doorway to the bedroom and nodded. Derek's first time should be in a bed, not on a couch. He deserved better. Scott stood up and helped Derek stand. Derek's legs were a little wobbly and he collapsed into Scott's arms. Scott smiled and kissed Derek's forehead.

"Let's get you into bed," he whispered.

He cupped the boy's ass and lifted, and Derek wrapped his legs around Scott's waist, letting him carry him into the bedroom. Derek snuggled his face into Scott's neck, planting kisses up and down. Scott set him on the bed gently but stayed nestled between the boy's legs. He was already getting hard, and both of their erections were pressed together. Derek rubbed against him but he placed a hand on the boy's chest to keep him still. Then Scott pulled off his shirt and Derek licked his lips. He seemed curious about Scott's scars but didn't comment on them.

"You're beautiful," he said. "Will you – can I see all of you?"

In response, Scott unbuttoned his pants and pulled them off, leaving only his boxers, which showed his hard-on quite prominently. He hesitated, a little embarrassed at the intensity of Derek's regard, then lifted the band on his boxers and revealed himself fully. His cock bobbed upward and Derek sighed as if in awe. Derek's legs were still sprawled on either side of Scott and Scott could see him getting harder despite being trapped inside his jeans. Derek had gotten his show, now it was time for Scott's.

He began by pressing the boy flat on his back on the bed and kissing him on the lips, then nibbling along his jaw line until Derek moaned in pleasure. He let his kisses trail down Derek's neck, constantly feeling for Derek's responses. When Derek's cock jerked against his body, Scott paused and paid special attention to that area until Derek squirmed and moaned and rubbed against him. He kissed his way down to the boy's nipples and couldn't resist lightly nipping at one, eliciting a soft cry of pleasure. They were beautiful, peaking in the cool air and beading tightly as Scott's tongue worked circles around them and his teeth gently caressed them. Derek's body spasmed.

"I can't-"

"You can," Scott said firmly. But he moved away from the nipples. They were too sensitive and he didn't want Derek to cum yet. But once they were naked together he knew he would be back to the addicting nubs.

He kissed down the boy's abdomen until he reached the button of his jeans. He unbuttoned them and pulled them down, revealing black boxers that already had a wet spot on them from Derek's precum. Very gently, he pulled off the boxers and Derek's penis popped out, straight and tall like a statue as it curled towards his belly, dripping wet. He heard Derek's indrawn breath and felt the boy's body tighten like a spring.

"You're beautiful," Scott said, letting his breath ghost along Derek's cock.

Derek relaxed, and Scott knew he had been afraid of ridicule or disappointing Scott. But he was anything but a disappointment. The boy's cock was a beautiful rose color and stood at a solid seven inches. He would never disappoint anyone.

Scott pulled Derek's clothes all the way off and then gestured for Derek to get fully on the bed so they could lie next to each other. Derek obeyed, but he looked shy.

"What's wrong?" Scott asked.

"Could we – um – turn the lights off?" Derek asked nervously, glancing at the overhead light directly over the bed.

Scott laughed. "Of course, but you have nothing to be ashamed of. You are truly beautiful."

But he reached for the switch and plunged the room in

partial darkness just the same. Anything to make the boy's first time more enjoyable and less frightening. He remembered his own first time and how terrifying it had been to have sex in the middle of the school under the florescent lighting where anyone could see them. He fully understood the need to hide, even for someone as daring as Derek could be. Because even though Derek was brave and outgoing, this was also new to him and he was probably frightened a little. Scott's first time had been riddled with fear and he wanted to make sure Derek's was as gentle as possible.

Scott climbed into bed and guided Derek so he was lying on his back with Scott balanced over him. Derek's breathing was shallow and he looked so nervous that Scott had to kiss him to ease his discomfort. Kissing seemed to help put Derek back on familiar ground, because as they kissed Derek regained his confidence and began stroking Scott's body. He started with Scott's back, but soon he became bold and one hand reached downward to cup Scott's ass while the other hand moved to the front to fondle his nipples. Everywhere he touched was like fire in Scott's veins and his cock pulsed with life. He lowered himself against Derek so that their cocks were touching and Derek cried out and began grinding against him.

Too soon, Scott thought as he felt Derek's rhythm quicken. He pulled away from Derek and heard Derek's moan of disappointment. He blindly reached for the bedside table drawer. It should be equipped with lube and yes, there it was. He sat up and applied the lube to his fingers.

"I'm going to prepare you, Derek," he said. His voice was huskier than usual and his cock was rock hard. He didn't know if he could make it; the kissing and rubbing had affected him as well as Derek.

He let his moist fingers drag along Derek's cock as the boy hissed and squirmed, then his fingers traced down his balls, under his balls, and finally came to rest at his opening. Derek trembled. Scott ran his fingers around the opening several times as Derek moaned.

"God, that feels good," Derek said.

Scott grinned. That was a good reaction. He took advantage of Derek's pleasure to slip a finger inside the boy and Derek gasped. Scott leaned forward to kiss Derek as his finger worked in and out of him, loosening him for Scott's cock. Their tongues met and danced together as fire filled Scott's veins. When Derek had fully relaxed, he slipped in a second finger and continued kissing. Derek sucked on his tongue, occasionally letting out murmurs of sheer pleasure as Scott added a third finger. Finally Derek pulled away from him and threw his head back.

"Enough," he cried. "I want you in me now! Fuck me, Scott!"

Scott's cock trembled and leapt to attention at the command. He used the lube liberally, not wanting to hurt the boy, then slowly pressed against the boy's opening. Derek bore down on him and grimaced slightly as Scott popped inside the tight ring of muscle. Both men gasped as Scott entered Derek for the first time. Scott moaned and leaned forward to kiss Derek again. He was so hot and tight, and it felt like silk as he gently pressed into Derek's body. Derek, for his part, had grabbed Scott's ass and was trying to pull him in faster, but Scott was determined to have a slow entry to make sure he didn't injure the boy. Derek's legs were drawn up to his hips and he was panting, his cock rock solid between them.

When Scott was fully seated inside Derek, he paused to catch his breath. Derek's eyes were shut and a look of pained pleasure was on his face. He was barely breathing.

"Are you alright?" Scott asked breathlessly.

Derek opened his eyes in surprise.

"Yeah," he whispered. "Yeah."

"Breathe," Scott reminded him.

Derek took a deep breath and smiled.

Scott kissed him, then began to move. Derek cried out and

Scott paused, wondering if he was in pain.

"No, don't stop," Derek shouted. "Keep going!"

Scott started moving again and Derek began moving with him until their rhythm became one. The bed rocked violently with the force of their motion and Scott idly wondered what the students next door must think before remembering that the room next door was empty. Good thing, too, because their rocking grew more and more violent as Derek seemed to come alive and demand more and more. His legs grasped at Scott's waist and pulled him closer, and his arms wrapped around Scott's torso as he rocked against Scott's cock and cried out for him to thrust harder, faster. Scott obliged, pleasure streaking through his body as sweat began to pour from his forehead and his chest. Derek too was shining with the effort of his exertions and he looked almost angelic, shining in the moonlight with an expression of bliss on his face.

Scott thrust harder and felt his balls tightening. He was about to cum. He shut his eyes and sat up, out of Derek's arms but still in full contact with his ass. His thrusts became erratic. He reached down and stroked Derek's cock from root to tip until Derek whimpered. He felt Derek quivering in his hand, but he kept his eyes closed.

"Are you ready?" he asked.

Derek was beyond words and Scott didn't open his eyes to see if he nodded. He just let his pleasure take control. He thrust one last time into Derek as his balls drew up and spasmed, and he felt his seed spray deep into Derek's body just as the boy let out a scream and his own cock jerked in Scott's hand and a stream of cum shot outward once, twice, and a smaller third time. Scott stroked the cock in his hand one last time before releasing it, a feeling of peace spreading over him. He opened his eyes and saw Derek sprawled before him with an expression of sheer bliss on his face.

Scott slowly pulled out, careful not to hurt the boy, then

got up and went to the bathroom. He cleaned himself up and brought a moist towel back to Derek. Derek looked puzzled until Scott began using the towel to wipe off the semen on his chest and belly. Then Derek looked embarrassed, ashamed almost, as if he had done something wrong by having an orgasm. Scott kissed him on the cheek and finished cleaning him off. He brought the towel back to the bathroom and returned to Derek's side. The boy was sitting up on the edge of the bed looking nervous and pale. Scott sat next to him and took his hand.

"Is everything all right?"

"Yeah," Derek said. "Just – did I do okay?"

Scott stared at him. He had been so worried about giving Derek a good first experience it had never even occurred to him that Derek might be worried about his actions.

"You were perfect," Scott said.

"Will you sleep with me tonight?"

Scott sighed. He had managed to put Jamie out of his mind long enough to give Derek the first time he deserved, but Jamie dominated Scott's life and he couldn't ignore his true love forever. They had never spoken about what was going to happen, but they had reached a silent agreement that Scott would have sex with Derek and nothing more. Nothing that hinted at intimacy, no touching that wasn't required, nothing except the sex. So even though it would hurt Derek to be refused so soon after his first time, Scott knew what his answer had to be.

"I'm sorry, Derek."

Derek looked down. "I know. Your boyfriend." Tears filled his eyes. "You don't feel anything for me, do you? I thought – just now – that there was a connection between us. That I was special. Was it all an act? Were you just using me?"

"No, Derek," Scott said. "You are special. And I do have feelings for you. That's why I can't sleep with you tonight."

"Who would know? I wouldn't tell anyone."

"I would know."

Derek's lip quivered and Scott was tempted to soothe it with a kiss. What harm could there be from sleeping with Derek, after all? It would certainly make his first time more positive, and that was Scott's goal. To leave him alone after what they had just experienced would be cruel. Scott sighed.

"Alright, I'll sleep with you. But just tonight."

Derek brightened as if a switch had been turned on.

"Thank you, Scott. You won't regret it."

Scott nodded, and hoped he wouldn't.

CHAPTER SIXTEEN

Obedience

Mike puzzled over Kale's behavior as they walked back to the dragon canyon to see how Jamie had fared. Kale felt some sort of attraction for him, but how could anyone be interested in Mike when they had Ashton's attention? Mike was nothing compared to Ashton. He wasn't sure what to make of Kale's story, either, about Ashton wanting to kill Kale. Surely the man had misunderstood. Ashton would never want his lover to die, and even if something had happened between Ashton and Kale, it would never happen between Ashton and Mike.

Mike fingered the collar around his neck nervously. He knew Ashton was secretive and deceptive, but he always seemed so open with Mike. They slept together, after all. Not just sex, but sleeping in the same bed through the night, with Mike cuddled against Ashton's strong body as they inhaled each other's breath and dreams. Ashton couldn't possibly wish him harm.

His ass twitched slightly and he was forced to amend that last statement – Ashton might wish him harm, but only in the service of granting him pleasure. And only with Ashton in complete control of the situation. Mike trusted him, body and soul, and he was richly rewarded.

He noticed Kale observing him and flushed, hoping his thoughts weren't too obvious. Luckily, they had just reached the bottom of the path up to Jamie's room. Eraxes sent him a brief warning that Ashton was angry with Kale and Kale should not come any closer.

"Thank you for walking back with me," Mike said.

"Let me guess," Kale said. "I'm not welcome anywhere near the queen's chambers."

Mike nodded.

"I should have known," Kale said with a sigh. "Well, it was a pleasure talking to you, Mike. I hope you'll remember what I've said. You're not alone, and if you're ever in a position where your life is in danger, remember that you have other options."

"Thanks, but I won't need the advice. Ashton would never hurt me."

Kale smiled sadly. "I truly hope so. Give my regards to Jamie."

Mike waved as he left, then Mike started up the path. Eraxes was antsy, eager for Mike to hurry up and reach Jamie's room, but he wouldn't tell Mike why. Mike knocked on the door and was surprised when Ashton answered it. He couldn't decide whether that meant Jamie's talk had gone well or poorly. Ashton looked upset, but a worn smile crossed his lips as he saw Mike.

"Ah, Michael, you're just in time," he said. "Jamie and Marisol are in need of some help."

For one brief moment, Mike thought Ashton had attacked the queen and needed his help covering the crime or helping them recover from his attack. Then he shook his head sharply and tried to rid himself of those thoughts. Ashton would never attack the queen. Ashton was the head of the council, head of all Tarragon society; he would never allow anyone to attack the queen.

Ashton must have caught the look in his eye in his brief moment of doubt because his faint smile faded.

"You've been talking to Kale."

It wasn't a question. Mike nodded.

"We will deal with that later," Ashton promised. "For now, go in and check on Jamie. He's in the bedroom. I will continue soothing Marisol."

"What happened?"

Ashton gave him a long, cold look before turning his back and heading to Marisol's room. "Marisol is suffering from morning sickness," he said over his shoulder. "Jamie should have been strong enough not to be affected, but because of his recent stress, he has become ill."

Then he was gone, into Marisol's chamber. Mike's eyes narrowed. Jamie had seemed a little off in their conversation before going to confront Ashton, but Mike had figured it was just anger and frustration, not illness. He went into the bedroom where he found Jamie cuddling a pillow with his eyes closed, but his uneven breathing and fluttering eyelids were a dead giveaway that he was wide awake.

"Jamie, it's Mike," he said. "How are you feeling? What happened?"

"I did it," Jamie said, opening his green eyes and fixing them on Mike. "I got Ashton to agree not to bother Scott again."

"Really?"

Mike frowned. He had wanted Jamie to win, of course, but he hadn't expected to find Jamie limp and feverish afterwards. Had Ashton just told Jamie what he wanted to hear to help the boy get better soon, or was it a sincere promise? And if Ashton had really agreed, why did it seem so easy to get him to change his mind about Scott? Unless Ashton had already decided that he wasn't going to make Scott sleep with anyone else, and this whole confrontation was useless. He imagined that Jamie had some strong arguments, especially since he was the queen, but Ashton's capitulation seemed far too easy.

"But he still has to go through with this weekend," Jamie said, shutting his eyes again.

Mike nodded slowly. Perhaps that was why Ashton agreed. He thought that this one betrayal was enough to shatter Jamie and Scott's relationship, so there was no need for future affairs.

And it did seem to be shattering Jamie at least. The boy was white as the sheets he lay in and trembling as if freezing, but sweat glistened on his forehead and upper lip. Mike laid a hand on his forehead and wasn't surprised that the boy was running a fever.

"Tell me about Derek," Jamie said. "I want to hear it from you."

Mike sighed and sat down on the bed, taking Jamie's hand. He didn't want to talk about Scott's required lover, but he knew that the jealousy and the unknowing was eating Jamie alive.

"I've told you most of what I know already," Mike said. "He has dark hair and dark eyes. He is attractive," Mike added reluctantly. "But I don't think he's Scott's type. Scott has always gone for men with lighter coloring."

"Like you?"

"More like you," Mike said with a pained smile. Jamie probably hadn't meant his comment as a barb, but it stung and reminded him that Jamie had never really told him what he thought about the fact that he had raped Scott.

"He seems nice enough," Mike continued. "Talkative, outgoing, but if he's anything like Ashton-"

Mike's breath caught. He couldn't say it. Couldn't say that Ashton was manipulative, devious, a liar. He knew it was true, Kale had confirmed that it was true, but he didn't want it to be true. Unconsciously he turned to Marisol's chamber where Ashton was taking care of the queen dragon. A sudden longing for Ashton filled him. He needed to breathe in Ashton's scent and feel the man's strong arms around him. He needed Ashton.

Jamie shifted in the bed and Mike returned his attention to the boy with a start. He had completely lost focus.

"It's okay," Jamie said. "I know how you feel about Ashton. I think I can get some rest now. Thank you for talking to me."

"I didn't help," Mike said.

"It's okay," Jamie repeated. "Why don't you make sure Marisol is still alright?"

"Thank you, Jamie," Mike whispered.

He was moved by Jamie's compassion. Even when Jamie was lying in bed with a fever, he was still willing to sacrifice his comfort in order to help a friend.

"The doctor will be in soon to get you some medicine, and you'll be up in no time," Mike said. Eraxes confirmed that the doctor was already on her way from the campus and would arrive in less than fifteen minutes. "I hate to leave you," he added, but Jamie made a shooing gesture.

"I think I can fall asleep," he said. "You don't have to stay."

Mike nodded and backed out of the room, making sure Jamie didn't change his mind at the last minute. He felt like he was abandoning Jamie, but the overwhelming urge to see Ashton was still flooding his mind and he couldn't fight it. Once he was out of sight of Jamie, he sprinted into Marisol's chambers and found Ashton rubbing Marisol's belly while she made whining noises and tossed her head like a five-year-old faking a stomachache. Ashton turned as he approached.

"Is Jamie asleep?"

"He will be soon," Mike replied, a little guiltily. But the sight of Ashton was so reassuring. He approached the older man and laid his hand on Ashton's shoulder, needing physical contact with him. Ashton placed his hand on top of Mike's and twisted their fingers together.

"Is everything alright?"

"Yeah," Mike said. "I just needed to come in here."

He was blushing, he knew, and he could tell that Marisol was extremely interested in what was going on between them because she had stopped whining and writhing around and was watching them intently. Ashton lifted their entwined hands and placed both on Marisol's belly.

"Well, you are welcome to help me take care of Marisol. She's feeling a bit under the weather. Her morning sickness and Jamie's illness are reinforcing each other and both are becoming more ill."

Her scales did feel a little warmer than usual, but it was hard to tell in a creature who always felt as if she had been soaking in sunbeams for hours on end.

"She hasn't shown signs of morning sickness before," Mike said, thinking back to previous mornings.

"Jamie's stress must have weakened her," Ashton said. "Or else it came on rapidly for other reasons. Either way, Marisol doesn't think it is harming the eggs. It seems to be a natural part of her pregnancy, though she's not happy about it."

Marisol whined and laid her head on the dragon bed, looking at Mike with pleading eyes.

Rub my belly? She asked. *It feels better when you do.*

Mike obeyed as Ashton stood and checked his watch.

"Mike, I need to speak with Jamie alone for a few minutes. I'll be right back."

"He's sleeping," Mike said.

"This can't wait."

"You're not going to go back on your deal, are you?"

Ashton stopped and turned to stare at Mike. "What makes you think that?"

Mike swallowed. From Ashton's predatory pose, it seemed like that was exactly what the man was preparing to do. "Can't you just let them be happy together until the next mating flight? If anyone needs to be seduced, I'll do it in Scott's place. You don't need him."

"You?" Ashton let out a bark of laughter and was suddenly at Mike's side, stroking Mike's cheek. "You belong to me, pet, and I will never let you sleep with anyone else."

Mike knew he should have felt threatened, or controlled, but instead a wave of love poured over him and he couldn't fight the proud smile that split his face as he leaned into Ashton's caress. He cautiously reached out to embrace Ashton and the older man allowed it. Briefly. Then Ashton pulled away and considered him.

"It really means so much to you?" he asked.

"Yes," Mike said. "The queen is suffering. Jamie is suffering. Scott is suffering."

"And you still have feelings for Scott."

Mike blushed. "He will always hold a place in my heart."

"I should be the only one in your heart," Ashton said in a low voice. "If I do this, if I choose to let Scott and Jamie be together after this weekend until the next mating flight, I want a promise from you."

"Anything for you," Mike whispered.

"That is what I want," Ashton said with a pleased smile. "I want your absolute obedience, no matter what I ask of you. Can you do that?"

Marisol growled and extended a claw to pull Mike away from Ashton.

You should not agree to something you do not understand, she warned.

But Mike's mind was already made up. He belonged to Ashton, and he would obey Ashton. He thought briefly of Kale's warning but it seemed so distant with Ashton here before him. Ashton would never hurt him. Ashton would never ask that of him. Ashton loved him, and Mike owed him obedience.

"I will obey you to the best of my abilities," Mike said, pulling away from Marisol's claws and bowing his head before Ashton.

Ashton grinned and kissed his forehead. "Good boy. Now go to my chambers and wait for me there. I will be along shortly."

"You don't need any help with Marisol?"

"Not anymore," he said.

Mike felt a weight lift off his chest. Ashton was not planning on confronting Jamie, then. He knew what would have happened if Ashton had confronted Jamie while the boy was ill. Ashton would have somehow gotten Jamie to agree to allow Scott to sleep with other men without realizing what he was agreeing to, and when he recovered and realized what he had agreed to, he would be devastated. All of that would be averted by simple obedience to Ashton, a man that Mike was already obedient to. As Mike left the room, Ashton called his name. Mike turned back.

"Remember, Michael," Ashton said. "You are not allowed to talk to Kale ever again."

Mike nodded, and some of the weight that had lifted settled back down. He had been drawn to Kale, the only man who understood what it was like to be Ashton's pet, but if Ashton didn't want them talking then they wouldn't talk. He wondered what he was supposed to do if Kale cornered him – say nothing and leave? Surely a few pleasantries were permissible. As he headed to Ashton's room, he nodded to himself. If Kale spoke to him, he would speak back, but there would be no more drawn-out conversations between them. It hurt a little, knowing that Ashton was limiting his life already, but he had sworn obedience and he would do his best.

He thought of Ashton's powerful form looming over him in bed and shut his eyes in imagined ecstasy. For Ashton, he would do anything. But he wouldn't quite cut Kale out of his life, not if the other man pushed his way in.

CHAPTER SEVENTEEN

Kissing the Enemy

Jamie heard Mike leave the room and turned over restlessly. Despite what he had told Mike, he knew that sleep was far away. He was too restless. He hoped the doctors arrived soon, because he felt sick to his stomach and weaker than he should. The door to his room creaked and Ashton's strong figure entered the room. Jamie rolled away from him. He did not want to see Ashton in his current condition.

"Marisol is feeling better," Ashton began, and Jamie was relieved that at least one problem was taken care of. He sent a thought to Marisol and found her in a deep sleep, happy and satisfied with the amount of attention that had been showered over her. "How are you feeling?"

"Not much better," Jamie replied, still turned away from Ashton.

He felt a weight on the bed. Ashton was sitting next to him. Then a hand pressed on his shoulder, forcing him onto his back where he couldn't ignore Ashton. Ashton smiled at him, but it was a predator's smile and Jamie shivered. Was Ashton about to go back on their deal? No, he couldn't. Weak or not, Jamie wouldn't let him.

"Our deal still stands," Jamie said, trying to sound as smooth and collected as possible. "You can't make Scott sleep with anyone else."

"Except for Derek, of course. It's night, you know. Do you

think your boyfriend is fulfilling his duty tonight?"

Jamie winced and shut his eyes, but shutting them only filled his mind with images of Scott kissing a handsome dark-haired boy, laying the boy on the bed and entering him with a sweet look of concentration on his face. Scott would be a gentle lover, Jamie knew, and would make sure that the experience was good for Derek just as he had made sure it was good for Jamie. That sweetness belonged to Jamie, however, and it was agony thinking of sharing it with anyone. Jamie quickly opened his eyes to block out the images, but found himself staring into Ashton's eyes. Ashton was only a few inches from his face and Jamie flinched.

"I could make you agree to go back on the deal," Ashton said. "It would be so easy. But I won't. I'll let you and Scott have whatever peace you can find in each other's arms until the next mating flight. But you will be mine next mating flight."

Ashton lowered his head and before Jamie could react, the man's lips were pressed upon his. He tried to struggle but he was too weak and Ashton overpowered him, grabbing his arms and pinning them to the bed, ignoring his futile kicks and instead running his tongue along Jamie's tightly shut mouth. Jamie shuddered. Ashton was good. He didn't want to react to the kiss, but there was something almost magical about the way Ashton was kissing him, as if his body was just waiting for the stimulation and was now going into hyperdrive.

He felt himself hardening embarrassingly fast, and even though he hadn't opened his mouth to Ashton his body was preparing itself for seduction. Only his mind was rebelling, and it was doing so loudly. Ashton ran his hand down Jamie's body and let it trace between his thighs, which opened of their own accord to give him access to the area between. Ashton cupped his hardening mound and smiled into the kiss.

"So responsive," he murmured.

Jamie whimpered. He didn't want to respond but Ashton

could light a stone on fire. Ashton placed one hand on Jamie's forehead to hold him still while his mouth traveled from his lips to his neck, kissing and nipping the skin as he went. His other hand stroked Jamie's lengthening cock as Jamie helplessly ground against him.

"No," Jamie whispered.

"Relax," Ashton said. "I'm only going to touch you, not enter you. I want you to know that you don't have to be afraid of your next mating flight, when I take you."

Then his lips were busy on Jamie's collarbone and Jamie whined and shifted uncomfortably at the sudden pleasure. His hands were free now, but they felt limp and unresponsive, as if he had been drugged or something. He wondered if perhaps Ashton had slipped something into the drink he had been given earlier that evening and that were the reason for this strange lust and the stranger inability to move. Jamie focused on his hands. He needed to push Ashton away before his body betrayed him further. Ashton might feel incredible, but he belonged to Scott and no one had the right to touch him this way.

He closed his eyes and tried to ignore the lips on his body and the hand stroking him through his pajama pants. Already a moist spot was forming on his pants and Ashton was massaging him gently as he reached his full length. All he needed was his hands. They tingled with pins and needles and he focused on lifting them. They lifted, but it was an enormous exertion. Still, anything was worth getting Ashton away. He dropped his hands on Ashton's back and pushed, trying to disrupt the man's rhythm and get him to stop.

It worked. Ashton broke off his kisses and looked up in surprise.

"Stop," Jamie said. "Stop now."

Ashton released him. Jamie hissed at the sudden end to the pressure and longed for more caresses, but he knew he had to be strong. For Scott, if not for himself.

"Are you sure?" Ashton asked with a knowing smile, tilting his head to indicate Jamie's hard on.

"Don't touch me," Jamie said.

The smile on Ashton's lips faded. He leaned and kissed Jamie on the forehead. "You've had a long day, little one, and perhaps it was wrong of me to push you further. But if you ever need more, just let me know."

Jamie tried to draw back from him, disgust welling up within him. Thoughts of Mike crossed his mind and he shivered.

"What would Mike think about this?" he asked.

"Michael knows who I am," Ashton said. "He knows I intend to take you during the next mating flight."

"But this is different."

"This is only to prepare you," Ashton said, running his hand through Jamie's hair with something resembling genuine concern. "I don't want you to be frightened, or hurt. I will be gentle with you at the mating flight, and before."

"Not before," Jamie said firmly. "Never before. And not at the flight, either. I already told you, only Narné and Scott will fly with me."

Ashton kissed his forehead again. "The innocence of youth. You will learn in time. I only hope the knowledge doesn't hurt too much."

He straightened and went to the door, checking outside as if looking for someone. Evidently he found what he was looking for, because his demeanor changed and he squared his shoulders before turning back to Jamie.

"Your doctor is here," he said. "Do behave. It is in the college's best interests to have you healthy and happy."

"The doctor can fix my health," Jamie said. "But you control my happiness."

"Indeed," Ashton said, letting his eyes linger on Jamie's body. "Then after this weekend, I expect no more episodes like this."

He left and was replaced by a woman in green scrubs. She looked vaguely familiar and introduced herself as Emma, one of the doctors who had helped Jamie after the first year exam. She examined from a distance and Jamie flushed when he realized his body was still in a state of full arousal. Cursing, he buried his hands in his crotch to hide his hard on, knowing that his face was bright red. The doctor didn't approach until he had himself under control, and when she did come closer there was a look of pity on her face, as if she understood what Ashton had tried to do.

"How are you feeling?" Emma asked, carefully resting her hands on his shoulders to push him back into the pillows.

Surprisingly, he felt a little better than before, or maybe he was just so panicked about what Ashton had done that there was no room in his mind to pay attention to his illness.

"Better," he said.

She placed a thermometer in his mouth, then examined the readout with a small crinkle in the middle of her forehead.

"You still have a temperature. I understand that this came on suddenly. Being as close to the queen dragon as you are, you're extremely susceptible to her health issues. You will need to stay very healthy in order to keep functioning during her pregnancy, when her health and temperature will vary from day to day. Otherwise, you'll get a fever and nausea every time she gets morning sickness."

"I'm trying to stay healthy, but I'm under a lot of stress," Jamie said.

The situation with Ashton hadn't helped the stress, even though he had Ashton's word that Scott wouldn't have to sleep with anyone else. Except Derek, as Ashton had pointed out. Jamie frowned. Something about the way Ashton had phrased that made it seem like Ashton intended to have Scott sleep with Derek again in the future, and because Derek was exempt from the agreement now, he would always be exempt. When

Jamie had enough energy, he would have to go to Ashton again and clarify that point. But the thought of seeing Ashton again, seeing the lips that had brought such forbidden pleasure to his body and the hand that he had ground against in helpless pleasure, was not a good thought and he wanted to stay as far away from Ashton as possible. At least he had the strength to resist Ashton, he thought. Even though his body had given in, his mind had remained strong and he didn't feel like he had betrayed Scott.

He wondered briefly how Scott felt, if Scott was able to do the same and let his body go through the motions of sex without an emotional connection. He somehow doubted it, but it was the only way Jamie could imagine Scott and Derek together without wanting to throw up. Scott was strong enough, so perhaps he would manage to sleep with Derek without forming any kind of emotional attachment. Jamie hoped so, because anything else would be a betrayal of their relationship, and Jamie was already in such a delicate state after his confrontation with Ashton that he didn't know if he could handle more.

"I understand," Emma said. "Your mate is with the prospective student. Well, you still need to take care of yourself. I'm ordering bedrest for the next day. Try to get as much sleep as you can; you need all your energy to recover. I'll be back to check on you tomorrow morning."

She felt his forehead with her hand, the way Jamie's mother used to, and sorrow welled up in Jamie's throat. It had been a long time since he had someone looking out for him like this. His aunt had never cared, and even though this woman was only a doctor and probably didn't have any emotion invested in him, it seemed like she cared as she tightened the covers around him and stood to leave.

"Wait," he called as she crossed the threshold into the corridor. She turned. "Thank you," he said quietly.

Emma smiled and waved, then turned off the light in his room and faded into the darkness.

CHAPTER EIGHTEEN

Visions

Scott woke with a familiar weight on his chest and he stroked the head resting on him without thinking, lifting the hair to plant a kiss on the forehead of his lover. His eyes were still shut with sleep and he was surprised when the body cradled against him stiffened in surprise and the head pulled away from him. He opened his eyes to ask if Jamie was all right and saw Derek instead.

His first instinct was to push the boy away, but Derek's sleepy gaze warned him that such a movement would be misinterpreted as hatred and ruin any goodwill built up between them. It would scar the boy's first time to be tossed aside so quickly, so instead Scott carefully extricated himself from Derek's arms in an attempt to stand up. Derek gripped him firmly, however, and refused to let go. Scott wasn't surprised to feel the boy's lust pressing against his leg, but he wasn't going to have sex with Derek a second time. He had slept with the boy, their bodies cradled together, and that was enough of a betrayal.

Derek refused to let Scott pull away and despite the sleep in his eyes, Derek was strong, even stronger than Scott since Scott was holding back some of his strength out of fear of hurting the boy. Derek pinned Scott to the bed and straddled him, looking down on Scott with victory in his eyes. He leaned down and kissed Scott's bare chest, his kisses working their way lower on his chest. Scott drew in a breath as his body began to respond against his will. The caress of Derek's lips and tongue across his abdomen was an aphrodisiac and his breath grew shallow as Derek's hands slipped to his hips and began working in circles, moving towards his inner thighs. Without thinking he spread his legs and Derek nestled between them, pulling the sheets away to expose his hardening cock.

Derek scooted down on the bed and Scott sat up abruptly, realizing what the boy was about to do.

"Derek," he said. "You don't-"

"Don't worry," Derek said, flashing him a smile. "I've never done this, but I know how."

Then he leaned down and hesitantly touched his tongue to Scott's cock. Scott let out a strangled moan. He needed to stop this immediately and he tried to pull Derek away, but Derek fought him off. Scott had just managed to get a grip on the boy and was about to toss him off the bed when Derek's hand snaked out and grabbed his balls, squeezing them threateningly. Scott froze.

"Let me do this," Derek warned, running his fingers over Scott's sensitive flesh. Scott moaned.

"Derek, don't do this," he whispered.

"Lie back down," Derek commanded.

When Scott didn't obey, Derek squeezed his balls again and Scott found himself flat on his back, waiting for the pain to end. Just like his father, Scott thought. Using pain and manipulation to get what he wanted. But why would he want this? What advantage would it give him? Derek's mouth returned to his softening cock and the touch of his lips started him hardening again. He moaned.

Derek may not have had experience but as he said, he did know what he was doing. He worked his tongue in small, concentric circles along his shaft, lapping up the precum that was escaping in small spurts with an expression of surprised pleasure. Scott's anger faded into pleasure and soon Derek's touches brought only bliss. He was so beautiful there, cradled between Scott's legs with his dark eyes glowing and his mouth stretched around Scott's cock. Scott's mind rebelled against the image – only Jamie should ever touch him – but he was helpless to resist Derek's caresses.

Derek lay Scott's cock against his tongue and then slid it into his mouth as far as it would go and Scott let out another moan, involuntarily grabbing Derek's hair and pushing against him to enter him further. Derek relaxed his jaw and let Scott control him, allowing him to dive into his throat as the sweet tightness enveloped him. He pulled out to give Derek a chance to breathe and thrust again. The pleasure was incredible. He couldn't even believe this was someone besides Jamie, because he was thoroughly aroused and wanted nothing more than for this to continue forever. What was wrong with him?

Derek took him into his throat again and rubbed his tongue along the vein in his cock and Scott curled around the boy, grunting in pleasure as the boy swabbed the sensitive spot over and over. He was so close to cumming. He didn't want to cum in the boy's mouth – that might be too much, no matter how adventurous the boy was – so he reluctantly pulled away from Derek.

"I'm going to-"

Words escaped him as Derek pulled him into his mouth again, again licking his sensitive shaft and drawing him further into his throat. He couldn't control it any more. He felt his balls draw up tight against his body and then semen spewed forth into Derek's willing mouth. For several long seconds all he knew was pleasure, and then he slumped forward.

Derek coughed and made a gagging sound, then laughed.

"I wasn't expecting that."

"I'm sorry," Scott said.

"Don't be," Derek said. "I wanted it. I wasn't expecting it to feel like that, that's all."

They were silent for several minutes as Derek leaned his cheek against Scott's thigh and stroked his fingers along Scott's skin. Then Derek stood up and stretched, a back-cracking stretch. His fingers nearly touched the ceiling as he rose up on his tip-toes. He grinned at Scott.

"You're incredible, you know?" Derek said in a seductive voice. "Better than I imagined. I want to try that again sometime. I think I can do better."

"Somehow I doubt that," Scott said, then pulled himself together. What was he doing, flirting with Derek? What would Jamie think? "We have a busy day today," he said, forcing his limp body to sit up and get out of bed. "Why don't you take the first shower."

As soon as Derek vanished into the bathroom, Scott began trembling and covered his face with his hands. This couldn't be happening. What was he going to tell Jamie? A tear ran down his face at the thought of his precious Jamie, the only thing that mattered in this world, being hurt because of his actions. He got up and went into the kitchen where the two glasses of water still stood, one of them laced with a drug if Derek had been telling the truth. If he had been drugged when he had sex with Derek, that would be understandable. But instead, he had had sex with Derek – twice, no less – and slept with him, all in less than twelve hours. He still had two more days with the boy and there was no way he could keep Derek off him if this morning was any indication.

Scott took a deep breath. He had been gentle with the boy because he hadn't wanted to ruin his first time, but that first time was long over now. From this point on, he would refuse any physical contact no matter how it hurt Derek. He nodded to himself and felt somewhat pleased with decision, even though he knew the damage had been done. He tried to reach Narné to see what the dragon thought of the situation, but Narné was still silent. Apparently Ashton and Arion wanted him to face this ordeal alone.

The water turned off and a few minutes later Derek emerged from the shower with only a towel wrapped around his waist. He was truly beautiful, Scott thought, though he could never compare to Jamie. But perhaps Jamie would understand why Scott was drawn to him and be a little forgiving.

"I half-expected you to join me," Derek said with a smile, shaking the moisture from his dark curls.

"There will be no more of that," Scott said. "I will be sleeping next door tonight."

The smile on Derek's lips faded. "I see. Well, the bathroom is all yours."

Scott had expected more of a struggle, and he could practically see the wheels in Derek's head spinning to turn this to his advantage. Clearly Derek viewed this as a temporary setback, much as he had viewed Scott's protests in bed this morning before he had manhandled Scott into staying still. Scott warily slipped into the bathroom and made sure the door was locked four times before he stepped into the steam of the shower.

He scrubbed himself thoroughly and roughly, longing for some way to erase the scent of Derek from his skin. But he knew Jamie would pick it up instantly. Jamie had developed an acute sense of smell ever since the first year exam and he would be able to tell that Scott and Derek had spent a considerable amount of time with their bodies pressed against each other, far more time than necessary for sex. He just hoped Jamie wouldn't be able to smell exactly what had happened between them.

His skin was red and raw from the scrubbing and the heat of the water by the time he was finished, and he toweled himself off with a sense of loathing. He was about to exit out into Derek's territory and he had no idea what to expect. He knew that Derek had a drug that could subdue him, so he shouldn't eat or drink anything in Derek's presence, but Derek had said that he didn't want to resort to such measures. The boy had seemed sincere, but was he? It was hard to tell with him. The sex and the cuddling were understandable, but the oral sex this morning was different. It was almost as if Derek were dominating him, even though Derek was the one pleasuring him. Still, Derek had been completely in control and had forced himself on Scott even though Scott had refused.

Scott left the bathroom with a towel around his waist just as Derek had, since there were no clothes to change into. Derek was nowhere to be seen, so he went to his small bag and grabbed some clothes and his bathroom supplies before returning to the bathroom. He was just rinsing out his mouth after brushing his teeth when he heard Derek in the other room. When he went out to greet the boy, he stopped short. Next to Derek stood Ashton, and the older man wore a smirk as Scott hesitantly joined them. He was thankful he was wearing clothes, because Ashton's gaze scoured him from head to toe and back again. Derek was dressed as well, and his dark hair had dried into a halo of curls that framed his face in much the same way Ashton's straight dark hair framed his.

"Ashton," Scott said hesitantly. "What brings you here?"

"Just spending some time with my son," the man said, turning to his son and putting a hand on his shoulder. He gazed at Derek and Derek's face lit up as if Ashton's regard were the best gift in the universe. Scott's heart went out to the young boy, who was clearly starved for fatherly affection and was desperate even for the simple gesture of a hand on the shoulder and a smile.

"I don't want to disturb you, then," Scott said, edging towards the door and hoping that Ashton was sincere in his desire for time with Derek and not just using this as an excuse to lord his power over Scott's head.

"You won't disturb us at all," Ashton said, turning to face Scott. "Why don't you stay?"

"Yes, stay," Derek said, still staring at his father with a goofy smile on his face. He looked absolutely besotted at the thought of his father spending time with him and Scott wondered if Ashton had ever paid attention to his child before. Probably not, since Derek had never had any value before. Now, Derek was his wedge between Scott and Jamie and only because of that did he have value. But Derek didn't know that, couldn't know that, and probably thought that his father's attention was sincere.

Ashton sat in the only chair in the apartment, forcing Scott and Derek to share the couch. Derek reached out and took Scott's hand without looking at him and Scott wondered if he was afraid of his father or trying to prove to his father that he was no longer a virgin. Either way, Scott tolerated the hand-holding for only a few moments before carefully withdrawing his hand. Ashton noticed everything and the smirk on his face grew more pronounced.

"I see you two have become well-acquainted with each other," Ashton said.

Derek blushed and ducked his head in an uncharacteristically modest gesture. Scott felt his face tightening into a scowl.

"You got what you wanted," he said. "My part in this is done."

He felt Derek's disappointment, but could still feel the wheels turning in the boy's head as he looked up at Scott with considering eyes. Scott ignored him and instead kept his focus on Ashton. Derek was a minor threat who would vanish tomorrow and not reappear until classes started in the fall. Ashton was the major force of evil on campus and would continue to challenge his relationship with Jamie for as long as the two of them lived.

Ashton stared at him coldly, then turned to his son.

"And you, Derek? Are you satisfied?"

Derek stared into his father's eyes as if trying to determine the correct answer, and Scott felt pity overwhelm him. He was so desperate to please his father, there was little else left of his own personality. Scott tried once more to reach out to Narné and suddenly a vision overcame his senses. He saw Derek, but it was a very different Derek with stress lines crisscrossing his face. His mouth was drawn into a frown and his right arm flung forward as if commanding an army. The vision zoomed outward and Scott gasped. Derek sat astride a magnificent dragon, larger than most, but what caught Scott's attention was the color. She was a queen dragon, crimson in the dying sunlight, and Derek was leading her into battle. The image vanished abruptly and Scott blinked as the sunlight became florescent beams from the ceiling and the strong leader astride a queen dragon became a young boy hesitant to answer his father's question.

Scott had never seen one of Narné's visions before, but the dragon had described them in enough detail that he recognized it instantly. It was a vision of a future that was likely to occur, if the world continued on its present course. But for Derek to partner with a queen meant that the campus would have two queen dragons, which had not occurred for thousands of years, since the time before dragons had to hide in the mists. And the older Derek had been leading other dragons into battle – what possible battle could this be? Surely dragons wouldn't be used against humans, but that only left a battle between dragons, and the thought chilled Scott's heart. Where was Jamie in the vision? Where was Scott?

"What did you see, Scott?" Ashton asked loudly, and Scott realized he had already asked that question twice while Scott was deep in thought.

Derek was being ignored completely and Ashton's focus was entirely on Scott. But Scott couldn't share the vision with Derek present, and he wasn't sure he wanted to share it with Ashton at all.

"I'm sorry," he said, raising a hand to his head. "I have a terrible headache. Perhaps it would be best if I went to my rooms to lie down for a while."

Ashton's lips tightened and his eyes narrowed. Would he let Scott return to Jamie's room or would he try to interfere? Scott held his breath, waiting for his reaction.

"Perhaps that would be best. I'm sure your headache will be gone by lunchtime, however, since my son needs his student escort for the afternoon activities."

"Of course," Scott murmured.

That meant Derek would be on his own for the morning, but Scott knew any of the upperclassmen would be willing to let the boy tag along as they instructed the prospective students in the history of the college and introduced them to some of the teachers. He would be fine, Scott thought, remembering how much of a social butterfly Derek had been at the opening ceremony. He would probably enjoy it far more than he would enjoy Scott's company.

Derek squeezed his hand.

"I look forward to seeing you then," he whispered.

Scott nodded and left the father and son alone, hoping that perhaps Ashton would show the boy some real compassion. He had just reached his shared room with Jamie when he remembered everything he and Derek had done, and that he didn't have an excuse for his actions. He took a deep breath to still his heart. Jamie had forgiven him before, but would he forgive him again? He pressed against the door with a heavy heart. Better to find out than worry.

CHAPTER NINETEEN

Seeds of Rebellion

Jamie lay in bed, watching the sunlight play on the pillows as he stretched and considered getting up. It was well into the morning. Emma had already come and gone, giving him permission to leave the bed for short periods of time. His fever was gone, but he got dizzy and nauseous if he stood for too long. Emma said something about his blood pressure, but he didn't know enough about medicine to understand. She said it had to do with Marisol and until Jamie managed to separate his mind from Marisol's more completely, he was going to suffer the same burdens of pregnancy that she went through.

Marisol was still asleep, and Jamie could hear her soft breathing from the dragon chamber next door. She emitted a slight whistling sound on her exhales that amused Jamie considerably and he was inventing melodies to go with the steady sound when he heard the door open.

"Jamie? Are you here?"

Jamie's eyes flew wide open. Scott!

"Yeah," he shouted, scrambling to his feet. Instantly black circled his vision and he fell backwards on the bed, trembling and unable to see. Two loving hands gripped him and he was enveloped by his beloved Scott.

"What's wrong? Are you ill?"

"A little," Jamie said. "I've been sharing Marisol's morning sickness."

Scott kissed Jamie and vision began to return slowly as Jamie first saw grays, then colors, then the oversaturated halos that he was growing accustomed to from being partnered to Marisol. He could see a cloud of amber worry around Scott and a foreign scent made him wrinkle his nose. Scott smelled like someone else.

Jamie withdrew from him to study his love. Scott looked worried and exhausted and at Jamie's regard, he ducked his head as if ashamed. The scent must be Derek's, but it was far too strong. He inhaled carefully, trying to understand the strength of the smell, and could sense two bodies pressed against each other for hours, twisting together in sex, rubbing pheromones and chemicals deep into Scott's skin.

"You slept with Derek," Jamie said slowly.

Tears welled up in Scott's eyes. "I'm sorry, Jamie."

Jamie took a deep breath. He had known this would happen. Oddly, he didn't feel upset, only resigned. There was more to Scott's story, he could tell, but he didn't want to know. He didn't want to know that Scott had feelings for Derek, that Scott had cradled the boy in his sleep and had sex multiple times. He couldn't bear to hear the words, and when Scott opened his mouth, Jamie placed his hand over it.

"Don't tell me," he pleaded. "Don't ever tell me."

Scott shut his mouth and nodded slowly. "I'm sorry," he said again.

Jamie shut his eyes and tried to push away the foreign scent on his boyfriend.

"Why are you here?" he asked.

"I needed to escape," Scott said. "And I had a vision, like Narné has, but I couldn't communicate with Narné. Arion has blocked me from my dragon."

"I can call Narné here," Jamie offered. "What was the vision?"

Jamie was grateful for the change in subject and listened

eagerly as Scott described his vision of Derek. But when he mentioned the queen dragon, Jamie's stomach flipped. Another queen dragon. If there were two queen dragons, then Jamie's status would be at risk and all of his bargaining ability would be gone. He couldn't stand up to Ashton if there were another queen dragon ready to take his place. Ashton would have no need for a rebellious queen with his own son to step in. But he would still need Jamie if he wanted to be the queen's mate. Surely he wasn't corrupt enough to sleep with his own son.

Narné arrived in the dragon chamber where Marisol slept and Scott took Jamie by the waist to escort him there. Narné listened as Scott repeated the vision he had seen. Because the dragon couldn't communicate telepathically to Scott, he was forced to resort to speech, which most dragons preferred to avoid.

"This was a true vision," Narné said. "I had the same vision when I first saw the boy."

"But what does it mean? Who is he fighting? Is he really going to end up with a queen?"

"When I first saw Jamie, I saw a similar vision. I saw Jamie astride a queen dragon, leading an army of dragons into battle. I was worried too, because there is never a good time for dragons to go into battle. The real question now is whether Derek will be on Jamie's side or fighting against him."

"Against him," Scott said. "He's Ashton's son, after all, and I can't imagine him taking the same side as Jamie on anything."

"Do not be so quick to judge," Narné said. "There is still good in him. And we do not know what battle this is. It may not be dragon against dragon."

Jamie gulped. Narné had seen him leading an army? That must be in the very distant future indeed, because he couldn't imagine such a thing. The very idea of fighting was anathema to his existence. He had been in a fair number of fights in his life, but only when he was getting beat up by stronger, older boys. He had never fought back, because there was never any point. The only time he had ever fought for anything was for his life during the first year exam and for Scott's freedom from Ashton's control, and neither of those were typical fights.

He felt a little reassured at Scott's instant decision that Derek would fight against Jamie – it meant that there was no real emotional connection between the two – but Narné's assertion that Derek was still a good person worried him. Not that he didn't want Derek to be a good person, and to be honest, if a war were being fought he wanted everyone possible to be on his side, but he didn't want to think of the person Scott had had sex with as a good person. He wanted to think of Derek as evil, as Ashton's son, because it made it easier to forgive and understand Scott's actions. It made Jamie believe that Scott still loved him, and wouldn't leave him one day for Derek.

"If it isn't a battle between dragons, what would it be? No one else knows dragons exist," Jamie said.

Narné shook his massive head. "I do not know."

Jamie caught something in Narné's mind, the edge of something sharp. He had never really looked into a dragon's mind, even though that was his gift, but now he followed that sharp edge and saw that it was a lie. Narné was lying. Jamie continued to follow the edge until he found an image of dragons in formation over a battlefield in what looked like the Middle East. There was a thick cloud cover that hid the dragons from view, but the dragons knew exactly where they were going. One at a time, each dragon expelled a fiery ball that struck a target building on the ground. People ran screaming from the burning buildings as the dragons elevated and returned to a secret hangar at a military base.

The image ended abruptly and Jamie stared at Narné, stunned. The dragon was unaware that Jamie had accessed the image. Jamie thought about what he had just seen. Were dragons used by the military? They would be powerful weapons in any war, that was for sure, but how could they possibly be used without anyone finding out about them? And how did the dragons decide which side to fight for? Tarragon Academy was in the United States, but according to Mr. Ferrin there were members of the Tarragon tribe across the globe. They all came to the academy to study and partner with their dragon, but then they dispersed, either going back to their home countries or else taking on jobs in foreign lands.

He thought of Kale and his job as bodyguard to the President of the United States. Did he know about dragons being used in modern warfare? He would have to. Jamie made a note to himself to talk to Kale at the soonest opportunity. If dragons were being used as weapons, he needed to know now, before Narné's vision came to pass and he led dragons into war.

Narné and Scott were chatting about the past few days, although Scott very carefully didn't mention anything about Derek, which took some effort since he must have been with Derek the whole time. Jamie was grateful for Scott's tact – he was still reeling from Narné's vision and the realization that dragons, whom he had previously thought of as docile creatures who all lived on campus, were in fact deadly weapons in the wars taking place around the globe. There was no way he could handle hearing about Derek on top of this.

Marisol slitted one eye to examine them. She had woken up some time ago and heard the conversation, but hadn't joined in. Now she rolled over on her side and sent a vague command to Jamie to rub her belly. He obeyed, and Scott moved to help. She was shedding scales again as her belly grew, and Jamie threw the discarded scales onto the ground where they could be swept up easily.

"There is another problem," Marisol said. "Mike is in danger."

"That's what Kale said, too," Jamie said.

He wondered why Marisol was concerned with Mike. She enjoyed Mike's company because he flattered her shamelessly and always rubbed her belly, but Marisol liked everyone who did that. He hadn't known that she liked Mike specifically, enough to worry about him.

"He agreed to a promise despite my warning," Marisol said, sounding disgruntled. "I told him to say no but he didn't listen. Now he is trapped in Ashton's web."

"I'm sure he had his reasons," Scott said with a bitter twist to his mouth.

Jamie patted Scott's arm, remembering what Mike had told him about his history with Scott. He still didn't know how he felt about the rape, and clearly Scott had mixed feelings as well. Even though Scott's words and attitude spoke of anger, his face showed concern and Jamie knew that he still cared about the man, despite what had happened between them.

The thought of being trapped in Ashton's web was terrifying to Jamie, but he could finally understand it. Before, he hadn't been able to fathom why Mike would possibly stay with Ashton. But ever since last night, when Ashton had kissed and caressed him, Jamie understood. Ashton's touch was addicting, almost magical. Ashton was at least a century old and he had clearly spent most of that time learning how to seduce young men, and if he had turned all of his charm on Jamie, Jamie knew he wouldn't have been able to resist. The only reason he had been able to push Ashton away was because of Scott, and because Ashton wasn't intending to seduce him, only touch him.

But for Mike, it must be intoxicating having Ashton as a lover. Jamie could see how he would be willing to overlook so many things about Ashton just to have him in his bed. Marisol's expression was apt; Ashton was a spider, weaving a web of seduction until his prey had strangled itself and was no longer capable of independent life.

"What can we do to help him?" Jamie asked.

Marisol was silent, then another vision filled his mind, far clearer than the vision of the battlefield. This was no memory, or image of the future. This was Marisol's desire put into pictures and Jamie could feel her longing in the green tint of the vision. At first it was simply Tarragon Academy, but then Jamie felt a lack of something but for some reason, this lack was welcome. The vision cleared even more and Jamie saw a gravestone in the adjacent cemetery with Ashton's name on it. Then the vision swooped to the dragon canyon, where an older Jamie and Marisol ruled over the academy fairly, the council finally fulfilling their duties without corruption, the population happy and content. The vision faded.

Jamie met Scott's eyes and knew he had seen the same image, as had Narné.

"Marisol," Jamie said slowly. "You want to-"

"Do not speak of such things aloud," Narné interrupted.

His head tossed and Jamie glanced around the room, realizing for the first time that Ashton had probably installed spy equipment to listen to his queen and her partner. A slow rage filled him at the invasion of privacy. So Ashton was listening to what they were saying, and watching their every move? Maybe Marisol was right. He had never wished for anyone to die before, but there was no other way to handle Ashton. The visions of Jamie and Derek leading the queens into battle suddenly made absolute sense. It would be dragon against dragon, Jamie against Ashton. But which side would Derek take? What about Kale? And what to do in the meantime, before they were ready for the battle?

Marisol was pregnant and couldn't move, so they were trapped at the academy for months while she laid her eggs and the eggs hatched. How could he possibly survive during that time, always knowing that he was destined to battle Ashton but never being able to act on that decision? Scott gripped his arm tightly and Jamie knew the same questions were going through his mind.

"We'll get through it," he said. "We got through this weekend, we'll get through this."

Jamie smiled faintly, not wanting to point out that the weekend wasn't over and Scott would soon have to return to Derek's side. They hadn't gotten through the weekend yet. But he took comfort in his boyfriend's touch and slid closer so they could embrace. He tried to ignore Derek's scent on Scott and wondered if Scott could smell Ashton on him. He shuddered at the thought of Ashton winning the next mating flight. Whatever war needed to be fought, it needed to be finished before Marisol mated next or else Jamie might enter into a nightmare beyond his worst imaginings.

CHAPTER TWENTY

Seen and Unseen

Mike couldn't help but notice how well Scott and Derek got along during the afternoon capture-the-flag game. He could tell that Scott was in a bad mood – and Mike could easily guess why, given the fact that Scott had seen Jamie earlier in the day – but even so the two seemed to be in sync far more than any of the other students and their upperclassmen. Mike wasn't the only person to notice this, either. Ashton stopped by towards the end of the game as Mike blew his whistle and had to separate two prospective students before a fight broke out. While Mike sorted out the mess, Ashton simply stood and watched, but Mike knew he was watching Scott. Scott must have known, too, because his cheeks tinted pink and he stumbled as he ran with the other team's flag and lost it to an aggressive redhead from the other team.

When the game was over, the students were all released to do whatever they wanted until dinner. Most, Mike knew, would return to the dorms and shower. Scott and Derek headed off to their dorm but Ashton remained. Mike smiled shyly and sidled up to the older man. They were the only two left on the football field and Ashton cupped Mike's face in his hand.

"How are the students doing?" Ashton asked.

Mike gave him a full account of the students, including the insights he had gained from Amar. The boy had a truly remarkable gift – he could see the potential strength that a boy had in forming a bond. Some boys had the ability for strong bonds and were almost certain to end up with a dragon, but Amar had pointed out several who had such a weak potential it was likely they would die in the attempt to bond with a dragon. The knowledge was invaluable and would hopefully help the university achieve a year without fatalities.

Ashton listened and nodded, one of his hands running over Mike's shoulder idly. Ashton might not have been aware of the gesture, but Mike was deeply aware of it and he stuttered a few times, longing for Ashton's touch to continue. When he finally finished his report, Ashton smiled at him and Mike stood up a little straighter, pleased to have earned a smile.

"You're very good to the students," Ashton said. "I'm glad you volunteered for this position."

"I love it," Mike said.

It was true; he loved taking care of the students and helping them through their myriad little problems while guiding the youngest members of the Tarragon society through their first year. Even though he had held the job for less than a year, he knew it was what he was born to do. He would miss his first batch of students in the fall when they became second-year students, but he knew the new batch of students – the batch he was meeting this weekend – would be there to replace them with a whole new set of faces and problems. It thrilled him and challenged him and he wouldn't trade it for anything. He had first taken the position grudgingly, because the rebellion had wanted him to infiltrate the council, but he had stumbled on a job that he truly loved and he wouldn't give it up for the world.

Ashton's smile grew wider and he leaned towards Mike as if to kiss him, but a scream rang through the football field coming in the direction of the dragon canyon. Mike went pale. Had some of the prospective students wandered in that direction?

He and Ashton both started running towards the dragon canyon and Mike noticed that the mist around the canyon, normally thick enough to completely block the view of the canyon, was unusually thin today. It had been thin a lot recently, he realized, thinking back to previous days. But this was no time to ponder that. In the center of the path, staring at the dragon canyon with expressions of rapt interest and some horror on their faces, were two prospective students and the limp body of a third. He must have been the one to scream before he fainted.

Mike immediately grabbed them and turned them around so they weren't facing the canyon. Their eyes, however, held the slightly glazed look of one who had seen too much, too soon.

"What did you see?" he asked gently. If they hadn't seen anything, perhaps dire action didn't need to be taken.

But Ashton was already on the cell with Margot, head of the women's university. In the rare circumstances like this where students saw too much, they were taken to Margot's dragon Yasmina who had the ability to remove memories from anyone not partnered with a dragon. Mike didn't trust Yasmina, however, and didn't trust that she couldn't steal memories from people with dragons. He had met her once and still wondered if there was a chunk of his life missing that he didn't – couldn't – know about.

One of the two students shuddered and finally answered Mike's question.

"I saw a movie set," he said slowly, as if trying to make sense of it all.

"That wasn't a set," the other student said.

They tried to turn around to look again but Mike stopped them. They had seen too much; Yasmina was the only option. Ashton picked up the third boy and gestured for them to walk.

"Why don't we take a drive and I'll explain the situation," he offered.

The other boys nodded and followed Ashton without a word, and Mike went behind them to make sure they didn't try to bolt. The damage was limited so far, but if they told anyone what they had seen, the whole Tarragon society would be in danger.

"I'll take your cell phones," Mike said, extending his hand.

He gave no reason, but luckily they were in enough shock that they didn't protest. While they walked, Mike went on their cell phones to make sure they hadn't sent any messages – they hadn't – or taken any pictures. One of the boys had taken a beautiful picture of the dragon canyon and Mike admired it for a time before deleting it. He had caught the light cascading down into the canyon with the forms of the dragons slicing through the thick light beautifully. But such a picture couldn't exist, so for the safety of the school, Mike deleted it.

Ashton didn't speak as they made their way through the campus to the road, where a black limo was pulling up. One of the boy's jaw dropped.

"We're driving in that? Awesome!"

He hopped in the car without a second thought. The other boy looked skeptical.

"Look, what's going on here? Did we see something we weren't supposed to see, and now you're trying to buy us off? It isn't going to work. If those things were really, well, were really dragons then the whole world needs to know! You can't buy my silence!"

"I'm not," Ashton said. "I'm going to explain what you saw, and then leave it to you whether or not you talk about it. But don't you want to know for sure what you saw before you start telling people?"

"What's with the limo then?"

Ashton looked at the limo blankly. "This is what I always drive."

The boy appeared as though he were searching for more arguments when Mike pushed him towards the limo.

"Ashton is the head of the council here," Mike said. "He always rides in luxury, so you should enjoy what he offers."

The boy nodded, seemingly reassured not just by Mike's words but by Mike's presence, and got in the limo. Ashton climbed in with the limp student, then gestured Mike to get in as well. Mike obeyed, even though he had other responsibilities on campus. A short ride to the woman's campus was all right. After all, the other students would be fine until dinner. At least he hoped so. He knew that Ashton was going to be pissed at the upperclassmen who left these three unattended. This was precisely why prospective students were assigned upperclassmen to escort them around while they were on campus, and they had failed miserably.

The unconscious student woke up on the ride and Mike confiscated his cell phone as well, even though it was unlikely he had time to do anything before fainting. Still, he might use the phone in the car ride to send a message, and that could be dangerous. He slipped all three phones into his pocket for the short ride to the girl's campus around on the other side of the mountain.

The dragon canyon lay between the campuses and both men and women lived in it, but other than that the campuses were distinct. There was a path running between the campuses on the other side of the mountain, opposite the dragon canyon, that freshmen frequently used to sneak over to the girl's campus for late night parties and other affairs, but it was discouraged. Still, the path was perfectly safe for the campus's secrets.

The drive was quick and Ashton was silent, even though Mike almost expected him to explain about dragons. There would be no harm in answering their questions since this memory would be erased, but Ashton seemed preoccupied. The boys, despite their questions, were too thrilled by the limo and the prospect of going to the girls' campus to insist that their questions be answered. When they reached the campus, they were greeted by two upperclassmen who escorted them into the largest apartment complex where Margot lived. She preferred to live in the modern apartments rather than the dragon canyon because she liked to be closer to her girls, or so she said, but Mike thought it was because Ashton lived in the dragon canyon and if both of them lived there, there would be too many conflicts between the two leaders.

Margot greeted them at the door to her apartment and invited them in. She was a commanding figure, with shockingly short, iron-gray hair and stylish black glasses. Most people who wore glasses before the first year exam found that partnering with a dragon improved their eyesight, but it was said that Margot enjoyed glasses so much she still wore them even though she didn't need them anymore. She wore a loose sweater over a patterned blue blouse, and jeans. It was a strange contrast to Ashton's formality, but it fit her and didn't diminish her at all; if anything, it gave her an air of supreme authority in her domain.

She escorted the three students through a hallway into Yasmina's room and all three students stopped, dumbstruck, as they saw the powerful blue dragon in all her glory before them. Mike tried to stay as far away as possible, but Ashton walked right up to Yasmina and stroked her eyebrow ridge.

"Yasmina, it has been too long," he said with far more affection than when he had greeted Margot.

Mike wondered if the rumors about the affair between Margot and Ashton were true, and that was why there was a frostiness in the air when the two looked at each other. According to rumor, the affair had ended badly and it was one reason Margot didn't live in the dragon canyon.

Yasmina turned her head into the caress, then returned her attention to the three students. She didn't say anything, just stared, and one by one the students collapsed to the floor, the last hour of their lives gone. Ashton went to the bodies and started to lift one.

"Michael, help me get them back in the car," he said.

Mike obeyed, and soon the three boys were sound asleep in the limo. Ashton gestured for Mike to accompany him back up to Margot's room and he followed, hoping Yasmina wouldn't try anything on him. His palms were sweaty with the stress of being in the dragon's presence and already he was wondering if he had forgotten anything, if she had stolen any memories.

Margot was waiting for them with glasses of wine, and they sat on one of her luxurious couches across from her. Mike downed his quickly to hide his panic at being so close to Yasmina. Ashton stroked the back of Mike's neck.

"Not so quickly, pet," he instructed as Margot refilled his wine with an amused smile.

"Yasmina has that effect on people," she said before sitting across from them. She didn't seem surprised by the display of affection between them, but she did study his collar carefully. "Now, Ashton, how did they come across the canyon?"

"The mist thinned," Ashton said. "They managed to wander through when they were unattended."

"Your upperclassmen are careless to leave so many students unattended."

"They will be dealt with," Ashton said, and for the first time Mike realized that he was partially to blame for the students being on their own. After all, he was in charge of the upperclassmen and he had failed to make sure that all of the students were under the direct supervision of their upperclassmen partners.

"We knew that the mist would fade soon," Margot said. "But I believe it is your turn to sacrifice. Why haven't you done so?"

"You know what happened six years ago."

"A set back. Unfortunate, but not permanent."

Mike's mind whirled as he attempted to follow the conversation. It was as if they were deliberately speaking in code, leaving out the vital information that would allow the conversation to make sense to him. They knew the mist would fade? And what sacrifice were they talking about? His mind flew to Kale, and Kale's story about Ashton wanting him to sacrifice his life, but surely they couldn't be talking about that. But that had happened around six years ago. Mike nervously fingered his collar. Was Ashton going to ask him to kill himself? He had sworn to obey Ashton, he realized. He would have to obey if Ashton ordered it.

Ashton glanced at Mike and seemed to sense his distress, because he waved his hand as if to cut the conversation off.

"Enough for now. We both know what needs to be done, and it will be done. In the meantime, make sure to protect your borders. If the mist is weakening, then we may start seeing campers and hikers wandering onto our grounds. We can't erase memories from all of them."

"My Yasmina is always up to the task," Margot said. "But I take your point. Still, this is not a situation that can continue. Do it quickly."

She stood and gestured for them to stand as well. "Thank you for coming to see me, but I have other affairs to see to. I wish you the best."

Ashton nodded, and Mike bowed, not knowing what else to do. She was such an imposing character despite her casual dress. She seemed amused by the gesture and placed her hand on Mike's shoulder.

"You should keep this one," she said.

"Yes, I should."

Mike beamed. Then they left to drive the sleeping forms back to the boy's college, where they would put the sleepers in their beds and tell them they slept through the capture-the-flag game. With any luck, all three of the boys would accept the story without question. Mike took the cell phones from his pocket and slipped them back to each of the boys, careful to give the right phone to the right boy. That would be a horrible mistake to make, and would raise too many questions if they awoke with someone else's cell phone. Then he took a deep breath and snuggled against Ashton as they finished driving back to campus.

CHAPTER TWENTY-ONE

Dreams

Jamie dreamed. He was a child again, lying in bed with a fever. His mother sang lullabies to him while she stroked his sweaty brow and took his temperature. She tutted at the result and went into the kitchen to make him some chicken noodle soup. As soon as she was gone, a creature entered the room. About the height of a dog, but this scaly creature was no dog. It was deformed, with what might have been undeveloped wings on its back, and its tongue hung out of its mouth as it crawled over to Jamie's bedside and stared up at him. Jamie stared back and saw something intelligent in those eyes, something tragic. A beautiful, sentient creature trapped in a barely functional body. Then the creature scuttled away and Jamie closed his eyes in the dream, sure that it was his fever.

Jamie awoke and pondered his dream. Was it a dream or a memory? He reached back into his memories and found several featuring the deformed creature. Looking back, it was easy to identify it as an underdeveloped dragon, but why would there be one in his house, and why wasn't it as glorious as Marisol or the other dragons he had seen at Tarragon Academy? His parents knew nothing about the academy, or so he'd been led to believe, so why did they have a dragon?

There was a knock at the door and Mike came in, looking flush as if he had been exercising. Jamie knew he looked pale and wan in comparison after lying in his sickbed all day and night.

He vowed to get out and take a walk sometime today. He felt a little better, and the mystery of his dream was a pleasant change from obsessing about Scott.

"How do you feel?" Mike asked, placing a hand on Jamie's forehead just like his mother had in the dream.

"Better," Jamie said. "How is Marisol?"

"Recovering," Mike said. "She just has morning sickness. You actually managed to catch something, but it seems like your fever broke and you're doing well now."

Jamie nodded, then bit his lip. Mike might know about deformed dragons, but it would be a strange thing to bring up. Still, he didn't know who else to ask and he knew he needed to know if it was a real memory or just the dreams of a child.

"Mike," he began slowly. "Do you know if it's possible to have a dragon if you didn't go to the academy?"

"No," Mike said.

"But the woods are right there, couldn't someone just walk in and find the eggs?"

Mike's brow creased. "I suppose. But the mist protects the mountain from intruders. And besides, even if someone found the eggs, they only hatch once per year. If someone somehow got the eggs to hatch some other time, the dragon wouldn't be ready and might come out underdeveloped and unready for life outside the shell. It probably wouldn't last long."

Jamie's mind flashed to the deformed creature in his dream and he knew that was what had happened. The mist must not have stopped his parents because they belonged to the Tarragon tribe, and when they reached the eggs, the eggs had hatched but the dragons weren't ready. But did both of his parents have a dragon, or just one? And how had they handled the knowledge that dragons were real? It must have been a shock, and then to be partnered with an underdeveloped dragon on top of every-thing else must have been life-changing. How had they adapted?

"Why do you ask?"

"I've been having dreams," Jamie said. "Memories from before my mom was killed. I saw a deformed creature that looked like a dragon. I just saw it sometimes but I always remembered it."

Mike's eyes widened. "Your parents were friends with several students at the academy, but I doubt any of them would have taken your parents to the nesting grounds. And you shouldn't have been able to see the dragon even if it was underdeveloped. Dragons are protected from view just like our mountain is protected by the mist."

"I saw Narné," Jamie said, remembering the two times he had seen the green dragon, first in the forest during his first kiss with Scott and again in Scott's apartment right before the mating flight.

"Did you?" Mike said in a pondering voice. He stared at Jamie speculatively. "Maybe you have a stronger gift than anyone guessed. You were destined to have a queen from the start."

"Do you really think my parents could have had a dragon?"

"I don't know," Mike said. "But it would make sense, given the nature of their- well, their deaths."

Jamie's head lowered. His parents had both died in fire-related accidents. His mother had died in a house fire, and his father had died in a car accident that exploded before anyone could reach him. In myths, dragons breathed fire but he hadn't seen any sign of that yet.

"I suppose dragons breathe fire, right?" he asked, hoping against hope that Mike would say no.

"That's right," Mike said. "They don't start until they're a couple years old and it takes time to master. Some dragons never learn mastery of it, and they're kept confined on campus to prevent them from hurting anyone."

"Then it's possible a dragon started both fires."

"I truly believe your father's death was an accident," Mike

said. "An explosion like that could only be caused by a trained dragon, and dragons do not kill people. But your mother... Well, if what you say about an underdeveloped dragon is true, then it's possible that dragon could have started a fire that led to your mother's death and the death of the dragon."

"But wouldn't someone have found the dragon's body? Wouldn't people ask questions?"

"I don't know," Mike said uncomfortably. "If there was a body, someone from the academy would have arranged to take it before anyone else knew about it. There would be no trace. The only person who would know for sure would be-"

"Ashton," Jamie finished. "And we can't ask him because he'll lie."

Mike flushed. Jamie shook his head, wondering why Mike was so entranced by the man. True, Jamie had thought very highly of Ashton for a long time, but now that Ashton wasn't bothering to hide his true nature around Jamie anymore, the man was despicable. Jamie understood the physical attraction now, at least, and could see how Mike could grow addicted to Ashton's touch, but he couldn't see how an intelligent person like Mike would let his body rule over his head. Surely good sex wasn't worth being with such a horrible person. Jamie tried not to judge, and told himself that he didn't have all of the facts, but he couldn't help but feel that Mike was being tricked by Ashton, just as Jamie had been tricked by Ashton at first.

Jamie thought of Scott and how Scott was even now taking care of Derek. It was late morning, and he wondered if Scott and Derek had slept together last night. He knew Scott had had sex with Derek multiple times already, and the knowledge cut him to the core. He tried not to think about it, tried to pretend it wasn't true, but he couldn't help but let his mind wander to unpleasant images of a dark-haired, dark-eyed youth stealing Scott's heart.

He shook his head and focused back on his parents, and the

mystery they posed. He hadn't thought about their deaths for some time and he felt a little ashamed, as if he had dishonored them by forgetting to think about them constantly. But he was so busy in his new life, and he could only mourn so much in any given day. Every night he caressed the snowglobe and thought of his mother and father and wished that they were still alive and looking over him somehow, but he no longer spent sleepless nights thinking of nothing else. He was beginning to accept their deaths and move on in his life, mourning them every day but also living his life. He thought that was what they would have wanted, but he had no way of knowing. The snowglobe was dark and broken, after all, and provided no magical answers no matter how he wished it would somehow speak to him in his father's steady voice.

Jamie was positive that the creature from his dream and his memory was a dragon, and if his parents were friends with people from Tarragon Academy then it was possible that those friends had told them about dragons and even brought them to the nesting grounds. He didn't think his father had the dragon, though, because he didn't have any memories of the creature from after his mother died. So the dragon must have died with her. How incredible, to have lived with a dragon so close by.

He wondered how other students felt, the ones who had parents who were graduates. They not only found out about dragons, they learned that their parents had been keeping a massive secret from them their entire lives. The betrayal they felt must be overwhelming. At least he had never been in that position. He wondered about Ashton's son and if Ashton had broken the rules and told him about dragons. Ashton didn't seem like the type to pay much heed to rules, even the rules he himself created, but he also wasn't the type to care about keeping secrets from people.

Mike had moved from his room into Marisol's, where he was rubbing her belly and pulling off loose scales. She was still expanding even though her belly was already enormous. Soon she would be bigger than the sleeping platform, although she assured Jamie that she would stop before she reached that point. He wasn't sure how she planned on flying to the nesting grounds, but she was confident in her ability to fly with a belly full of eggs even though she was in a state of forced immobility now.

Jamie dressed and followed Mike into Marisol's room, greeting her with a kiss and a rub. She nuzzled him and greeted him warmly. They hadn't seen each other since Jamie had fallen ill the day before and she was happy he was feeling better. She was feeling nauseous, and a little warm, but Ashton had said it was morning sickness and would go away in time. Jamie was doing his best to keep a wall between his mind and Marisol's so that her sickness didn't spill over into him again.

Mike seemed deep in thought, and he turned to Jamie after pulling off another loose scale. "I can talk to Ashton, you know. Ask him about your parents."

"No," Jamie said. "I don't want to cause you trouble."

"It's no trouble."

"We don't know that," Jamie said.

It was true. Asking Ashton might turn out to be an innocent question that led to a dark, insidious plot on the part of the council and if it was, Mike would surely be punished for asking. Jamie didn't want to be responsible for anything that happened to Mike and he knew that no matter what the truth was, Ashton would give the same response. Ashton was a liar, and would never change.

"I don't want you asking," Jamie repeated, and Mike nodded.

"Well, if you have any other questions, I'll do my best to help."

"Thanks," Jamie said.

He rubbed Marisol's belly and felt the lumpy eggs under the scales. She seemed so close to having the eggs, but she assured him that she was not ready yet. A few more weeks, maybe. She had a good sense of her body, but she was also young and doing this without help from others of her kind so her predictions were never completely accurate, and Jamie worried that she would go into labor at any moment. She snorted in amusement.

I am not that big yet, and the eggs are not developed, she said.

Jamie smiled, and Mike, who had also heard the comment, laughed.

"You are beautifully large, my queen," he said. "But you may take as long as you want to lay your eggs."

"You're not worried they're about to pop out?" Jamie asked, his hand still on Marisol's warm scales.

"Marisol will know when it's time," Mike said with complete confidence. "Dragons have had eggs successfully for thousands of years and she'll be no exception."

Marisol fluttered her eyes bashfully and rested her head on her large front claws.

Mike is right, she said. *Do not worry about me.*

Jamie nodded, but his heart didn't feel any lighter. He might not be worried about her, but there were still plenty of things to fill his mind. He couldn't bear to think about Scott, so perhaps he would focus on the mystery of his parent's death a little longer. A new thought popped into his head and he blinked in surprise that he hadn't thought of it before: he would ask Kale. Kale would know if dragons had killed or been killed in the area, and Jamie was already planning on talking to him about the vision he had seen in Narné's mind about the fighting dragons. Kale would have the answers, he decided.

"I think I'm going to go for a walk," he announced. "Emma said I was strong enough."

"That's a good idea," Mike said. "You look too pale, and you need exercise. Lying in bed all day will just make you sicker. Do you want me to go with you?"

"No," Jamie said. "I just want some fresh air and quiet."

"Alright," Mike said. "I'll stay with Marisol a little longer, I think."

"Thanks," Jamie said, flashing a smile.

He left the room and began heading towards campus. He didn't know where Kale was but by reading the minds of the nearby dragons he could vaguely sense where the stranger had been recently and track Kale's movements. He located a spot where he thought Kale would be and set off, determined to learn more about how dragons were involved in war and in his parents' deaths.

CHAPTER TWENTY-TWO

Questions and Answers

Kale wandered near the entrance to the dragon canyon. There was nothing for him to do with Vestis gone. Vestis reported that everything was under control at the White House, but tensions had been rising since the mating flight. People wanted to know who the boy in their vision was, and why they had all been summoned to a mating flight in Portland. Kale was surprised that Tarragon Academy hadn't already announced the birth of a queen dragon, but perhaps they were waiting to make sure she would survive her first few months.

Everyone had been devastated when the last queen had died so quickly because she had been unable to properly connect to her human. But the bond between Jamie and Marisol was one of the strongest Kale had ever seen, and Marisol was even pregnant. Surely there was no reason to keep it a secret. Except, of course, that announcing a queen would mean announcing her mate, and then Ashton would be required to give up some of his power to Scott. And Ashton was having far too much fun toying with Scott to give up his control yet.

Kale wondered if Ashton was planning on waiting until the second mating flight to announce the queen to the world, assuming he won the next mating flight. Kale rather thought Ashton would win the mating flight. Scott had won with the element of surprise and Jamie's unexpected invitation to the other dragons, but it would not happen again. The second mating flight would be highly controlled and it was unlikely that Scott would be able to outfly Ashton in a fair flight.

Waiting to tell the world would have serious consequences, however. Already people were on edge and worried about the powerful newcomer who had woken them with a vision of a mating flight in which they could not participate, and people were worried that Jamie could interfere in other things as well. After all, Jamie's mating flight had wreaked chaos across the globe on everyone partnered with a dragon. If one person had that kind of strength, what else could he do?

Kale was debating having Vestis tell the White House dragons about the queen in order to spread the word quickly and undermine Ashton's authority, but he wasn't sure how Ashton would respond. It was easy enough to disobey Ashton with thousands of miles between them, but now, with Ashton a stone's throw away, disobedience was a less desirable option. Ashton and Arion could cut him off from contact with Vestis, for one, and he would lose the most important creature in his life. That was a serious threat in and of itself, but there were plenty of other ways Ashton could threaten and hurt Kale.

A lone figure appeared on the walkway leading out of the dragon canyon and Kale was surprised to see Jamie. He had heard that Jamie was ill, an effect of his close bond with Marisol, and didn't expect to see the boy outside walking around. Jamie looked a little paler than usual, but otherwise fine. His pace picked up when he spotted Kale and he looked like the pointer of a compass if Kale were true north. Jamie stopped a few paces away and hesitantly smiled.

"I was hoping to talk to you," he said.

"Of course," Kale said, extending his hand to shake Jamie's.

Kale shook Jamie's hand and the boy tensed and pulled his hand away quickly as if the touch burned. Kale could have kicked himself; the boy was undoubtedly uncomfortable with physical contact after the mating flight, and being ill probably exaggerated the effect. Kale still remembered the image of Jamie that had been burned into his mind the night of the mating flight: Jamie sprawled on a bed, writhing in pleasure, begging Kale to touch him. He and Vestis had nearly taken flight right then and there if Kale's self-control hadn't been as strong.

He suspected that every dragon and partner in the world had received that image and Jamie was probably having a hard time adapting to a world where everyone had seen him in that state. From what Kale could tell about Jamie, after all, it seemed that Jamie was a chaste and shy boy who would never willingly project himself like that to the world. He wondered if Jamie even knew how far that image had spread, and how every dragon and partner would react to seeing him in the flesh.

So for Jamie to be jumpy about touch right now was not unusual, even though Jamie had shaken his hand without a problem when they met earlier. Jamie seemed deep in thought and clearly had questions for Kale, but he took a long time preparing the questions and they walked nearly a quarter mile towards the forest before he finally spoke. When he did speak, it was a question that Kale never could have anticipated.

"Does the military use dragons as weapons?"

Kale blinked in surprise, especially because it sounded as if Jamie already knew the answer and was just testing Kale.

"How did you find out?"

"I saw it in a dragon's mind," Jamie replied, and Kale drew in a sharp breath. Jamie could read the minds of dragons? Kale had known that Jamie could communicate with all dragons, a valuable and rare gift in itself, but being able to read their minds was unheard of. It was incredible.

"Wow," Kale said, still processing Jamie's ability and forgetting the boy's question for the moment. The possibilities of such a gift! Jamie might even be able to read Arion's mind and see what Ashton was planning. And it was well-known that dragons regularly hid things from their human partners, who they thought of as weak and intellectually delicate; could Jamie learn the secrets of dragonkind? Had he tried already? Did he know things that no other human could know?

"You haven't answered my question," Jamie reminded him, and Kale pushed his awe away and focused on dragons in the military.

"You've heard of drones being used in combat, right? Unmanned drones? Well, most of them are drones, but for high profile or delicate work, dragons are used instead. They're called stealth drones and not even most of the military knows what they really are. They just know that if they call in the stealth drones, the job will get done."

"Which armies have access to dragons?"

Kale hesitated. He had so many guesses, but he knew so little for sure.

"I don't actually know. But I know that the United States isn't the only nation that uses them. There have been suspicious attacks between other nations, but I don't want to name names."

"If I'm Queen, shouldn't I know where all of my dragons are and what they're doing?"

Kale shook his head. "That's the job of the Queen's mate. You're in charge of domestic affairs and looking after the young dragons, the eggs, and the academy. Your mate takes care of everything else, and since there hasn't been a Queen or a mate in so long, the council has taken over both duties."

In reality, the council had shoved all of the Queen's duties onto Mike, who was performing admirably, and Ashton had claimed all of the foreign affairs. Jamie and Scott were figureheads, and unhappy ones at that. They were too intelligent and too involved to be happy going to school and letting the council take care of everything – eventually they would want to take on their responsibilities and it looked like Jamie was ready for his already, even though he had been partnered to his dragon for only a couple of months.

Jamie rubbed his hands against his pants and seemed very vulnerable all of a sudden. He glanced up at Kale swiftly, then cast his eyes back at the ground.

"Have dragons ever been used to kill people? Individuals, I mean? Here?"

Kale's brow furrowed. It was an odd question, but clearly a personal one for the boy. He wondered if Jamie had known someone who was killed by a dragon, but it was highly unlikely because dragons never left any trace of their presence – and if they did, the council covered it up before anyone else found out.

"It's possible," Kale said. "But there would be no way of knowing. Besides, the dragons who remain here at the canyon aren't killers. Any dragon with a penchant for death is sent to the military."

Jamie let out a sigh. "I see."

He looked so vulnerable that Kale couldn't help but place his hand on the boy's shoulder to comfort him, and to his surprise the boy allowed it. Perhaps his reading of Jamie was wrong, and he wasn't afraid of human contact after the mating flight. But he had definitely been eager to pull away from the handshake when they had met, so perhaps Kale had passed some sort of test and now physical contact was acceptable. No matter what, Kale didn't press his luck and removed his hand after only a few seconds.

"I'd like to be alone," Jamie said, gesturing to the forest around them.

Kale nodded. He understood the need to be at peace and isolated within nature. He said goodbye and headed back to the campus. He had just left the forest when another shape began heading towards him, but this one was unwelcome. He stopped and let Ashton come to him, not willing to take one step in Ashton's direction. The man smirked and extended his hand. Kale hesitantly took it, but instead of shaking it, Ashton cradled it and turned so that they were side by side as they started walking. Kale tried to hide his fear. He was a bodyguard to the President and had been in far more dangerous situations than this, but somehow Ashton made him feel like a child again, lonely and afraid.

"The mist is thinning, just as I told you it would," Ashton said.

Kale remembered that day long ago on the volcano when Ashton had explained how the school would fail if he didn't sacrifice his life. First the mist would fade, Ashton had said, and outsiders would swarm, learn about the dragons, and destroy the school and hatching grounds in their attempt to understand and acquire the dragons. The scientists would want to perform invasive and fatal experiments on the dragons and their partners, and the military would view them as threats and weapons and seek to destroy them. Dragons worldwide would be slaughtered out of fear, and their partners would be slain out of mistrust and misunderstanding. The entire world would turn against the Tarragon tribe. All because a sacrifice was not made to the old gods who protected the mountain.

Kale hadn't believed it, not really, but he had been so eager to please Ashton that he would have killed himself regardless. In the years since he had often thought of the argument that Ashton had made and he had to admit that it was probably what would happen if people did find out about the academy, but the mist was always there to protect the campus. No one got through the mist; it disoriented people and turned them around so they never got close to the dragon canyon or anything important. The only way to get into the campus and onto the mountain was to be accompanied by someone partnered with a dragon. The mist had always been there, so why would the mist ever thin?

But at Ashton's words he had to admit that the mist did seem a little thin as they walked towards the dragon canyon. He hadn't noticed before, because he had been gone for so long and just assumed this was what the mist had always been like, but the memories from his time at the academy were always shrouded in a deep mist that prevented him from seeing more than a few feet in front of him whenever he went off one of the approved paths. Now the mist made it difficult to see, but not impossible, and the shortcuts were just as easy to traverse as the main paths. The mountain was changing, that was for sure, but Kale doubted it had anything to do with human sacrifice.

"You swore once to give your life to the mountain," Ashton said. "The mountain will keep you to that promise."

Kale flinched. He had sworn, but he had broken his vow. Surely Ashton didn't expect him to complete a vow he had broken six years ago.

"The mountain doesn't need my life or my blood," Kale said, trying to sound sure of himself.

Ashton smiled. "That's where you're wrong. If you want the mist to thicken again and the campus to be protected, blood must be spilled. Whether it is your blood or someone else's is all that's left to be decided."

Mike, Kale thought. Ashton was talking about Mike. Would Ashton really trick Mike into taking his own life? It seemed as though Ashton were trying to make this into a cruel game to see who would take their life, Kale or Mike. Would Kale be willing to end his life to protect Mike, or would he selfishly stand by and let Mike die? Neither, Kale vowed. Neither of them would die, and the mist would thicken on its own.

"The mist will return on its own," Kale said, but even he could hear the question in his statement.

"You know that's a lie," Ashton said. "We have a few months, maybe less, before the mist won't protect us at all. Even now a determined hiker could find us. Is that what you want? For the academy to be exposed, for dragons to be eradicated?"

"Of course not," Kale said. "But human sacrifice is not the answer. Surely there's some other way to restore the mist. Shouldn't you have scientists working on it or something?"

"The blood and life force of a partnered human is the only thing that will restore the mist."

Kale was silent. This was not an argument he wanted to engage in, because Ashton thought he was absolutely correct. But Kale knew there had to be another solution. It just didn't make sense that in this age of technology and civility, human sacrifice was the only means for survival.

Ashton finally released Kale's hand that he had been holding the entire conversation and turned to leave.

"I see you're thinking. Well, you have some time. I encourage you not to take too long, however. There are others willing to do the job for you."

Kale grit his teeth. Ashton clearly didn't care for Mike at all and only viewed him as a potential sacrifice. But Kale had seen Mike and knew that Mike was deeply in love with Ashton. It ought to be a crime, what Ashton was doing to Mike. And no matter what Kale said, he knew Mike would never believe him. He needed to talk to Mike again and try to explain the danger he was in, or else neither of them would survive Ashton's machinations. Kale took a deep breath. He needed to talk to Mike, and he needed to talk to Jamie again. He needed to make sure that Jamie was on his side against Ashton so that when the war came – and it was coming – he would have the queen to back him up.

CHAPTER TWENTY-THREE

Gold Medals

Derek and Scott slept together Saturday night, but only because the room next door was still locked. They didn't have sex; Scott was adamant about that. Derek seemed content to have the other man's arms wrapped around him all night and, surprisingly, didn't push for more. When Scott woke up in the morning, he nearly tossed Derek off the bed in his attempt to leap off and ensure that Derek couldn't ensnare him in sex the way he had the previous morning. Derek looked confused and sleepy, but Scott didn't apologize. There was no way he was having sex with Derek ever again, and he wasn't going to give the boy any chances to manipulate him.

Scott went straight to the shower and soaked himself in the scalding water. He felt a little bad for waking Derek up in such a rude fashion, but he knew there were no other options. He still remembered the previous morning, waking up with Derek cradled against him so sweetly, and then Derek turning and grabbing his balls until he submitted and allowed the boy to suck him off. Not today, he vowed. He may have slept in the same bed as Derek and perhaps they had held each other in sleep, but not when they were awake.

He dressed and prepared for the day. His last day with Derek. The prospective students would have a final day of contests and fun before returning home. He was actually looking forward to it, if he were honest with himself. He had never escorted a prospective student before but he had heard that the last day contests were a lot of fun. Plus, most importantly, they didn't involve sex, so he could get to know Derek outside of the forced intimacy the rest of this experience had held.

When he left the bathroom, Derek was waiting, still with a sleepy look on his face. Scott squeezed his arm in apology before letting him in the bathroom. Perhaps leaping out of bed like that was unnecessary, but he wasn't taking any more chances. He wanted to be able to go back to Jamie without secrets.

The morning passed in a blur as they ate breakfast with the other prospective students and upperclassmen. Scott had to keep reminding himself that sex was not a part of most prospective students' experiences as they raved about how much fun they were having while their assigned upperclassmen beamed, but he had to wonder how many of the upperclassmen had taken advantage of the students. Not that they would hurt the students, but many of the students would probably welcome the advances of an older student. Scott wondered how many people knew that he and Derek had slept together as Derek told stories of his adventures during capture-the-flag. Derek wisely didn't mention anything about sex, but Scott could almost feel the eyes of the upperclassmen watching the two of them with amusement and too much knowledge.

The contests began immediately after breakfast and took place in the football field. With forty prospective students and forty upperclassmen filling the field, not to mention about twenty instructors and volunteers, the field seemed completely full as Scott helped Derek maneuver towards the three-legged race. It was the first contest of the day and Derek had informed Scott that he was determined to win. Derek looked so sincere that Scott had smiled and agreed.

Derek kept looking around as if searching for someone and at first Scott couldn't figure out who he was looking for, but then he realized the boy was looking for his father. A lump formed in Scott's belly. Derek wanted to win in order to impress

Ashton. Cold determination filled Scott. Derek wouldn't just win the three-legged race, he would win all the contests and Ashton would be forced to acknowledge his wonderful, talented son. His hatred of Ashton grew a little deeper at the thought of Ashton ignoring his son for so long, especially a son who was so clearly enamored of his father. Derek deserved better, and Scott would do everything in his power to make Ashton take notice.

They sailed through the three-legged race with almost no competition. Most of the other couples stumbled and tripped at some point, but Scott and Derek moved as one person, with Scott paying close attention to every shift of Derek's body to tell when he was about to move. They were given gold medals with pink ribbons, and then Derek led him to the javelin throw. Both the prospective student's throw and the upperclassmen's throw were averaged together for the competition and Scott didn't want to admit that he'd never thrown a javelin before, but he knew that for Derek, he would do his best. He wanted Derek's neck to be covered with gold medals so Ashton would have to be proud.

Derek threw the javelin skillfully and it fell farther than anyone else. Then it was Scott's turn. He had studied Derek when he threw, and now he reached out to Narné for help. Luckily, the dragon was available to him – Arion had stopped his interference – and Narné coached him on his position. But the final throw was his alone. His throw was mediocre, but combined with Derek's excellent throw they were the best pair and gold medals with green ribbons were hung around their necks.

The whole field was alive with various contests and there was a constant roar of students cheering. Several food stands offered free elephant ears and hot dogs, and water stands were everywhere to keep students hydrated as they competed. Derek pointed to the outside of the field where a race was about to start. They headed over and signed in, then removed their medals so the bouncing tin circles wouldn't get in the way of their speed.

Again, the speed of both partners would be averaged together but this time Scott knew he would be a help, not a hindrance. He had been a sprinter in the academy's track team up until a few months ago when he had sprained his ankle and been forced to take a break, but he had never gotten back into practice because of Jamie and everything else going on in his life. Still, he should have an advantage during the race.

A gun went off and he bolted forward, easily outpacing the rest. He zoomed forward, luxuriating in the feel of the wind against his cheeks as his legs seemed to sail through the air. He loved the feeling when his feet struck the ground and then shoved him back into the air like a gazelle galloping through the savannah. He sprinted as though his life depended on it, circling the track and then feeling the ribbon of first place breaking against his chest. He finally allowed himself to slow and stop, and heard cheering from the audience.

"That's how he caught the queen," he heard an upperclassmen mutter to his friend.

Scott blushed. It was true, he did have speed on his side, but it had been a trap that let him capture the queen. He was surprised the upperclassmen was talking about such matters here, in front of the prospective students, and he made a note to tell Mike about it. Mike would be sure to chew out the student for potentially revealing their secrets to the students, and Mike was surely somewhere at the football field enjoying the success of the visit.

The other students petered in, some of them out of breath. Derek was third and slightly out of breath. He looked at Scott with awe in his eyes.

"Wow," he said. "You're really fast."

"That might be a school record," another voice said, and Scott turned to see the track coach come up behind him. "Looks like your ankle healed just fine. Are you coming back to the team?"

"I hope so," Scott said. "I just don't know if I'll have time."

"Oh, you have to!" Derek said. "You're way too fast not to be a pro."

The announcer then called them forward to receive more gold medals, this time on red ribbons, and they looked at the assortment hanging from their necks.

"Maybe we should take a break for a little bit," Derek said with a laugh.

"Are you hungry?"

They wandered over to the food, Derek constantly keeping watch on the crowd as if searching for Ashton's face, and Scott's heart went out to him. He was so eager for his father's attention and affection, but Scott knew that Ashton would never give it. Ashton didn't even care that Derek existed except that Derek gave him control over Scott. If Scott didn't exist, Derek wouldn't matter at all and Scott doubted that Ashton would have even contacted him, let alone invited him to the prospective student's weekend. Derek would be allowed to come to the academy, surely, but he wouldn't be given any special treatment.

Scott, for his part, was keeping an eye out for Mike to report the upperclassmen's behavior. His quest was more fruitful because after they had gotten hot dogs, Mike appeared at the edge of his vision. To Scott's surprise, Amar was with him and Amar looked like he was having the time of his life. Amar had been with Mike during the first night of the prospective students' visit, but he had looked withdrawn. Something had clearly happened to the boy and Scott wondered what it was.

As soon as Mike saw him, he and Amar headed in his direction as if they had been looking for Scott just as Scott had been looking for him. Scott introduced Mike and Amar to Derek, who had already met them, of course, but had probably forgotten their names. Amar asked Derek about his gold medals and Mike pulled Scott to one side.

"You look like you're having fun," Mike said.

"Is that a surprise?"

"A little. I just wanted to make sure you were alright."

"Yeah," Scott said. "It's almost over. Hey, there were some upperclassmen talking."

He explained what he had overheard and who had been talking, and Mike's mouth puckered into a frown.

"Thanks for letting me know. We've already had trouble with those particular students."

"Trouble?"

Mike shook his head and fixed a smile on his face. "Ask me later."

Scott nodded. Here in the middle of the contests surrounded by prospective students was no place to talk about trouble. He said goodbye to Mike and returned to Amar and Derek, who were comparing javelin throwing techniques and laughing. Amar looked uneasily at Scott and Scott knew he still hadn't figured out how to treat Jamie's boyfriend, probably especially when that boyfriend was escorting another man around, but at least Amar was polite and seemed friendly. He was definitely more relaxed than he had been the other night.

Derek laughed and turned to Scott. "Amar thinks we should try to win all the medals."

"The other students might get angry."

"Let them be angry. Let's get more medals."

"I'm not even finished eating yet," Scott protested, but his tone was playful. He wolfed down his hot dog as Derek and Amar talked, and soon they were heading towards yet another contest.

They won three more medals before they were banned from entering any more contests, for a total of six. Their chests glittered with a rainbow of ribbons and the sparkling gold of the painted tin medals. Other students stopped them to talk, and soon Derek seemed to have forgotten his goal of winning all the medals because he was having such a good time showing off the ones he already had. But he always kept an eye elsewhere, always watching the field, waiting for Ashton. Scott wanted to find Ashton and shake him viciously for what he was doing to his son.

And then, finally, with only fifteen minutes before the last contest ended, Ashton appeared. Derek spotted him immediately and yanked on Scott's arm, dragging him towards the man. Scott tried to hide his scowl and instead feel happy for Derek. Maybe Ashton did care about his son. Or maybe Ashton was here to gloat over Scott, as he had done before. Either way, Derek seemed to be on cloud nine and his steps were light and airy as they practically flew to Ashton's side.

"Father," Derek said, out of breath from the race to Ashton. Derek puffed up his chest so Ashton could see the kaleidoscope of ribbons and medals on his chest, but Ashton simply looked at him, then looked at Scott.

"I see the two of you are a good team," Ashton said, reaching out to finger one of Derek's medals. The boy's face nearly split with his smile and Scott wondered how Derek didn't see that the comment wasn't even directed at him but rather at Scott.

"Your son is a good person," Scott said, placing his arm around Derek's shoulders and pushing him forward.

"Indeed," Ashton said, running his eyes briefly over Derek before returning his attention to Scott. Derek was beaming. "I hope the two of you remain friends when Derek comes to the campus in the fall."

Scott flushed. Was that some sort of command? Was he telling Scott that he would be required to have sex with Derek in the future as well? It wouldn't happen, Scott knew. The sexual part of their relationship was over, but today had proved that they could be friends without sex. They had spent all day engaged in contests, having fun, laughing, without even thinking about sex. When Derek did return in the fall, that was the part of the relationship Scott hoped to rekindle, not the sexual part. No matter what Ashton said, it wasn't happening.

"Scott's a great friend," Derek said, rising up on his tiptoes as if to stress the point. "I couldn't have won this many medals with anyone else."

Ashton turned his attention back to his son and his face relaxed. "You have done very well."

Scott thought it must have been the first time Ashton had ever complimented the boy because Derek turned pink and looked absolutely tongue-tied. It was almost sickening how much control Ashton had over him, far more than he had over Mike, even. At least Mike knew what he was getting into, but Derek was trapped by genetics, by the unfortunate circumstances of his birth. Scott wondered who his mother was, and why his mother hadn't warned him about Ashton. But then he remembered some of Derek's comments about Ashton from earlier, and Derek's instant understanding of the situation Scott was in. Derek knew that Ashton was manipulative, but he was still enthralled by the man. Just like Mike. What kind of power did Ashton wield over certain people that allowed them to be so blind?

Ashton excused himself from their presence and Derek watched him go with a proud smile on his face as he fingered the gold medal that Ashton had touched.

"Thank you, Scott," he said. "And I hope we do remain friends in the fall."

"We will," Scott said. He thought about reminding Derek that he had a boyfriend and that the relationship between them would be totally different, but he didn't. It seemed like too much information, and it would ruin the ending of this interlude. Instead, he left it with those words.

The contests closed up and the prospective students returned to their dorms to pick up the bags they had packed that morning and get on the buses that would take them back to civilization. Derek hugged Scott firmly and Scott resisted the impulse to kiss him on the cheek. Instead, he wished him well over the summer and said he looked forward to the fall. To his surprise, he wasn't lying. Derek might not be perfect, but once they sorted out the sexual tension between them he was a good person. He thought of the vision he had seen and felt even more resolved to become friends with the boy. If a war was to be fought, he wanted Derek on his side, not on Ashton's. Derek deserved better.

CHAPTER TWENTY-FOUR

The Strong One

Jamie rubbed Marisol's head. She was complaining of a belly-ache again. It was worst right after she ate. Arion was in charge of bringing her food every day, since she couldn't fly to the pasture, and he carried in a live cow. Jamie didn't have the stomach to watch his delicate Marisol devour a living creature, so he always left her alone during feeding but he came in to visit her immediately after ever since the two of them had gotten sick.

She complained that the meat tasted bad and made her feel icky, but she couldn't put it into better terms. Ashton explained that pregnancy was probably affecting her taste buds and making her crave food other than what they had available, and even though Ashton was a liar it seemed like good reasoning. Jamie had never known any pregnant women, but he knew they craved strange things.

He rubbed her belly and was a little nervous when no scales fell off. She had stopped growing. Soon, she would be laying eggs, but where would she lay them? How would she lay them? Would she bring Jamie along or do everything herself? So many things were up in the air and even Ashton didn't have a good explanation. No one had been alive the last time a well-bonded queen laid eggs, and the books told conflicting stories. Everyone had theories, but the only expert was Marisol and she was young and inexperienced, operating off instinct rather than knowledge.

Today she was feeling especially sick, and Jamie was concentrating on keeping the wall between their minds sturdy to prevent him from getting sick as well. Her nausea would fade, he knew, and soon would just be a general sense of unease, but right now she was suffering and there was little he could do.

He was feeling sick as well, but for entirely other reason. Scott was coming back today after spending a second night with Derek, and Jamie had the sinking suspicion that they had had sex. After all, they had had sex multiple times already, what was once more? He was frightened and confused by the thought of seeing Scott again. He loved Scott with all of his heart, but Scott hurt him so much. First it had been the revelation that Scott had been assigned to seduce him, and now this. Maybe his love for Scott wasn't enough. Maybe he needed someone who wouldn't hurt him, someone who would stand up for their love and not let Ashton dictate the terms of their relationship. After all, Jamie had been able to stand up to Ashton. Why couldn't Scott?

But the thought of losing Scott was heart-wrenching. Scott was the only thing he had to hold onto in the world, and he knew that whatever happened, Scott was his. Jamie knew they were destined to be together and they would be once everything worked out. It wasn't Scott's fault for any of this, after all, it was Ashton's. Jamie couldn't let Ashton win; he had to stay with Scott. He had to stand up for Scott, and be Scott's support.

It was strange, but even though at first Scott was the strong one in the relationship, now it seemed the positions were reversed and Jamie was making all the hard decisions and choices. Maybe it was because Jamie was queen now, and had taken on a lot of responsibility that Scott couldn't take on, but it was an unfamiliar feeling. Jamie had always stood up for himself, of course – it wasn't like anyone else in his life cared about him – but he had assumed that for once, someone else would take care of him when he entered into a relationship with Scott. Now, though, it was clear that he would have to be the responsible one yet again and be strong while Scott wandered and lost himself.

He wasn't sure he was happy with that kind of relationship, however. He kind of wanted to be taken care of. He wanted someone to check on him, and make sure he was okay, and see that all of his needs and wants were met. He had thought that person would be Scott but Scott could barely take care of himself, let alone Jamie. Jamie sighed. Well, he wouldn't have his ideal relationship, but he would take what he could get just to be with Scott. Scott was worth anything to him, because Scott loved him. No matter what, he could feel Scott's love like a physical thing and when they had sex and their minds melded together, he knew they belonged together no matter what else happened. As long as he had that, nothing else mattered.

It was evening before Scott knocked at the door and came in, and Jamie was waiting on the couch. He had been waiting for nearly an hour, but he didn't want Scott to know so he tried to look surprised to see him. Scott's face, which was closed and dark when he opened the door, broke into a glorious smile at the sight of Jamie and the whole room felt brighter. Scott's scent was heavily mixed with the other scent Jamie associated with Derek, but he didn't smell sex. So they had been in very close physical contact, but they hadn't had sex. A hesitant smile lit his lips as well. Scott had been strong for him, just as Jamie had been strong for Scott.

Scott sat beside Jamie on the couch and took his hands, stroking his palms lightly in a way that had Jamie's breath hitching unexpectedly.

"I need to take a shower," Scott said, "And wash this scent off of me. You have no idea how happy I am to see you, my love."

"And I you," Jamie whispered.

He and Scott both stood and Jamie followed Scott into the bathroom. Scott lifted an eyebrow. Jamie flushed.

"How will you know when the scent is gone if I don't tell you?" Jamie asked in as innocent a voice as possible. In reality he was just desperate to see his lover, to be in his presence. And the stroking of his palms had lit another hunger in him. Once Scott was free of Derek's scent, Jamie wanted to cleanse his lover with his body and reaffirm the bond between them. Jamie noticed a small bulge in Scott's pants as Scott blushed.

"You want to watch?"

"I want to help," Jamie said, surprised at his boldness. But he had been bold several times the past few days and he was getting used to asking for what he wanted rather than waiting for other people to offer.

Scott seemed speechless and his hands trembled while he stripped. His body was far more beautiful than Jamie remembered, a dark tan with black hair circling his half-hard cock. Jamie self-consciously removed his own clothing, knowing he was nothing compared to Scott. He wondered if Scott was comparing him to Derek in his mind as he pulled off his shirt and revealed his scars, then slipped off his shoes and socks before sliding out of his pants and boxers. His nervousness must have been obvious because Scott reached out to embrace him. They leaned against each other and Scott cupped his ass.

"You are far too beautiful for words," Scott whispered.

Jamie lifted his face to Scott's and they kissed, a deep, passionate kiss. Jamie could taste Derek in Scott's mouth but he chased the taste away, claiming Scott as his and eradicating all traces of his rival. Scott didn't seem to mind; based on how he was massaging Jamie's ass and grinding against him, he was enjoying it thoroughly. When they finally broke away, they were both out of breath. Scott reluctantly let go of him and turned around to flip the water on, giving Jamie an excellent view of Scott's ass.

Then the water was on and Scott was stepping into the steam, extending a hand for Jamie to join him. Jamie was grateful the showers in the queen's chamber were built for two; they didn't have to worry about space as they both embraced again in the fiery water. Jamie reached to turn the water down a little and soon there was a pleasant steam fogging the mirrors as they kissed and kissed like they would never stop.

While they kissed, Jamie grabbed some soap and ran his hands all over Scott's body to rid his boyfriend of the enemy scent. Occasionally they broke apart as Jamie lathered up areas that were hard to reach. Jamie dropped to his knees to clean Scott's legs and thighs, carefully not touching his erect cock. Yet.

He waited until the very end of his erotic cleaning before he finally ran a soapy hand up Scott's shaft. Scott cried out in pleasure and his cock twitched. Jamie turned his full attention on the beautiful creature, massaging and stroking every centimeter, working his fingers into every crevice while Scott clutched the wall and grunted in pure pleasure. Jamie fondled Scott's balls carefully, cleaning and ridding them of Derek's scent, and let his hands work backwards until they reached Scott's opening. Playfully, he stroked a circle around the opening and then pressed against the hole.

Scott bit back a howl as Jamie's finger entered him and massaged his opening just as Scott had done to him before. He didn't add another finger, however, but he was pleased that Scott had enjoyed it so much. Water was streaming down Scott's body and Jamie arranged Scott so that all the suds were rinsed off and he was beautifully clean before Jamie stood back up. Scott immediately swept him into a rough kiss, pressing his back against the cold wall as he forced their bodies and their cocks together and began grinding. Jamie's eyes opened wide at the ferocity he felt in Scott's body, at the desperation.

"Purify me, Jamie," Scott whispered, then he was grabbing Jamie's ass and lifting him up.

Jamie was lifted up, his back pressed against the tile and his ass hovering just above Scott's erect cock. He gasped as he realized what was about to happen. Scott slowly pressed against his opening with no lube, no preparation, only the water running down their bodies. The first pulse of Scott's body into his was painful, but then the pleasure started. Scott kept him pinned to the wall as he pressed into Jamie's willing body, both of them moaning as Jamie's tight body was stretched wide to accommodate Scott's. Jamie wiggled and the motion was incredible. Then Scott pushed into him completely and their minds connected as they had ever since the mating flight and Jamie tilted his head back against the tile and exhaled in wonder.

He was Jamie, held up only by Scott's arms and his cock. He was Scott, thrusting into his lover. He was strong, he was weak, he was submissive and dominant. Jamie's eyes closed and he let himself experience the physical sensations fully. Scott readjusted him against the wall so that he could push against his prostrate with every thrust and the effect was powerful – Jamie held back a scream and settled on a low wail instead. He opened his body to Scott, willing the man to enter him fully and rid himself of memories of Derek in Jamie's loving flesh. There would be nothing left of Derek after this, Jamie knew. Derek could offer sex, but Jamie could offer his soul.

In and out, in and out, strong, slow thrusts that Jamie felt in every fiber of his being and he knew that Scott felt it too. Scott wasn't just making love; he was claiming Jamie as his. There was no rush towards orgasm, although the constant stimulation of his prostrate was making Jamie feel an intense pressure in his balls that would need to be relieved soon. Instead, this was a slow race to the finish line, a gentle rocking motion designed to lead both of them through a valley of pleasure before finally reaching pure bliss.

Scott must have sensed Jamie's building need for orgasm because he altered his strokes to only hit Jamie's prostrate every other stroke, and Jamie sighed and went limp as pleasure overtook him. They stayed that way for what might have been hours or minutes, but eventually Scott's arms must have grown tired from holding Jamie because he pulled out and set Jamie down.

"Turn around," he said, and Jamie obeyed, instinctively putting his hands on the tile and jutting out his ass to give Scott better access. They had never had sex like this before, when they weren't facing each other, and it was strange. But as soon as Scott was fully seated inside of him again, the mental connection sparked back to life and Jamie could feel Scott inside him. Scott's hand snaked around to Jamie's cock and began stroking it, and Jamie knew the end was coming. Scott began striking his prostrate again with every stroke, and his hand matched the pattern as he tightened his grip on Jamie's cock.

Heat began building in Jamie's belly, a familiar heat of passion, and he leaned against the cool tile in an attempt to dull his pleasure and let the experience last longer. But now Scott was growing close to completion as well; his breathing was short and stuttering and he was moaning as his thrusts became staccato. Jamie gave himself over to pleasure again and let his own orgasm build until it was unbearable and his own breathing was punctuated by little whines. He twitched in Scott's hand and finally he could take it no more: his body seized and his balls seemed to explode as semen poured out of his cock. His orgasm was the trigger for Scott's because just as Jamie began to cum, he felt a long shuddering thrust into his body and his insides felt deliciously moist.

Both of them remained where they were, the water washing away the remnants of their lovemaking, until Scott slowly pulled out. He turned Jamie around and kissed him, and Jamie could feel all of the need and passion and love that Scott had for him. He remembered his doubts about their relationship, and those doubts vanished. Maybe Jamie would have to be the strong one in the relationship, the one who stood up to Ashton and earned their freedom, but it was worth it. Anything was worth having Scott at his side.

CHAPTER TWENTY-FIVE

Blood Sacrifice

Kale took a deep breath and closed his connection with Vestis. He had done it. He had told Vestis to inform the other dragons about the queen dragon at Tarragon Academy. Ashton's little secret was out, and it was only a matter of time now before everyone in the world knew. Soon, other dragons would start showing up at the academy to start paying homage to the queen and many would view Jamie as the leader of the Tarragon tribe, not Ashton. It would drive Ashton insane, Kale knew, but it needed to be done. Something had to be done to end this depressing status quo where Ashton had complete control over the queen and her mate. He only hoped Jamie wouldn't pay the price for Kale's actions.

Vestis was on his way back to the academy but it would take nearly a week since he had to avoid airplanes, satellites, and anything else that could identify him. He was skilled at making himself invisible, but lately his abilities – and the abilities of dragons across the world – were starting to fade. Kale thought of Ashton's warnings about the volcano losing its ability to protect the Tarragon tribe, but surely it was a myth. A human sacrifice in Portland could not have an affect on dragons worldwide.

Kale observed the campus while he waited for Vestis to return. Jamie and Scott had been reunited and it looked like Ashton was finally leaving them alone, at least for the time being. Jamie still had lessons with Ashton every day and Kale wondered what those lessons were like now that the boy had realized Ashton's true nature. Mike avoided Kale even when Kale went out of his way to find the man, and he suspected Ashton had something to do with it. And the queen dragon continued to be ill, even though dragons were supposed to be immune to diseases. Still, morning sickness was not really a disease, Kale thought, and no one knew what was normal for a queen dragon.

She had stopped growing and was due to lay her eggs soon, although no one could guess when exactly. There was high-stakes pool betting on when and where she would lay her eggs, but Kale hadn't made a bid. There was just no telling when it would happen. Now that the prospective students were gone, though, the entire campus seemed to have turned into a waiting party for the eggs. All of the students had become obsessed with Marisol and the teachers were, too. Girls snuck over from the sister campus just to see the queen, and Jamie had started to have bags under his eyes from being woken up so many times in the middle of the night by visitors wanting to see Marisol.

At least people seemed to have gotten over their obsession with Jamie, Kale thought, although a good many of the people who went to see Marisol secretly wanted to meet Jamie as well. Jamie was a good sport, much better than Kale would have expected. He seemed to have matured since Kale had met him. Perhaps being forced to watch his boyfriend sleep with another man had given him the strength to stand up for himself in a way he hadn't been able to before. Whatever it was, he seemed much stronger than before even though Kale knew he was barely getting any sleep with all the interruptions.

Vestis was due to arrive in one day when Ashton came to see Kale in his apartment. Kale was surprised when he opened the door to see the man; normally Ashton avoided him as if wanting to wait for Kale to make the decision to kill himself and save the academy. But today Ashton wore a grim expression and Kale knew something was not right. He couldn't sense danger to himself, but he didn't need to in order to know that he was in a very bad situation.

"We've received word from Portugal that they are sending an envoy to meet the queen dragon," Ashton started without preamble.

Kale nodded. So his message to the White House had finally reached an international audience. It had happened faster than he expected and he was a little frightened. He had hoped to have Vestis nearby when Ashton found out what he had done.

"I never announced the queen dragon, and neither did anyone else on campus," Ashton continued. "After all, her health is so delicate. We were waiting until she laid her eggs."

No, Kale thought to himself. You were waiting until you were the queen's mate. But Kale said nothing.

"The only one who could have spread such a rumor is you. Did you?"

Kale swallowed. "Yes," he said. "But only a few people at the White House, and I asked them to keep it a secret. They needed to know what happened and why I was staying here."

"Why are you staying here?"

"To serve the queen," he said, but as soon as he said it he knew it was a mistake. Ashton's eyes flashed and the man lashed out, his fist landing squarely behind Kale's ear. Kale fell to the floor, dazed and confused as the world seemed to spin out of control.

"You serve me," Ashton said. "No one else."

Kale tried to gather his wits but Ashton grabbed him like he weighed nothing and tossed him over his shoulder. Ashton carried him outside, where Arion was waiting, and flung him on Arion's back before climbing up himself. Arion had spikes on his back but Ashton carefully wedged their bodies between the spikes as the dragon took flight. Kale returned to his senses mid-air, but there was nothing he could do.

The volcano loomed large in front of them and Kale flashed

back to the day six years ago when Ashton had taken him on a similar flight. Only then, Kale had been eager to be with Ashton. He would have done anything for Ashton, even give his own life. Now, the sight of the clearing at the top of the volcano filled him with terror. Was Ashton going to force him to take his life? Was Ashton going to kill him?

They landed and as Ashton pulled Kale off the dragon, he slashed Kale's wrist with a long dagger Kale hadn't even noticed. Blood began to flow immediately and as it hit the ground it was absorbed instantly. Kale was ready, though, and whirled to face his opponent.

Kale and Ashton circled each other while blood poured down Kale's arm. He was at a major disadvantage: he was unarmed and severely injured. If he didn't attack soon the blood loss would make him weak and Ashton could easily kill him. He circled and waited for an opportunity. Even though he couldn't waste time, he couldn't lunge too early either or he would skewer himself on Ashton's blade.

A loud blast from the air deafened them and Kale leapt forward, taking advantage of Ashton's surprise to roll under his guard and grab the blade. He swiped at Ashton but the man was quick; his robe was torn but he was unharmed. The dragon above who had emitted the loud noise came closer and Kale thought he recognized it. No time; he had to focus on Ashton who was still a formidable threat. Kale's hand quaked with the blade in it; the blood loss was getting to him. It frightened him how the earth seemed to gobble up his blood and leave no trace. He swayed and Ashton lunged, but Kale sidestepped out of the way and Ashton rushed past him, off balance. Kale swung the blade at his back and scored a hit, ripping into the man's back and leaving a red trail on the ground that was absorbed instantly.

Ashton whirled and his face was pure rage. He charged at Kale, nothing held back. Kale tried to back up and fell, the blade falling from his hand as he tried to shield himself. The dragon that had distracted them earlier grabbed Ashton before the man made contact and hauled him back. Kale opened his eyes that he had unconsciously closed and saw that it was Vestis, come back early. He nearly cried in relief. Vestis held Ashton at bay while the great dragon hissed at Arion as if accusing the dragon of standing by and doing nothing while the humans fought. Arion shrugged, a surprisingly human gesture.

Vestis grabbed Kale with his other claw and held him high in the air before releasing Ashton, who looked furious. Then Vestis flew away from the volcano and Ashton, carrying Kale someplace far away, hopefully someplace safe. Kale tried to put pressure on his wrist but he was seeing stars and knew he wouldn't last long.

Kale dropped to the floor when Vestis released him, and Kale was barely aware of hands turning him over and grabbing his wrist. A bandage was applied while something sharp was inserted into the inside of his other elbow. Must be giving him a blood transfusion to replace the blood he lost, Kale thought idly. He wondered if the doctors would get in trouble for helping someone Ashton had tried to kill and hoped not. After all, they were just doing their job. Everything was gray and fuzzy for a long time, but soon color returned and he was able to make out faces. Mostly nameless doctors, but there were two faces that stood out among the rest.

One was Eric, and Kale knew that Vestis had flown him to Eric after rescuing him from Ashton. Eric was the one who had saved Kale six years ago as well. He hoped Ashton didn't take his anger out on Eric this time, since Ashton had let the incident go six years ago. The other face was Jamie, and Kale was shocked to see him there. Vestis informed him that Jamie hadn't been feeling well again and had been seeing a doctor when Vestis had brought Kale in. Jamie looked to be on the brink of tears but when Kale tried to move to greet him, a smile lit his face.

"You're alive," he said.

"Barely," Kale said. "Only because of Vestis."

"We have to get you out of here," Eric said. "Again. And the White House won't work this time. We have to send you somewhere Ashton won't be able to follow."

"He can follow anywhere if he's determined," Kale said, feeling despair choke his heart.

"Marisol says he can't follow into the nesting grounds," Jamie suggested.

"Humans aren't allowed there," Eric said dismissively.

It was an impossible suggestion, Kale knew. The eggs in the nesting grounds were extremely fragile and ready to hatch at any time, but if they hatched at any time before the first year exam then the dragons inside ended up deformed and malnourished. And having a human wandering around was exactly the way eggs ended up hatching.

"Marisol says as long he's careful not to disturb the eggs, he'll be fine there."

Eric looked at Jamie for a long time in silence with the slightly glazed look of someone communicating with their dragon.

"You're sure the queen would allow this?" he finally asked.

"Yes," Jamie said without hesitation. "You can ask her yourself if you want."

Eric's lips twitched. "I can't talk to other dragons, but I take your word for it. And it is the only place safe from Ashton. Well, Kale? What do you think? Can you be careful not to touch the eggs?"

"How long will I be there?"

Both Eric and Jamie were silent, and then a strange dragon's voice filled his mind. He didn't need to ask to know it was Marisol, speaking directly to him.

Only until the war begins, she said.

Kale nodded, a tinge of excitement running up his spine. So Marisol recognized that there would have to be a war to get rid of Ashton. That meant Jamie was surely in on it, too, even though the boy couldn't speak of it in front of Eric. And with the queen dragon on their side, they actually had a chance of winning, a chance no one had ever had before. Finally, there might be a way to get rid of Ashton permanently.

"Alright," Kale said. "I'll go, and I'll be careful."

The doctors unhooked him from the machine and warned him against strenuous activity for the next week until his own blood restored itself, since they had been unable to restore all his blood. He agreed and mounted Vestis with hope in his heart. He had nearly been killed, but at least it had triggered something. The council would know what Ashton had done, and Jamie knew what Ashton had done. No matter what Ashton said or did, there would be consequences for him. Eric and Jamie would see to it, and all Kale had to do was rest and recover, and wait for the war to begin.

CHAPTER TWENTY-SIX

Wary Friendship

Scott watched Jamie leave for the doctor with a heavy heart. Jamie was sick again and headed to see Emma. He was glad that Jamie had a doctor he connected with, but upset at how many times Jamie needed to see her. Jamie worked hard keeping the wall between his mind and Marisol's secure, but Marisol's constant illness was taking its toll on Jamie, not to mention the endless visits from people wanting to see the queen. Scott would have just turned everyone away, but Jamie insisted on letting everyone in to see Marisol and meet him, even when it was the middle of the night and the visit seemed designed to prevent him from getting sleep. Sometimes Scott wondered if it were a trick by Ashton to ensure that Jamie never felt strong enough to take him on again.

Jamie had finally told Scott about his confrontation with Ashton and how he had gotten Ashton to promise that Scott wouldn't have to sleep with anyone else. Scott had been so proud of his boyfriend, but a little worried, too. Ashton wasn't the type to give in so easily and Scott wondered if he were somehow behind Marisol's illness. He didn't know how, but he had his suspicions. After all, Arion was the one to bring Marisol her food every day. It wouldn't be too hard for Arion to slip something else to Marisol at the same time. Marisol hadn't mentioned anything, but would she even know to notice it?

Scott set out to his dragon-training class with Eric. It was one of the few parts of the day he looked forward to. Narné was quite skilled with fire now, and would master the craft in a matter of weeks. Even though Eric was on the council and Scott had to watch what he said around the man, Eric was still a good person and Scott enjoyed hanging out with him and learning about Narné's abilities.

Today, though, instead of seeing Eric in the football field Scott saw Amar. Amar kicked the ground as Scott came closer, looking around for the instructor.

"Um, Eric was called away for an emergency," Amar said. "I said I'd stick around and tell you."

"Thanks," Scott said. The awkwardness was almost palpable. "How are your classes?"

"Great," Amar said.

Silence.

"So what did you think of the prospective students?" Scott asked, desperate to get some kind of conversation going. Amar had asked to remain behind so clearly he wanted to talk to Scott, but he wasn't making it easy. But at this question, Amar seemed to brighten.

"I liked most of them. Tephis is able to see if they'll be able to bond with dragons, you know, so I was there to help with recruitment."

"That's pretty cool," Scott said.

"Yeah," Amar said. "I was the only first-year student allowed."

"I was wondering how you got in," Scott said with a smile. "Any potential dragon partners in the bunch?"

"Most of them," Amar said. "Especially the boy you were with."

"Derek," Scott said slowly.

It had been a week since he was with Derek but at the boy's name all the memories came flooding back. He felt ashamed of what he had done. While Jamie had been standing up to Ashton and demanding that they be allowed to live their lives freely, Scott had been seducing and having sex with Ashton's son, and even enjoying it. He wasn't sure how or why Jamie had forgiven him, since he would never forgive himself. He thought of the fall semester, when Derek would be on campus full time, and wondered what it would be like. He hoped they would be able to be friends like they were on the last day, without any of the sexual tension.

"I've never seen anything like him, except for Jamie," Amar said. "He and Jamie look the same."

Scott nodded, but didn't tell Amar about his vision of Derek with the queen dragon. It was interesting, however, that Amar seemed to be able to sense what type of dragon the person would partner with. He wondered if Amar could sense green versus blue dragons as well, or at least if Amar would learn to be able to do so after he honed his skills.

Amar took a breath. "How is Jamie?"

"Still sick," Scott said. "Marisol's morning sickness is getting worse. Ashton thinks it's because she's getting ready to lay her eggs, but it just doesn't seem right. You haven't been to visit Jamie lately," Scott said, realizing that in all the various visits they had had over the past week, Amar had not been among them.

"I had some issues," Amar said. "I worked them out, but I still feel kind of awkward around Jamie."

"You mean the mating flight."

"How did you know?"

Scott shrugged. "Your best friend has a mating flight and you see him in a way you never thought you would. It's sure to cause some friction in your relationship. You should still go and talk to Jamie, though. He needs a friend, especially now."

"Because he's sick?"

"No, he's going through a lot. Trying to be the queen, trying to take on all these responsibilities, trying to keep up in his classes, it's a lot of work. Being sick just makes everything harder, and he could use a friend right now."

"He has you, though, right?"

Even though the question was asked casually, Scott could hear the threat under it.

"Of course he does," Scott said. "But he'd really like to see you, I'm sure."

Amar nodded and scuffed his shoe on the grass. "Maybe I'll go see him. When will he be back from the doctor?"

"Pretty soon. Do you want me to walk over with you?"

"Don't you have class?"

"If Eric's this late, I can safely skip," Scott said, hoping it was true. He didn't want to hurt Eric's feelings, but on the other hand, if Eric had a true emergency then who knew how long it would take. Narné was circling overhead and didn't care if Scott left, so he and Amar started walking to the doctor's offices.

They talked about classes, and Scott gave him advice for each of his teachers based on his own experiences. They talked about their dragons, a subject everyone in Tarragon society loved, and Amar became unusually expressive when he talked about Tephis and everything Tephis could do. Scott even got to brag a little about Narné, since Amar didn't know anything about his dragon or green dragons in general. They talked about all sorts of things and finally made their way into the doctor's office, where there was an unusual rush of people for a quiet Monday afternoon. Scott asked where Jamie was, and an orderly pointed without saying a word before rushing off.

Jamie wasn't alone, and it was with surprise that Scott saw Eric with him. The two of them were standing next to an empty bed and both men looked shaken. Scott ran up to Jamie and cradled him.

"Is everything okay?"

"No," Jamie murmured, speaking so softly only Scott could hear. "Ashton tried to kill Kale."

Scott went rigid and his eyes riveted to the empty bed. Had Kale lain there on the brink of death? Where was he now? He reached out to Narné and the dragon informed him that he was getting the information from Marisol, but Marisol didn't seem concerned. He wondered why Ashton had tried to kill Kale, what had driven Ashton to such an extreme.

He didn't understand the motive, but if Ashton wanted to kill someone, Kale was the ideal person to kill. Kale had no close ties at the academy and kept to himself. Everyone knew he had to return to the White House eventually, so if he and Vestis vanished people would just assume he had left. No one would ever suspect that Ashton had killed him. And the people in the White House would just assume he had decided to stay at the academy indefinitely, so they wouldn't question it either.

Kale had to be safe now, or else Marisol would be worried about him. He wondered why Eric was here, and knew that this was the emergency that had pulled Eric away from his class. Eric looked at Scott and Amar as if he had just been caught somewhere he shouldn't be. If he had helped Kale escape and word reached Ashton, then Ashton would surely retaliate. Scott knew Eric's secret was safe with him, but he didn't know about Amar. Would Amar even know to keep quiet about this?

"What's going on?" Amar said, moving into the room and studying Jamie and Eric with curiosity.

They couldn't even tell Amar that Eric had been helping Jamie, because if news reached Ashton that Eric and Jamie were together when Kale disappeared, Eric would be implicated and punished. Scott wondered what the doctors and nurses did, then he remembered confidentiality and wondered if that extended to the other people in the room, not just the patient. He suspected it did, because Eric didn't look concerned by the nurses who walked past the open door.

"I have to leave," Eric said. "Just stopping by to check on Jamie."

"Was that the emergency?" Amar asked.

"Amar," Jamie said. "We need to talk."

Eric scooted out of the room and shut the door behind him, leaving Scott, Jamie, and Amar alone. Amar looked around nervously.

"Um, what do we need to talk about?"

"I need you to swear to keep something secret."

"Sure."

"No, really swear. It'll be difficult to do, but if my friendship means anything to you, I need your absolute silence."

Amar looked at him and Scott wondered what he saw. Amar no doubt still had the image of Jamie from the mating flight burned into his memory, but he also had memories of their whole first semester together to balance out that single image. Would the memories of friendship be enough?

"Anything, Jamie. I swear to keep your secret."

Jamie smiled and the room seemed brighter. "A friend of mine was hurt and Eric and I had to help him. But you can't tell anyone that Eric or I were involved, or else we'll be hurt too."

"Who would hurt you? You're the queen."

Jamie's expression darkened. "There's a lot that goes into being the queen, and it's not all good. You won't tell anyone that Eric was here? That I was here?"

"I won't tell anyone, but I don't understand."

"I'll explain it all, Amar. I promise. Someday soon, I'll explain it."

Amar nodded. "I'll keep you to that promise. Are you at least feeling better?"

Jamie let out a little laugh. "You know, I am? Why don't we return to my rooms and you can see Marisol? You haven't seen her since she was little and she's changed so much. Tephis can come too."

Scott watched Jamie and saw that shadows still hung over his eyes, but he was making a strong effort to be carefree and happy and Scott didn't want to ruin that, so he offered to cook up dinner for the three of them. Amar asked if his girlfriend could come so they could make it a double date and Scott smiled. Amar seemed to be far more accepting of his relationship with Jamie than he had before.

Nikki, Amar's girlfriend, was waiting at dragon canyon when they arrived and the first thing Jamie did was show off Marisol just as he'd been showing off his dragon to all of the guests and visitors the past week. Only this time he seemed genuinely excited and proud of his dragon, and Amar and Nikki were properly impressed. Nikki rubbed Marisol's belly as the great dragon's eyes half-closed in contentment. Then Nikki and Amar's dragons showed up and there wasn't enough room for all of them in the dragon chamber, so the humans retreated to the living area. Scott headed to the kitchen to cook up some hamburgers and one veggie burger for Nikki and he listened to the others talking and laughing as he cooked.

It had been a long time since he heard Jamie laughing, he thought. It was nice. The pressure of being queen and then the prospective students had eaten away at all of Jamie's reserve energy, but hopefully this double date would revitalize him. Scott added his special blend of seasonings to the burgers and began to grill them on the special minigrill he had bought a few years ago, then began slicing up vegetables. As he sliced, his mind turned to Kale. The man had to be alright. There was no way Jamie would be so relaxed if Kale were still in serious danger. But why had Ashton attacked, and what would the repercussions be?

There wasn't much Jamie and Scott could do to punish Ashton, after all; it was in the hands of the council and Eric hadn't seemed to eager to share what had happened with the council. After all, that would then expose his role in helping Kale escape and then he would be at Ashton's mercy. No, Ashton would get away with this, just as he got away with everything. Scott doubted there was anything he could do that would make the council sit up and take notice, and the council was the only recourse they had. The entire system was corrupt and designed by Ashton to benefit Ashton. The only way to fix it was to get rid of it completely, but that would be nearly impossible to do.

He remembered the vision of Derek astride the queen dragon and once again he wondered which side Derek would be on. He would do everything in his power to make sure that Derek was on Jamie's side, and that it was two queens against one corrupt council member. After all, the world would follow the queens, not Ashton, right? He shook his head and flipped the burgers. Everything was up in the air and it felt like another ball had been added to a marathon juggling game. Kale was gone, for now at least, but perhaps Amar and Nikki would help fill the void. He could only hope.

CHAPTER TWENTY-SEVEN

Sedative

Two weeks had passed since the prospective students were on campus and everything was going smoothly. Classes were back to normal, students were back to their usual dramas, and Mike could sit back and let the semester glide by him. Marisol and Jamie were still getting sick regularly, however, and it was preventing Jamie from joining the rest of his class. He had been getting private lessons from Ashton, Mike, and a handful of other teachers who offered to help various days of the week, but he wasn't getting a consistent education. Mike was determined to find the source of Marisol's illness and put an end to it, no matter what it took.

He started at the library, naturally enough, researching morning sickness in dragons. There were no mentions of it, no mentions, in fact, of any type of illness in dragons except for poisons and injuries. He wondered if perhaps Marisol was unknowingly ingesting some type of poison along with her food. Perhaps Marisol was allergic to something in the cows she ate. There were no mentions of allergies in the books, either, unfortunately, but it seemed reasonable.

Mike went to the fields where Arion chose Marisol's daily cattle. Perhaps Arion was choosing cattle who strayed too near a certain type of plant that she was allergic to. After all, dragons tended to chose prey from the same area again and again. He studied the field where the cattle roamed. Occasionally a dragon would soar down and chaos would ensue as the panicked animals ran for cover before one would be lifted into the air and taken away to be eaten elsewhere. Mike swallowed. It was not the prettiest sight in the world and he had a distinct desire never to eat beef again.

He noticed a man out with the cattle, running his hands along one of the largest cattle on the field. The man tied a gold ribbon around the cattle's neck and Mike knew that indicated that this cattle was intended for Marisol. He studied the location of the cattle but saw no unusual plants, nothing to account for the unusual illness. Then the man pulled out a massive syringe and stabbed it into the poor cow's back, pumping its body full of a strange yellow liquid. When the syringe was empty, the man walked away. After less than a minute, the cow fell to the ground as if dead.

Mike sent a message to Eraxes to prevent any other dragons from entering the area, then he cautiously climbed the fence and got in the pen with the cows. He prayed any nearby dragons would listen to Eraxes, because he didn't want to get crushed or trampled in a stampede. He made his way to the limp cattle with the golden ribbon and stared at it.

Its eyes were open and it was clearly alive, but paralyzed. Mike had brought a few test tubes to put flowers in to test for allergies, but now he took out a knife and slit the beast's skin slightly, filling one of the tubes with blood before sealing it. He removed the yellow ribbon and tied it on the neck of one of the standing cattle. There was no way Marisol could be expected to eat a cow that couldn't even stand. The man had poisoned this cow, and that was poisoning Marisol. Eraxes belted a warning. Arion was coming.

Mike ran to the nearest fence and darted over it just as the other dragon came into view. Eraxes hid in the forest, not wanting to be seen by his superior. Arion circled and seemed to enjoy the chaos he caused. He paused over the limp cow and nearly picked it up, as if he knew that it was the cow that was supposed to be for Marisol, but then he grabbed the running cow that Mike had tied the ribbon to instead and carried off that cow. Mike sighed. At least Marisol wouldn't be poisoned today.

But if Arion had seemed to expect the limp cow, then that meant this had been going on for a while and wasn't a one time poisoning. It also indicated that perhaps Ashton knew about it, although Mike tried to push that thought from his mind. He would take the blood to the medical lab and see what they found, and then he would worry about who was doing what to Marisol. After all, he didn't even know that the yellow liquid injected into the cow was dangerous to dragons. Perhaps it was a form of dragon vitamins that were dangerous to cows but not to dragons. He would stay positive, he decided, until he had proof otherwise.

Proof came after three days of tests. Emma, the doctor taking care of Jamie, had offered to run the blood in the labs. On the third day after Mike had dropped off the blood without saying where he got it, she called him into her office with a concerned look on her face.

"Where did you get this?" she asked. "It's a heavy sedative used on dragons that can cause severe side effects. This isn't even allowed anymore except in emergency cases."

"A sedative?" Mike asked with a frown. Marisol didn't seem sedated, but then again she barely moved because of the eggs. Maybe the sedative was designed to encourage her not to move in order to protect the eggs.

"With severe side effects," Emma repeated. "Where did you get it?"

"In a cow," Mike admitted.

"Was this cow intended for Marisol?"

"What makes you say that?"

"Because it fits her symptoms perfectly, and Jamie's as well. This sedative was banned not only because of the side effects to the dragon but also the side effects to the partner."

Mike was silent for a moment. "What are the side effects?"

"Nausea, exhaustion, fuzzy thinking, overall weakness, lack of self-control, hypersexuality."

"Wait, what? Hypersexuality? Lack of self-control? Fuzzy thinking? Those are just for the dragon, right?"

Emma shook her head and Mike's breath caught. He hated thinking poorly of Ashton, but it sounded exactly like something Ashton would do. In fact, it sounded like something Ashton would do in order to seduce Jamie, and he thought of all the private lessons Ashton had given the boy. If Jamie weren't strong enough to fight, if his body were reacting on its own without him being able to control it, then who knew what would happen? What if Ashton were having sex with Jamie regularly, while Mike thought that Ashton was true to him? Jealousy bit into his heart and as he thought of Jamie as he had been in the mating flight, vulnerable yet desperate to be touched, Mike knew that he would never forgive Ashton if the man had touched Jamie.

"Mike, if Marisol is regularly consuming this sedative, then all of her symptoms and Jamie's are explained. But we need to get her off the sedative. I think you would know how to go about that better than me."

She glanced meaningfully at the collar around his neck and he blushed. She was asking him to go talk to Ashton about this. He would rather let Marisol remain on the sedative than talk to Ashton, but he knew his first responsibility was to his students, and Jamie was his student.

"You're right," he said glumly. "Thanks for helping me."

He walked toward the dragon canyon with a heavy heart. He nearly stumbled into someone walking the opposite direction and when he realized it was Jamie he nearly cursed. The boy looked surprised to see him, and even more surprised that Mike didn't appear happy to see him.

"Good evening, Mike," Jamie said politely.

"Jamie," Mike said.

"Is everything okay?"

"Fine," Mike said blandly, but his lying skills must have been not functioning because Jamie looked highly suspicious. "I have to go," Mike added, then hurried off. He thought he heard a gasp from Jamie and hoped his sudden departure wasn't too sudden, but he couldn't stand the thought of talking to Jamie with this new knowledge he had. There was no way he could keep it a secret. He needed to talk to Ashton and see what Ashton wanted him to do first.

Ashton was finishing dinner when Mike arrived, and Mike waited beside the table while the man finished, clearly enjoying his dominance over Mike as he made Mike wait for every slow bite. When it was finally done, he kissed Mike gently on the lips.

"What do you need, pet?"

"Did you know that Marisol is being sedated?"

The words just flowed out of him without thought and it was too late to take them back. He had thought of better ways to say it, more discrete, practical ways, but this way would have to work. Ashton stared at him for a long moment, then reached out and grabbed his collar. He led Mike into the bedroom and Mike tensed. This was where he received pleasure, but also where he was punished and he suspected punishment was more in store for him tonight.

"Marisol is being controlled for her own good," Ashton said.

Mike relaxed. So Ashton did have a reason for sedating her. "There are side effects to the drug you're using," Mike said, hoping to sound helpful and not accusing. "Perhaps another sedative would be better."

"Who all knows about this?"

"One doctor, that's it. And me."

"And our doctors never share secrets," Ashton said with a smile. "You were good not to tell anyone else. You're sure Jamie or Scott don't know?"

"I passed Jamie on the way here but I didn't say anything."

Ashton nodded and stroked his cheek. "Good. You will never tell anyone. And the sedative will remain as it is. Side effects or not, Marisol needs to be contained to protect her eggs. You believe me, don't you?"

"Yes," Mike said without hesitation. But the more he thought about it, the less he did. He would just have to try not to think about it.

"You're so obedient," Ashton said, leaning in close so his breath tickled Mike's ear. "But it was wrong of you to investigate in the first place."

"I'm sorry," Mike said, his voice hitching. It would be punishment, then.

Ashton pointed at his bed and Mike began stripping. As soon as he was completely naked, he climbed onto the satin coverlet and waited for whatever was coming. Ashton stripped slowly, never taking his eyes off Mike and watching as Ashton's nude body had its usual effect. Ashton was perfection under those clothes, and Mike often wished that he would go around naked all the time. More people would worship Ashton if they saw him naked, he knew. Ashton climbed onto the bed with him, positioning himself over Mike with his elbows pressing the pillow on either side of Mike's head and his face just inches from Mike's.

"What are you afraid of, pet? Why did you have so much fear in your voice when you spoke of the sedative?"

"Are you sleeping with Jamie?" Mike asked, and felt the tension rise between them like an unstoppable tsunami. When Ashton didn't reply, Mike felt a tear form in his eye.

"No, Michael," Ashton finally said. "But I will, during the mating flight. Will you be able to let me sleep with him then?"

Mike shifted uncomfortably. He had known that Ashton would try to win Jamie in the mating flight, but he had never put the pieces together and realized that it would mean that

Ashton would be sleeping with Jamie. Of course, Mike dreamed about sleeping with Jamie all the time. If it hadn't been for Narné's sneaky maneuver, Mike would be the queen's mate and everything would be easy. Instead, everything was chaos, with Scott and Ashton at odds and even Jamie turning against Ashton and the queen being sedated without her knowledge. None of this would have happened if Eraxes had been just a little faster to grab Marisol during the mating flight. He would be trying to win Jamie in the next mating flight as well, he realized, so he couldn't blame Ashton for doing the same.

"It's a mating flight," Mike said, trying to sound like he didn't care even as the words cost him everything. "You're free to pursue Jamie."

"And other mating flights?"

Jealousy leapt up in Mike's throat. "No," he said without a second thought. He would make an exception for Jamie, but not for anyone else.

Ashton laughed. "My loyal pet. You have been good to me, and I will be good to you. You'll see. But I will be sleeping with Jamie at the mating flight, and you will have to get used to that idea. In the meantime, let this soothe you."

He kissed Mike and instantly Mike's body was aflame. Every point of contact between them was on fire and he grabbed Ashton to pull him closer. Ashton lifted Mike's legs to his waist and began pumping his own cock until it was hard, then he aimed himself into Mike. Mike tried to relax. He had been penetrated by Ashton without any preparation before and while it hurt immensely at first, he had grown to enjoy it. Mike was only partially hard when Ashton pierced him and he cried out in pain. It almost felt like something were ripping as Ashton continued to enter him, ignoring his continued cries as the pressure mounted and he squirmed to try and acquaint himself with the immense object inside of him.

His cock began pulsing with need and Mike pushed down

against Ashton in a steady rhythm, a rhythm that helped ease the pain as Ashton began thrusting more easily in and out of him. With every thrust he seemed to reach a place deep inside Mike that needed to be filled, that could only be filled by Ashton, and he moaned as sweat formed on his chest and forehead and he wrapped his legs around Ashton's waist to encourage him to go deeper.

Ashton kissed him deeply, his tongue tracing the contours of his mouth as if creating a map, and the sensation of his warm tongue penetrating his mouth was nearly as good as his cock penetrating him below. Ashton kept his hands near Mike's face, stroking his hair and wiping the sweat from his brow. His thrusts came faster and Mike knew Ashton was close, even though he was still a ways from his orgasm. They didn't always cum together, although when they did it was magical, and Mike suspected that he would be left hungry as punishment once Ashton took his pleasure.

Ashton's thrusts became erratic and he moaned and pressed his head against Mike's neck, then he jabbed Mike once, twice, and Mike felt something explode inside him. His own cock was hard but not near orgasm, and Ashton gave him a teasing caress before pulling out. Sure enough, Ashton stood up, leaving him unfulfilled. Mike's hand strayed to his cock, since sometimes Ashton allowed him to jerk himself off after Ashton was finished, but Ashton shook his head and Mike removed his hand and bit his lip. He was so aroused, and it was beyond cruel to be left like this. But he had disobeyed his master, and his master had the right to punish his pet.

"You will say nothing of the sedative to anyone," Ashton said as he dressed. "If anyone finds out, I will know that you talked and you will be properly punished."

Mike nodded but remained on the bed. He knew he would not be allowed to get up and dress until Ashton was gone. Ashton liked to see him naked on the bed for as long as possible, especially when he was in need like this. Finally, Ashton turned and left, and Mike sprang for the shower where he turned the water as cold as it would go. He didn't touch himself, even though he could have without Ashton knowing. Instead, he let the cold water sluice away his lust as he washed away the evidence and thought of the sedative. Jamie and Marisol deserved to know, but Ashton was right. Emma would never tell anyone; the doctors were renowned for their secrecy. If anyone found out, it would be because of Mike. Ashton hadn't punished him today, not really, but if anyone found out, Mike knew he would be ruthless. He shivered in the cold shower and vowed not to tell anyone, no matter how much they deserved to know.

CHAPTER TWENTY-EIGHT

Realization

Jamie watched Mike leave and wondered why he had lied. It was highly unusual that Mike would lie to him. He couldn't read Mike's mind to find out the lie, but he could read Mike's dragon's mind and he prodded Eraxes carefully so the dragon wouldn't notice. Just as he had with Narné, he felt the sharp edge of something not lining up, the sharp edge he had come to associate with a lie in the mind of a dragon. He followed the sharp edge and expected to see an image, like he had with Narné's mind when he had seen the dragons flying in formation in a war, but instead he found a conversation with Emma and suddenly the knowledge was in his mind: he and Marisol were being sedated.

He gasped as the information slid into place and suddenly everything made sense. Even Ashton's attempts to seduce him made sense. Ashton had thought that he was weak and vulnerable when he had kissed Jamie, and Jamie had been suffering from the side effects of a drug that made him highly susceptible to sexual contact. That was why he had been turned on by Ashton, not for any other reason. He felt immensely relieved even while the shock worked its way through his body. He had been headed to Emma, but now he knew he needed to be with Marisol. She was going to be eating soon, something he usually avoided, but today he needed to be there to see for himself if the cow looked drugged.

Marisol was picking up on his distress and it didn't take long before she figured out why he was so distressed. He heard her trumpeting call of anger when he was still climbing towards his chamber and wondered what the other dragons thought. They all babied her, and if they thought she was angry they would surely try to find out why. But how would they react when they knew the truth? Would they turn against Ashton, or turn a blind eye? He had to control knowledge of the sedative carefully to use it to his greatest advantage. He instructed Marisol not to tell anyone, but had Narné and Scott meet him in her chambers. They were at class with Eric, the instructor who had been so kind to Kale, so surely Eric would let them go early if Jamie requested it.

He reached Marisol right as Arion was presenting her with the cow. The beast was completely limp and unmoving except for its eyes and there was a scent of ammonia that overpowered the natural animal smells that should have accompanied the best. Arion seemed surprised that Jamie appeared, and nodded in greeting to him. Jamie gestured to the cow.

"This cow is sick," he said. "Marisol wants a cow that can move. Go and get her another one. I'll wait here."

Arion nodded and picked up the limp cow, carrying it towards the pasture without a word. Jamie reached into Arion's mind carefully and saw that the dragon intended on catching a normal cow, not a drugged one, because he knew that Jamie would be checking. Arion didn't seem to think that one cow would make a difference and was willing to humor Jamie, but he didn't know that Jamie intended on being present for every feeding from now on. He had been a fool to leave Marisol alone before. The clues were all there: Marisol grew ill immediately after eating, so naturally he should have checked her food. But he hadn't wanted to see the animals she gobbled down, so he had stayed away.

Arion returned with another cow, an ordinary cow, and Marisol devoured it in a single bite. Arion waited until she finished, then flew away just as Narné and Scott appeared in the doorway.

Arion hesitated midair as if studying them, then continued to head towards Ashton's rooms. Jamie didn't care what Arion thought; it was common for Narné and Scott to come to the dragon cave instead of using the walkways and after all, it was their room.

Scott hopped down off Narné and embraced Jamie.

"What's wrong?"

Jamie and Scott had scoured their rooms for listening devices and found and destroyed several, and they were fairly certain that this room at least was clean, even if the rest of their quarters were not. So Jamie explained what he had seen in Eraxes's mind and how Marisol was being fed a sedative that had drastic side effects on both her and him. Scott's lips tightened as he spoke, and the man's hands curled into fists.

"That bastard," Scott finally hissed when Jamie was done. "What about tonight? She just ate."

"A clean cow, I made sure of it. But they tried to give her a drugged one first."

"One of us will have to be here every feeding time."

"And they'll grow suspicious."

Marisol swung her head down next to them. Her eyes whirled with rage and Jamie could feel how tightly she was keeping her emotions so that they didn't spill over into Jamie.

Ashton must pay, she said. *He might be harming the eggs. We do not know what this sedative will do to my eggs, or how it will affect my nesting.*

"She's right," Scott said. "We have to say something this time. We can't just sit back and hope it all works out. Even if we stay for every feeding, Ashton'll just think of something else."

"But what can we do? The only person with authority here is Ashton, and he's the one doing it."

Scott and Jamie were both silent. Narné nestled his head into Marisol's side and began licking the golden scales as if he could clean away the poison in her system. She nuzzled him sweetly and licked his cheek in return, but her anger was undiminished.

Silence had fallen for several minutes when Jamie leapt to his feet. "I can't take this," he said. "I can't take living like this. It's impossible. I need to be free. Free of these stupid rules and responsibilities but most of all free of Ashton. But we can't leave because Marisol can't fly."

Marisol ducked her head and Jamie could feel shame mixed with her anger.

"It's not your fault, Marisol," he added quickly. "You'll be able to fly soon, but we'll still be trapped here."

"There has to be another way," Scott said.

Jamie paced and tried to think of anyone with as much power as Ashton. His mind lit on the girl's school, and the headmistress who was rumored to have had an affair with Ashton once.

"What about the girl's school? The head of the school? Wouldn't she be as powerful as Ashton?"

Scott tapped his lips. "She's on the council, but Ashton is head of the council. Only if the entire council voted against him would they ever act against him."

"That's it, then," Jamie said. "We'll approach the council, not Ashton, and we'll try to get Ashton removed as head of the council."

"I don't think students can meet with the council."

"I'm not a student, I'm the queen," Jamie said with confidence.

He thought of his solution and knew it would work. Once the council found out what Ashton was doing behind their backs, they would have no choice but to remove him from power. Their dragons would be able to confirm everything that Jamie said, giving him extra credence. He was positive that the council did not know what Ashton was doing, because the one thing that all of the council members he had met so far had in common

was a reverence for Marisol. They might not treat Jamie well –
in fact, most of them ignored him because he was too young to
warrant their attention – but Marisol was sacred. They would do
anything for her, and if they found out Ashton was threatening
the lives of the eggs and sedating Marisol against her will and
knowledge, they would turn against him in a heartbeat. It was
part of Tarragon society: the queen before the council.

Jamie didn't know where to start, however. He didn't even
know how many people were on the council. The only person he
knew for sure who was on the council was Eric, and he wasn't
sure he wanted to go to Eric for help since that might make
Ashton suspect that Eric had to do with Kale's disappearance.
But Eric was also Scott's teacher, so maybe it was a natural
choice. He explained the problem to Scott and Scott nodded.

"I think Eric is a good first step, but are you sure you want to
do this, Jamie? I'll be with you every step of the way-"

"No," Jamie said. "You won't. The council won't listen to you,
they'll only listen to me. I have to do this alone."

"Are you sure?"

Jamie thought about what would happen if Scott went with
him. The council would see it as an attempt by Scott to get back
at Ashton for the hell Ashton was putting him through. It would
be seen as simple, petty revenge and nothing more. The council
wouldn't even listen to the complaints. But if Jamie went alone,
Jamie who had no real qualms with Ashton, then the council
would have no choice but to listen. It wouldn't be revenge but
the truth. It was funny to think that even a month ago such a
decision would have terrified him, but he had aged in the past
few weeks and now felt strong enough to take on the council by
himself. He could do it alone. He could stand up for himself as
he had never been able to do before.

Jamie left Scott and Narné with Marisol in case Arion tried
to return with a drugged cow for dessert, and headed to Eric's
quarters. The light was on and Jamie knocked, hoping Eric

was home. The door opened and revealed the council member dressed casually in jeans and a black t-shirt, his spiky brown hair disheveled and his brown eyes widening at the sight of Jamie.

"Um, come in," he said, welcoming Jamie into his rooms. They were mostly neat, but Eric had stacks of papers on nearly every horizontal surface. Jamie was tempted to snoop, but managed to keep his eyes off the papers. They looked like student papers, anyways. Not interesting. "To what do I owe this pleasure?"

Something about the way he said it made Jamie think he was deeply concerned that Jamie was going to ask about Kale, and he did not want to answer questions about Kale. Luckily, Kale was not even on Jamie's agenda today, even though he wished he could make Ashton pay for that crime as well.

"I would like to speak with the council," Jamie said. "The whole council, men and women. But I don't know how."

"Why?"

"Because Ashton has been doing things that they aren't aware of, and I want him to pay."

"Jamie," Eric began in a warning voice, but Jamie cut him off.

"It isn't about that. It's about Marisol and her eggs. Ashton has put them in danger and I need the council to protect me."

Eric frowned. "I doubt Ashton would do such a thing. You and Marisol mean the world to him."

"If you let me talk to the council, I can tell you exactly what he's done. I just need the council's protection."

"I suppose I could convene a meeting for you," Eric said. "You're sure it has nothing to do with... with him?"

"I won't mention him at all."

"Alright," Eric said. "If Ashton is threatening you, then you probably do need the council's help. Just don't expect too much. They may turn you down."

Jamie nodded, but couldn't help the pulse of adrenaline coursing through his system. He was going to talk to the council. He was finally going to meet the people who, collectively, had as much power as Ashton. He couldn't wait to stand in front of them and finally have someone listen to him and help him. He was so tired of helping himself, it would be nice to have someone else be on his side for once.

Eric went to the phone and started making calls. After nearly twenty minutes of talking on the phone while Jamie sat at the kitchen table and fidgeted, he turned to Jamie.

"Well, you have your meeting. Tomorrow at noon in the council chambers. I'll escort you, since students aren't allowed there. I just hope you know what you're doing."

CHAPTER TWENTY-NINE

Jamie's Demands

Jamie stood in front of the council and tried to look strong. When he had requested the meeting, he hadn't realized how large the council was, or how intimidating they would look in their dark robes with the dragon sigil embroidered on the breast. He tried to talk, but the council members were talking to each other and ignoring him completely. The female students were starting their mating flights soon, and there was an air of excitement and anticipation among the council members as they gossiped about who would go first, and who would catch whom. One of the council members turned as if to listen to Jamie, but then his neighbor asked a question and he turned away. They were completely absorbed in each other.

"Excuse me," he said loudly, trying to get their attention. After all, he had called this meeting. Shouldn't they be listening to him? But they continued talking loudly, laughing and joking and ignoring him completely. Anger began to boil in his blood. This was not a time for jokes and laughter. He was here for serious business and he deserved to be heard. He stepped up on the dais at the front of the room, where they could all see him, and called for their attention again. No luck.

"I am your Queen," Jamie shouted, furious now that no one was listening to him. "You will listen to my demands."

At that reminder of his position, the council grew quiet, finally, and turned toward him. Ashton took a few steps towards him and stretched out one hand.

"And what are your demands, little one?" Ashton asked in a deliberately cloy voice, as if he were pacifying a toddler. Jamie hadn't expected Ashton to be here and he knew it would make his arguments weaker, but apparently Ashton was required to be present at all council meetings, a fact Eric had neglected to mention.

"I want Ashton removed as head of the council."

There was silence around the circle of council members, then one let out a chuckle.

"And why would we consider that?" a woman asked. Her voice, too, was soft as if speaking to a child.

"He has threatened to harm Marisol and her unborn eggs."

Another silence, but this one was frosty and several glares were directed at Ashton.

"Is this true, Ashton?"

Ashton spread his hands out as if to prove his innocence. "Of course not. I told you before that the queen and her partner were ill; this is just hysteria speaking."

"The only reason we're ill," Jamie said, leaping into the conversation before they could dismiss him again, "is because Ashton has been putting sedatives into Marisol's food."

A third silence, this one angry.

"Ashton would never do such a thing," one man said.

Jamie glared as he realized the anger was directed at him, not Ashton. But he was in the right, he knew it. "Ask your dragons," he said. "They know the truth."

He had discovered by looking into the council's dragons' minds that they were all aware of what Ashton was doing, but because they disagreed with it so strongly they pretended it wasn't happening and didn't tell their human partners. But now, he could hear the conversations around him as the dragons reluctantly confirmed Jamie's words. Jamie stood as tall and straight as he could while Ashton glared venomously. He didn't think Ashton would attack him, not in front of the council, but he felt exposed and vulnerable.

Once the council members had affirmed the truth with their dragons, they began talking to each other, leaving him and Ashton alone to face each other. Ashton closed the short distance between them with a few simple strides and Jamie tried not to quake.

"This will never work," Ashton said so quietly no one else could hear. "They belong to me and will never get rid of me. And next mating flight, you will be mine too."

"Never," Jamie said. "I will never be yours."

Ashton said nothing, just smiled in a way that had shivers running up and down Jamie's spine. He self-consciously tugged at the sleeves of his shirt as if that would shield him from Ashton's knowing gaze, but it did no good. He remembered when Ashton had pinned him to the bed and kissed him. He remembered growing hard from that kiss, and Ashton's hand stroking him through his pajamas until he was fully aroused. Ashton had set his body on fire and he knew that if Ashton caught him in a mating flight, he would willingly give himself to such a skilled lover. There had to be some way to ensure that Ashton wasn't in his mating flight, some trick like he had used last time that guaranteed that Ashton would be distracted and unable to properly race for Marisol.

Ashton reached out to brush a strand of auburn hair out of Jamie's eyes and Jamie visibly shivered. One of the council members, Eric, must have seen the movement because he left the group and came over.

"Is everything alright?" he asked. "Are you okay, Jamie?"

"Yes," Jamie said automatically, but he took advantage of Eric's presence to take several steps away from Ashton.

Ashton returned to where he was standing before, and Eric was absorbed back into the council's circle. Jamie rubbed his hands on his pants nervously. He had been doing that a lot lately. It was a nervous habit from high school that he had worked hard to lose, but the stress of the past few weeks had brought it back. He divided his attention between Ashton, who watched him with a predator's gaze, and the council, whose low voices were entirely unintelligible from his distance. Finally, the council fell silent and turned to face Jamie.

"Jamie," one of the older men said. "Your health, and the health of your dragon, are the top priority in our council and any threats to either of your will be taken seriously."

Jamie's heart sank as he could almost hear the 'but' at the end of the sentence.

"We will send a representative to ensure Marisol's safety, and your own. But we do not think it wise at this point to remove Ashton from his current position as head of the council. He will be disciplined for his actions, rest assured, but it will be handled by the council according to council rules."

Which probably meant a slap on the wrist, Jamie thought. Ashton would be scolded and then given absolute control again. He wondered who the representative would be, and if he would have any choice in the matter. He wondered if the representative would have the authority to protect Jamie from Ashton, if necessary. He wondered if the representative would try to sleep with Jamie, as Ashton had tried to do. Jamie shivered. Why was it so cold in the council's chamber?

Ashton strode into the council's circle and turned to face Jamie with the might of the council surrounding him. Jamie felt outnumbered and alone, and he realized that truth was not the ally he needed in this battle. He needed people on his side, people to protect him and fight for him. He thought of Narné's vision and grimly realized it needed to come true. If Ashton was going to remain head of the council even after he harmed the queen dragon, then only a true revolution would rid Tarragon society of its corruption. He needed an army to face this threat.

Ashton smiled and gestured to the council around him.

"I do not have any hard feelings about this, Jamie," he said. "You were acting to protect your dragon, just as any partner should. Perhaps once the two of you have settled down after your next mating flight, you will understand why things need to be how they are."

Jamie clenched his hands into fists. Fury swept over him, but he contained it. He managed to smile. "Thank you for hearing my complaints," he said stiffly. "I expect to see my representative shortly."

He turned on his heel and left the room before his anger exploded and the council's opinion of him dropped even further. Why hadn't they listened to him? Well, they had listened to him, and to their dragons, but why hadn't it done any good? Why were they following someone they knew was a threat to their queen? He slammed one fist into his other hand again and again as he walked blindly towards his chambers. He could feel Marisol reflecting his anger and tried to contain it. He didn't want to trigger any strong emotions in her and risk the eggs, but it was hard to control. Why didn't they see how evil Ashton was? And if they did see, why did they allow him to continue? Surely all of them couldn't be blind.

He scanned the minds of the council's dragons for signs that they disagreed with Ashton and he found five that secretly resented the man. Five. Still, if Jamie were forming his own army, five council members would be an immense help if he could convince them to leave.

As he entered his rooms, Scott stood up. Scott must have been able to tell what happened just by looking at Jamie because he didn't say a word, just embraced him. Jamie clung to his boyfriend, inhaling the scent of honey and dandelions. They stayed that way for what seemed like hours, until Scott picked Jamie up as if he weighed nothing and carried him to the couch and cradled him on his lap. Jamie let his head fall into the crook of

Scott's neck and his anger began to fade into sorrow.

He had done everything in his power to get rid of Ashton, and now the only solution left was war. Marisol silently confirmed this, and when he reached out to Narné, the older dragon confirmed it as well. But they couldn't build an army at the academy; Ashton would notice and they would lose before they even started. They needed someplace safe and secret, where only those friendly to the cause could go.

Anything relating to the rebellion was out, because Kale had mentioned that Ashton and the council monitored the rebellion. They couldn't go anywhere public or they would risk humans finding out about dragons, which would lead to chaos and potentially the end of all dragons. Only the mountain with its mist was safe, but Ashton controlled the mountain.

He does not control all the mountain, Marisol said.

Jamie sat up and turned to Marisol's room. Scott kissed his cheek and they both went to visit the enormous crimson dragon with the golden belly. She was so near to giving birth. Scott couldn't hear what she was saying, but he knew Jamie was talking to her so he remained silent.

Ashton does not control the nesting grounds, Marisol continued. *When I go to give birth, we will be somewhere he cannot go.*

Jamie frowned. *But Marisol, other dragons can't go there either, nor can their humans. We need somewhere a large number of humans and dragons can hide.*

You need the nesting grounds, she insisted. *Each site is as big as it needs to be, and can be entered by invitation. My eggs will survive exposure to other dragons and humans because my eggs will be new, not old eggs that are ready to burst at any moment.*

Jamie felt his brow furrowing. If it was true and dragons and humans could be around new eggs without harming the eggs – and he had to trust Marisol on this – then the nesting grounds were an ideal place. It was where Kale was hiding, after all. No one really understood how the nesting grounds worked, or at least no one had been able to explain to Jamie properly, but it almost seemed like each nesting ground existed in a different dimension, all connected at one fork in the path up the mountain. One person traveling that path ended up in one nesting ground, another person on the same path ended up in another nesting ground. If there were some way to control who entered the nesting ground, it would be ideal. Plus, if any students entered the nesting ground when Tarragon Academy held their first year exam, they could be recruited to join the cause. Another thought entered his mind and he stared at Scott, then back at Marisol.

Will the mating flight be protected? he asked.

Marisol slowly shook her head. *No, we would have to fly with all the dragons.*

A weight settled in Jamie's heart, but he tried to stay strong. They would just have to end the war before Marisol's next mating flight, that was all. She didn't think she would need to fly again until the eggs hatched, which gave him some time, but she also wasn't entirely sure. Still, the nesting ground seemed like the best idea so far. He hated the secrecy, but he told himself that it wouldn't last forever. Soon, he would be in a place without Ashton. Soon, he would be leading a war. He didn't know whether to laugh or cry.

CHAPTER THIRTY

Repercussions

Eraxes warned Mike about Ashton's mood moments before Ashton stormed into his room and grabbed him by the collar. Ashton slapped him across the face, hard. There was no pleasure in this pain and Mike knew it was only intended to hurt, but he didn't know what he had done wrong. Tears sprang to his eyes as Ashton slapped him a second time, then shoved him to the floor and kicked him.

"You told Jamie," Ashton said, kicking him so hard he fell over on his side. Mike curled into the fetal position to protect himself while he tried to figure out what was going on. "You told him about the sedative."

"No," Mike cried. "I told no one. When would I have time to tell him? I've been here all day."

"He knew," Ashton hissed. "How else could he know? Get up and get on the bed."

Mike trembled but obeyed. He had never seen Ashton angry before, he realized. He thought he had, but compared to this it was nothing. Ashton was furious. His eyes glittered and his cheeks were flushed, and he was already stripping and stroking his cock as if just waiting for the punishment he was going to inflict on Mike. Mike stepped out of his clothes more slowly, hoping that if he took more time Ashton would realize that Mike was telling the truth.

"What happened?" Mike ventured, not sure if it would enrage

Ashton or calm him to talk about it.

"Little Jamie tried to get me thrown off the council," Ashton said. "And those numbskulls actually considered it. They're putting me on probation – probation! – as head of the council and all of my decisions have to be checked by another member before I can act. On the bed, now."

Mike finished undressing and got on the bed with a heavy heart. Jamie certainly knew how to stir the pot. Getting Ashton kicked off the council? The fact that the council had even considered it was monumental; they must have been really upset about the sedative. And the only way Jamie could have known was from Mike. Or Eraxes, Mike realized.

"My dragon," Mike said, flinching as Ashton raised his hand to strike him. "Maybe Jamie learned it from Eraxes."

"You would implicate your own dragon rather than face punishment from me?" He leaned down until his breath ghosted over Mike's face. "I've taught you well, pet. Your dragon will be questioned, but it won't affect what happens to you."

Mike shivered as Ashton pulled out a blindfold and tied it securely, covering most of his face. He couldn't see anything, not even the little pinpoints of light he could usually see when Ashton blindfolded him. He felt wind across his body and flinched. Ashton laughed. Then a hand grasped his cock and something tight and cold was being squeezed onto it. A cockring, he thought. Ashton had never used one on him before, instead relying on his own self-control to stop him from cumming. Then Ashton grabbed him and hauled him up from the bed. He was positioned by a wall, with his hands and forehead leaning against the wall. He expected to feel Ashton's hands on him but instead there was a hissing sound and something thin tore through his skin. He jumped and cried out. It felt like he had been whipped. Ashton ordered him to stay still and there was another whistling sound and another tearing sensation. He was being whipped. He grit his teeth as lash after lash struck his back and his bare ass, and occasionally his legs, which made him jump and Ashton laugh cruelly.

His entire back side stung and he was relieved when Ashton finally touched him, but then Ashton began tracing the cuts on his skin and pressing into them.

"Tell me what you told Jamie," he said, digging his finger into an especially large cut running across his ass.

"Nothing," Mike pleaded. The pain was incredible and he longed for it to stop, but he couldn't lie to Ashton.

Ashton ran his finger along another injury and asked the same question, to which Mike gave the same answer. Again and again until Mike was sobbing and repeating himself regardless of what Ashton was saying. Finally, the torture stopped and Ashton gripped the sides of his hips. His backside was slick with blood and he felt faint. He was glad he could lean up against the wall, because otherwise he would have collapsed. Ashton reached forward to grab Mike's cock and began stroking from the base of his cock where the cockring clenched tightly to his skin to his sensitive tip that quivered with each flourish of Ashton's wrist.

Ashton let his other hand open Mike's crack as he guided himself into his body, slicked only with blood from the whipping, and penetrated Mike without any warning. Mike shouted at the pain, but also the pleasure as he was starting to grow hard despite the cockring trying to strangle all the pleasure out of him. He could imagine enjoying the cockring under different circumstances, but not like this. Ashton dove into him and began thrusting and Mike was caught in a rhythm between Ashton's hand and his cock, a delightful rhythm under most circumstances but not now, not like this.

Ashton came very quickly and Mike suspected he had been getting off on the torture before the sex, because normally he took longer. When he was finished, he pulled off of Mike completely, took off the blindfold, and left him there, panting, sweating, bleeding. Ashton went to the bathroom to wipe himself off but Mike was too scared to move. He didn't want to get into more trouble. When Ashton returned, he scowled at Mike as if at a piece of meat that had fallen onto the floor. He grabbed Mike's hands and pulled out handcuffs from a drawer. Mike thought he was going to handcuff him to the bed – they had done that before – but instead Ashton reached up to a chain in the middle of the room that Mike had never noticed and tied him to that instead, so that his arms were raised above his head and he had to stand on tiptoes.

Then Ashton left the room, completely naked, and returned with a student, a girl. She looked to be in a mating flight daze because she didn't react to Mike's presence at all, she just wanted to touch and be touched by Ashton. Ashton looked at Mike pointedly before taking the girl to his bed. A tear slipped down Mike's cheek as he watched the two begin kissing. His back stung, but it was nothing compared to this. His master was having sex with someone else. The ultimate punishment. He tried to walk forward to stop them, but the chain gave him no slack. He moaned and whined and called out to Ashton but by now, both Ashton and the girl were in the thick of the mating flight and Ashton's eyes were blown wide with arousal, his senses focused entirely on the girl. They were completely unaware of him.

Mike watched in agony as they touched each other and then the girl pushed Ashton flat on his back and pinned herself on top of him, sighing with a completion that only Mike had the right to know. He was crying openly now as they moved together and slowly, far too slowly for Mike, climbed towards bliss. They cried out together and the girl collapsed against Ashton, who waited several long moments before sitting up and looking at Mike with an expression of anger mixed with pity.

"Do not disobey me or lie to me again, pet," he warned, then he picked up the girl and carried her to the other room.

He returned and untied Mike, who collapsed to the floor in tears. He clutched at Ashton's knees, begging for forgiveness. Ashton kissed him on the forehead and removed the cockring, then ordered him to bathe his wounds. As Mike obeyed, a flare of unusual anger flashed through him. He shouldn't be begging for forgiveness from the man who had just tortured and humiliated him. He ought to be fighting back. That was what Kale would do. He remembered Kale telling him that Ashton had asked for something he couldn't give, and so he had run away. Well, it was about time for Mike to think of what he would and wouldn't give to Ashton. He had given Ashton everything and still been punished, so what was the point of obedience?

As he bathed, he looked into the mirror at his back and saw a series of long lines leaking blood. Never again would he let Ashton hurt him like this. Ashton had gone too far; he had crossed the line. Mike would be his pet, but only when it suited Mike's needs. He thought of the council considering getting rid of Ashton and for the first time, he wished that Jamie had succeeded. Even if Ashton had come back and killed him, at least the rest of the campus would have been safe. There had to be some way to make the council reconsider, to show them that Ashton truly was unworthy to be head of the council.

He took a deep breath and tried to remember what the rebellion had taught him before setting him loose. Ashton was dangerous. He had known that all along, but he had never seen it until tonight. He had been too enthralled by Ashton's allure, but under that beautiful exterior was a cold-hearted bastard. He couldn't stop being Ashton's pet, but he could at least be an informed pet. He longed to talk to Kale, but apparently Kale had returned to the White House without saying goodbye because no one had seen him in quite a while. At least he had somewhere to run to. Mike was trapped here, alone at Ashton's mercy.

He returned to Ashton and tried to smile, but he knew it came off fake. Ashton cradled him in his arms.

"You don't have to pretend to be happy, pet," he said. "You're just as beautiful when you're angry."

He longed to shove away from Ashton and punch the man, or slap him as he had slapped Mike, but he didn't. He let Ashton hold him because he knew that if he ran away, Ashton would only replace him with someone else and he couldn't let anyone else suffer his fate. For better or for worse, he was Ashton's pet and there was nothing he could do about it. He just needed to bide his time until he could strike back and earn his freedom.

CHAPTER THIRTY-ONE

Golden Eggs

Three weeks passed after the council decided to keep Ashton as head of the council. Luckily, Jamie no longer had to take lessons from Ashton every day; they were taken over by Eric, the council member who was appointed as his representative to the council. Jamie was grateful that he didn't have to see Ashton, because he had heard that Ashton flew into a fury after the council meeting and beat Mike. It was only a rumor, but Mike had been sporting a black eye and limping for days afterwards and Jamie prayed it wasn't because he had lifted knowledge of the sedative from Eraxes's mind. He hadn't intended for Mike to be blamed for the incident.

Mike avoided Jamie and Scott since then, staying mostly at Ashton's side. He barely seemed to have time for students even though that was his passion before, and Jamie knew that whatever had happened to him had broken something inside him, and Jamie was somehow to blame. But Ashton had to take most of the blame, Jamie reminded himself. Ashton was the one who had hurt Mike, not Jamie, so there was no reason for Jamie to feel so guilty. But Jamie missed Mike stopping by to check on Marisol, and Marisol missed him as well.

Marisol was flourishing now that she was eating proper meat. Jamie, Scott, and Eric were all present every time she fed, although Eric always had to leave immediately after to get to his classes. She was no longer sick and neither was Jamie, and she had enough energy to walk around the room instead of being confined to bed. She insisted that walking around was good for her and would help her when she had to fly off and have her eggs, and Jamie rejoiced because it was the first mention of how she would have her eggs. Several people had speculated that she would have them right in the room since she couldn't move, but that was back when she was drugged.

People still came to see her, only now Jamie was beginning to get international envoys. Guests from all across the globe were converging on Tarragon Academy and the council had its hands full trying to accommodate all of the VIPs. It was a good thing the council had assigned a representative for Jamie, or else he would have been forgotten in the chaos and completely at Ashton's mercy. But Ashton seemed happy escorting guests around campus and speaking in various languages to the visitors. Jamie wished he had taken another language in school because he didn't understand what most of the visitors said, and he didn't always trust the translators.

Everyone was quite taken with Marisol, even if they were less than impressed with Jamie, and he didn't mind. He understood that he was extremely young and not what they wanted in a queen, but one day he would be. Scott was occasionally introduced to people, but he mostly kept a low profile. Eric had recommended that announcing him as the queen's mate would only cause more trouble, and Jamie trusted him.

Two French women were admiring Marisol as the dragon preened and fluttered her eyes when she suddenly sneezed and went rigid. Jamie, who had been at the back of the room where he wouldn't get in the way of the important people, rushed to her side. Her eyes were entirely black and her claws extended completely. Without a word, she picked Jamie up and put him on her back, then she edged towards the large opening to the dragon canyon.

"Jamie!"

It was Scott. He and Narné were just outside and had seen

Marisol's movement. Jamie waved and felt the beginnings of excitement deep in his belly. Was this it? Was Marisol about to go to the nesting grounds? She extended her wings and the French women gasped in awe. Eric and another council member in the room raced after Marisol, shouting for her to stop. But biology was driving her now and Jamie was just glad he was being brought along for the ride. She slowly lifted her wings, testing them, and for a moment Jamie wondered if she would even be able to fly with the additional weight of the eggs burdening her. Maybe he shouldn't be riding her when she was already struggling. And she hadn't flown in so long, would she be able to get airborne?

She leapt out of the window into the dragon canyon and all of the dragons cried out as one as she fell nearly twenty feet before her wings snapped into place and she soared upward. The other dragons, Narné included, flew with her towards the nesting grounds, calling to each other in a way that sounded like singing and Jamie wondered if it was a birthing song, or a good luck song to their queen. When they reached the air above the nesting grounds, the other dragons scattered except for Narné. Marisol's wings flapped heavily and Jamie could feel her exhaustion, but he couldn't see the nesting grounds, only endless forest.

Marisol opened her mouth and a beautiful melody poured forth, and everything around them grew misty. Then, in an instant, sun pierced through the mist and they were above a lake with a large island in the middle. It looked like the island where Jamie had found Marisol's egg, only much larger than he remembered. She coasted down to the shore and landed delicately, keeping her belly above the ground. He slid off and moved away to give her space. She wasn't speaking and he could feel her concentration. Now was not the time to talk to her. She turned towards the wooded area at the center of the island and began lumbering towards it, careful to keep her belly above the fallen trees and other dangers of the forest floor. Jamie scrambled along beside her, barely able to keep up and frequently falling behind. Luckily, she left quite a trail and was easy to spot.

She found a clearing in the middle of the woods and settled down with a sigh, then began using her tail to uproot the grass. Jamie leapt backwards as the tail began sweeping back and forth, back and forth, clearing the land until it was only dirt and there were piles of soil and uprooted grass on either side. Then she stood and squatted over the fresh dirt. Jamie knew he should look away but he couldn't. This was his dragon giving birth. Something shiny emerged and in moments a golden egg was shimmering in the sunlight. Marisol crouched beside the egg and soon another one appeared. She continued laying eggs all through the dirt patch she had made, thirty-two eggs total. When she was finished, she ran her tail over the mounds of dirt that she had made and scattered the dirt over the eggs, covering most of them in a fine brown mist.

Marisol then inhaled deeply and blew fire at her eggs. Jamie jumped in fear at the sight of his dragon using fire, especially when she hadn't been trained, but she seemed to know exactly what she was doing. The eggs turned black, then began to glow blue or green depending on the egg and Jamie realized he was seeing the color of the dragon. Then her fire died out and they were golden brown again.

She wasn't finished yet, however. She went to the other side of the clearing and used her tail to create another dirt patch. He marveled that she had so many eggs still left, since her belly looked distinctly empty now. She crouched and grunted as a massive gold egg emerged, far larger than the others. She dumped a little dirt back on it and breathed a single stream of fire at it. The egg went black, then began to glow a brilliant red and Jamie knew that this was the queen egg, the egg Derek was destined to partner with. The fire ended and the golden egg looked normal again. Marisol laid down in the dirt patch beside the queen egg and curled around it.

Thank you, Jamie, she said.

"I didn't do anything," he said.

You didn't interrupt. You must not touch the eggs, she instructed. *But other humans may come to this island if you need a safe place to go.*

"Thank you, Marisol," Jamie whispered. He thought of Kale and wondered whether or not the man would be able to find his way here from whatever nesting ground he was at.

Anyone may enter if they know the song and you approve of them, she said.

A song filled his mind and he knew it was burned into his memory. He would be able to share it with others and if they wanted to help in his revolution against Ashton, they would be welcome to come.

I would like to stay with the eggs for a while, she said, resting her head on her front claws. *If you wish to leave, you must ask Narné.*

Jamie nodded. He should go back just to let everyone know the nesting had gone well, and he reached out to Narné and sent him the song. In a few moments he felt a nudge against his mind and he allowed Narné to enter the nesting ground. Narné flew over the clearing once, no doubt to give Scott a view, then he landed at the beach where there was room for a dragon to land. Jamie hiked back down to the beach and embraced Scott when he arrived.

"It was magical," he said. "And there's a queen egg."

"We should tell the others," Scott said, lifting him up onto Narné's back. "And then we should return here."

"Return here? Why?"

"Because here we can live freely," Scott said. "There is no council here, no Ashton. No one to make us do anything. We can be at peace."

"Not forever," Jamie said, thinking of his mating flight.

"No, not forever," Scott acknowledged. "But surely we've

earned a vacation, don't you think? Some time away from the world?"

Jamie chewed on his lower lip. It sounded wonderful, but he would have to think about it. Narné lifted them up into the sky and soon they were surrounded by mist. When the mist cleared, they were high above Mount Tarragon.

"The mist has returned," Scott said. "Perhaps it's because of the eggs."

"Perhaps," Jamie said, but he was thinking of Kale and the blood Kale had shed. Maybe the mountain had been hungry for a sacrifice and Kale's blood was enough to restore it. Either way he was relieved that the mist would continue protecting the dragons a little longer. After all, now that Marisol had laid eggs, she was tightly woven into Tarragon society. Soon her children would be students at the academy, and after that they would be out in the world with the rest of the dragons. Jamie would always be bound to Mount Tarragon and the Tarragon tribe, and it was his responsibility to make sure that it was led by a just and virtuous ruler, as unlike Ashton as possible. He clutched Scott tightly as they flew back to the dragon canyon surrounded by other dragons singing a song of joy.

CHAPTER THIRTY-TWO

Conditions of Release

The council convened a second time and invited both Jamie and Scott to attend, and Scott was nervous. Jamie had told him all about the first meeting and he knew that the council was liable to take Ashton's side in everything. But now that the eggs were laid, he didn't even know what Ashton's side was. All he knew was that he wanted to be at the nesting grounds with Jamie, free from Ashton's control. And Ashton was very unlikely to allow that.

Eric met them in their chambers as soon as they returned from the nesting grounds and shared the council's request that they join, and Jamie and Scott didn't even have time to talk about a plan before Eric was leading them to the council chambers. Narné instructed Scott to be calm and speak plainly, but he was having no visions of the outcome and couldn't give specific advice. Narné's visions were hit and miss; when he had them, they were extraordinarily useful, but they were also quite rare.

Jamie whispered to Scott that Marisol was sound asleep after giving birth and wouldn't be able to help them, either, so they were on their own, without dragons. It didn't matter, though. Scott knew what he wanted and he was going to get it. He and Jamie were going to live freely in the nesting grounds until at least the start of summer, preferably until the fall semester started. After all, spring semester was past the midway point now and Jamie had essentially been out of school thanks to his illness, so what was a little longer without formal instruction? Scott could teach him what he needed to know, and Jamie would be a lot happier learning from Scott than one of the teachers on campus who still looked at Jamie with lust left over from the mating flight.

When they entered the council chambers, Scott's steps faltered for a moment. Jamie hadn't mentioned that it looked like a medieval tomb, or that all of the council members wore dark robes with crimson dragons embroidered on them. It looked like a cult, not a council. But he pulled himself together and followed Jamie to the dais at the front of the room. Whereas before Jamie had said he couldn't get anyone's attention, now everyone was watching them silently, with eager anticipation. Jamie's back was stiff, the way it got when he was nervous, but Scott didn't dare caress his lover in front of everyone.

They reached the dais and turned around. Scott couldn't think of anything to say, and it seemed like everyone was waiting for them to speak. But luckily Jamie seemed to know what they wanted to hear.

"The Queen has laid her eggs successfully," he said simply, and the tension in the room vanished, replaced by celebration. Instantly the buzz of conversation filled the room as the council members began talking to each other, no doubt sharing relief and joy at the event as well as comparing bets.

Jamie lifted his arm and the room fell silent. Scott was impressed. Jamie had clearly learned how to handle this group since the last time he had met with them, or else the council was desperate for more details.

"She will remain with the eggs on the nesting ground," he continued. "And Scott and I will stay with her."

There was another buzz of conversation, this one not as pleasant. Ashton, who had been hiding in the crowd until now, strode to the front of the crowd.

"You have your classes, Jamie," he reminded them. "And it is dangerous for humans to be near unhatched eggs."

"Marisol assures me that the eggs will be safe," Jamie said. "And I would be willing to allow my representative to visit me and instruct me once a week."

Eric looked shocked, and a little uneasy. He glanced at the council members around him, who were staring at him with a mixture of jealousy and anger. Ashton was staring at him with thinly concealed rage and Scott hoped Jamie hadn't just signed Eric's death warrant. They had been so careful not to reveal Eric's part in Kale's disappearance, but now Jamie was calling him out in a similar way and the consequences could be equally devastating.

"You need someone skilled at teaching first-year students," Ashton said, turning from Eric dismissively. "In addition to weekly visits from Eric, you would need daily visits from a real teacher."

"Every other day," Jamie said. "And I will allow it only if Mike is the teacher."

A wicked smile lit Ashton's face. "I would have it no other way. So, then, you will live in the nesting grounds with weekly visits from Eric and Mike visiting you every other day. How long will you remain there? You will need to start school in the fall with the other students, you know."

"I know," Jamie said. "I expect to be ready to return by then."

Another council member pressed her way to the front. She was imposing and even without having seen her before, Scott knew she must be Margot, head of the women's college.

"We cannot go for so long without having the queen here," she said. "We have visitors every day coming to meet the queen and even with the dragon gone, they must meet someone. Either the queen or the queen's mate needs to remain here to greet the foreign dignitaries."

Ashton's mouth twisted at the mention of the queen's mate.

Scott took a step forward. "I would be willing to return every once in a while to greet people, but Jamie stays at the nesting grounds with Marisol. It will help Marisol to have Jamie with her," he added, knowing that was an argument no one could deny.

"Scott is hardly acceptable as the queen's mate," Ashton said. "He's too young, and it is unlikely he'll remain her mate."

"But until then," Margot said, her glasses glimmering in the dim light, "We need someone and he is the queen's mate. You cannot deny it forever, Ashton."

Scott paled a little at the anger in Ashton's eyes and was grateful it wasn't directed at him. No wonder the men and women's schools didn't get along. The two remained locked in a staring match as Jamie and Scott uneasily stood by. The rest of the council seemed uneasy as well, and Eric especially looked ill at ease. Scott sincerely hoped he wouldn't get in any trouble, but he was their representative and it was perfectly natural to suggest that he visit them, as opposed to someone else on the council.

He thought of Mike and hoped Mike didn't get in trouble either. He knew Ashton had lashed out at Mike several weeks ago – Mike had been bruised, which had never happened before – and he prayed it wouldn't happen again. But no, Ashton had seemed pleased when Jamie suggested Mike, not upset, so perhaps this was playing into Ashton's hand. Scott's simple plan of living at the nesting grounds had quickly become complex with all sorts of visitors, and it was hard to tell who was benefitting now. But as long as Jamie was kept safe from Ashton, all would be well.

And once they were alone and away from Ashton, they could begin planning their war against him. The nesting grounds was an ideal recruiting ground, after all. Jamie would only let in dragons who hated Ashton, so everyone could be controlled, and they would start building their army without Ashton's knowledge. Perhaps it was good that Scott come back to the campus every once in a while, especially if foreigners were coming to visit. News of the war would need to be spread somehow in order to get recruits. It was only a matter of time before Ashton found out, but until then Scott needed to question all of the visitors carefully and invite the chosen few to join the queen in her battle against Ashton. Once Ashton found out, of course, Scott wouldn't be safe at the academy, but until then the council would protect him just as they protected Jamie. He was the queen's mate, whether they liked it or not.

Ashton grimaced as he looked at Scott. "I suppose Scott could greet the visitors, but I would need to be present as well."

"As head of the council, that is your right," Margot said.

Scott knew Ashton wanted to be present because he expected to be Marisol's next mate, but that would never happen. No matter what, Marisol would never fly with Arion. Scott would rather die than see Jamie with Ashton.

The council petered out after that. Most of the council members swarmed Jamie asking for details of the egg laying, and he volunteered a few, holding back only the number of eggs and the fact that a queen egg had been laid. He was good to keep back those details, Scott thought. Jamie had grown wise in the past few months, even while Scott had barely grown at all. Ashton was trying to get close to Jamie, but Eric was intercepting the movements, and Scott backed away from the noisy group until he was alone. Or he thought he was alone. He was surprised when a hand touched his sleeve and he saw Margot right beside him.

He trembled, remembering her dragon's gift for stealing memories, but apparently Yasmina couldn't steal memories from anyone bonded to a dragon. Still, it was unnerving being so close to Margot, a woman he had never met before but one with as much strength as Ashton, though she chose not to use it the way he did.

"Take advantage of your freedom," she advised. "You'll only have so much time before he realizes what you're really doing."

"What is that?" he asked, puzzled.

"Building your army," she said with a small laugh before returning to the rest of the group.

Scott's feet felt planted to the ground and he shut his jaw quickly, hoping no one had noticed his shock. Margot knew? She knew but she was saying nothing? Did that mean she would be on his side, or on Ashton's? He somehow suspected that she would be on neither side and would simply watch the conflict from the comfort of the girl's college, but this was no ordinary power struggle. This battle would involve everyone in Tarragon society and eventually she would have to pick a side. At least she wouldn't tell Ashton, Scott thought. She may not have decided to join his side, but at least there was that.

He lifted his head high and went to Jamie's side. He shouldn't be slouching in the corner. He needed to get used to going into groups and determining who had the right to join their cause, and that meant going out of his comfort zone just like Jamie was doing right now. He placed a hand on Jamie's shoulder and Jamie looked up at him in relief, as if the boy had secretly been wishing for him to do just that. He felt bad that he had left Jamie to answer the council's questions on his own. Just because Jamie was capable of standing on his own didn't mean he liked it, and Scott realized that a lot of the strength Jamie had shown recently had been coming at a high cost.

They both needed a break, a vacation, a time away from everyone else. They needed the nesting grounds. They would stay at the nesting grounds alone for a time before even telling Kale where they were, because once Kale arrived the battle would start in earnest and Scott would have to do serious recruiting. And before they could do that, they needed a break.

Jamie seemed to gather his courage and went to Ashton, confirming the details of their arrangement before he and Scott left the council chambers. They climbed on Narné and flew to their quarters first to get clothes and other supplies to last them their summer in the wilderness. As soon as they were alone in their quarters, the tension seemed to bleed away from Jamie and he went limp in Scott's arms.

"Just hold me, Scott," Jamie said, and Scott was more than willing to oblige.

He cradled his beloved Jamie and kissed his forehead, his cheeks, and finally his sweet lips. Jamie melted into him as they kissed and their tongues met and playfully sparred. Scott lifted Jamie up and carried him into the bedroom. It was going to be months before they had a good bed, and he wanted to take advantage of it while they could.

Jamie didn't move as Scott undressed him, then peeled off his own clothes, but the hunger in Jamie's eyes was unmistakable. Scott kissed Jamie again, then let his kisses work their way down Jamie's neck to his collarbone, an area Jamie loved that had him whining as Scott nipped and licked, then lower to his nipples, another area that had his lover gasping for breath, then even lower to his belly.

Jamie was hard and erect and his cock was furled tight against his belly, and Scott lovingly took it into his hand and let his tongue trail over its tip. Jamie gasped and arched his back. Scott lapped up the precum that was escaping Jamie's tip and licked his shaft, then set Jamie's cock on his tongue and let the entire length slip down his throat. Jamie moaned and Scott could see him fisting the blanket as Scott took him in his mouth. Scott tongued his cock while it was in his throat, and he swallowed, the suction skyrocketing as Jamie keened in pleasure.

Scott kept him inside for as long as he could until he had to release Jamie to breathe, but as soon as he had taken a breath he swallowed the young man again and again Jamie began moaning and writhing above him helplessly. Scott loved the control he had over Jamie's pleasure and began testing different touches to see which created the most pleasure in his love. He soon discovered that Jamie adored having the thick vein on his cock massaged and he shamelessly lathered his attention on it while Jamie gasped and stuttered for breath, his hand reaching down to grab Scott's hair and keep him in place.

Scott could feel a trembling in the base of Jamie's cock and knew he was about to cum, so he ran his tongue over the vein one last time and planted himself firmly as Jamie cried out and his cock spasmed again and again, heavy liquid pouring into Scott's mouth as he swallowed as quickly as he could. Some of it dribbled onto his lips and he licked it up with a pleased smile, then he kissed his way back up to Jamie's face.

Jamie had an expression of pure bliss on his face and his eyes were half-closed. His skin was flushed red across his body and his hands were still clutched tightly to the blanket. Scott eased his fingers off the blanket and arranged Jamie so they were spooning, with Scott cradling his lover. Jamie was still breathing heavily as if he had just run a marathon and Scott was extremely pleased with himself.

This was what Jamie needed. This was what he deserved. Bliss. No worries, no fears, only happiness in his lover's arms. There was so much in the world to worry about: Ashton's machinations, the council's inability to stand up to Ashton, the upcoming war that Jamie was destined to lead, the eggs at the nesting ground and their safety, Kale's health and survival, Mike's health and survival, too, and the constant threat of Ashton winning the next mating flight. But in this moment, Scott knew that none of those things mattered for Jamie. Scott had been able to give him a moment where all of his fears vanished and only happiness remained. And Scott would fight to give him such moments for the rest of his life.

Jamie finally stirred in his arms and turned to face him.

"I love you, Scott," he said, his eyes wide and earnest.

"I love you, Jamie," Scott said, hoping Jamie could hear his heart speaking the words in addition to his mouth.

A little smile appeared on Jamie's lips and he kissed Scott chastely. "I'm going to love being stuck on an island with you."

Scott laughed, and felt some of his own tension melt away at last. "What are we waiting for?"

ABOUT THE AUTHOR

Elizabeth James

Elizabeth James hails from Portland, Oregon and spent many hours of her childhood tucked away in the Gold Room of Powell's Books, reading science fiction and fantasy masterpieces and hidden treasures. She writes romance with strong elements of science fiction and fantasy as a result, focusing on LGBT characters.

THRALL OF DARKNESS

science fiction and fantasy
romance publisher

Thrall of Darkness was founded because there is a shortage of good, quality literature featuring gay protagonists that does not reduce gay characters to stereotypes or dismiss them as secondary characters. Every story seeks to challenge the status quo by focusing on gay characters and combining drama, action, and sex into an addicting blend of fun-filled narrative.

You can find more information on Thrall of Darkness novels and short stories at thrallofdarkness.com.

BOOKS BY THIS AUTHOR

Demon Season

Taylor just wanted to bond with a regular demon during his first demon season, but instead he ends up with the prince of demons, an incubus! He fights through his fears of intimacy while battling past enemies as he and his demon come to a new understanding.

A Vampire's Desire

Kairos takes a job in an ancient vampire house knowing nothing about them and their society, and immediately falls in love with his boss, a powerful but cold vampire. As he tries to get closer, threats from a rival house threaten to tear them apart.

Dragon Tamer

Luke has heard dragons all his life and when a dragon summons him to raise her dragonlings, he runs away to help her. But the world he enters is fraught with danger and he knows little of the outside world. As the dragons begin dying off and dragon tamers like him become scarce, a rival tribe kidnaps him and everything he knows is thrown into question.

Sagent

Gabriel is a sagent, a sex agent, at the start of his career, but he is already scarred by his previous agency. When he is sent on a dangerous mission to the underbelly of Destiny, everything starts to fall apart. Isolated from his agency and not knowing where to go, Gabriel must choose between returning to safety and Destiny, or staying and forging his own path.

First Prince

Wren is the beautiful yet rebellious first prince of Fontain, forced to move to the Imperial Palace as part of a treaty. Upon arriving, he receives a frigid welcome and realizes his stay will be fraught with danger. When he finds romance in an unexpected place, he realizes that his life may not be as dire as he imagined and pleasure can be found where it is least expected.

Prisoner Of Love

When Prince Tristan is captured in battle, he fully expects to be tortured and killed. But the torture turns to erotic pleasure as he learns that his enemy, Prince Ryan, is in love with him and has been planning his capture with meticulous care for years. Will Tristan hold firm to his principles, or will Ryan's forceful seduction overpower his senses?

Dark Offering

Nightmares are a nightly occurrence on the planet of Ylse, and they're strong enough to lure humans to be fed on by the creatures who haunt the night. Jarl is charged with risking the night to feed the colony. He comes across one of the creatures offering peace. Is the creature sincere or is this just a new way to lure the humans to their deaths on this inhospitable planet?

Bride Of Albis

Sam and his small crew of space-faring traders have their usual routine permanently shattered when they are kidnapped by pirates. Sam makes a deal with the head of the pirates: he will be sold as a slave in exchange for the freedom of his crew. But when he discovers that the pirate lied and sold his crew as well, he vows vengeance.

Seeking More

Seeking More is a collection of eight contemporary gay romance stories that range from the deeply emotional to action-packed, from hapless MFA students to couples on the brink of a new relationship. Each story is focused not only on steamy romance, of which there is plenty, but also on character development and an emotional connection between reader and character.

Eve Of Eternity

Sabine is a young woman searching for her identity while fleeing the powerful man trying to steal her heart and mind. She's almost under his control when she is kidnapped by a man with conflicting loyalties and a mysterious past who claims to kidnap her in order to rescue her. Will she break free from the men around her?

Treacherous A Dragon's Love

In the middle of the final battle against the great dragon Arostrath, a woman appears bound in golden chains. The King claims her as his reward but the youngest son has an unusual fondness for her that could cast the kingdom into ruin. Will his love for the beautiful and strange woman destroy the kingdom, or does her mystery hide the answer to all of their prayers?

www.ingramcontent.com/pod-product-compliance
Lightning Source LLC
Chambersburg PA
CBHW020057180626
46812CB00006B/2370